WHITE WATER FALLS
UNDERWATER FERRIS WHEEL
EMPLOYEE PARKING
WET & WILD BA
HUMAN CANNON
SPRINKLER CITY
KIDDIE POOL
GO KARTS VILLE
THE RIPTIDE

SCREAM RIVER
RAPID DANGER!
JUNGLE SWINGS
TSUNAMI POOL
MEDIC STATION
DOGGON IT!
COOLCONE
ADMIN BUILDING
Welcome to
BREAKNECK BAY

BREAKNECK BAY

A THRILLER

FAITH GARDNER

Be the first to learn about Faith Gardner's upcoming releases by joining her newsletter!

*For my dad, who's always excited to go out to lunch
and talk about serial killers.*

HELP WANTED

SUMMER JOBS AT
BREAKNECK BAY WATERPARK!

Looking for a fun summer job that moves at breakneck speed?
Breakneck Bay Waterpark is NOW HIRING for the 1982 season!

We need lifeguards, ride attendants, snack bar workers, and
ticket booth staff to join our team.

- ✓ Competitive hourly pay
- ✓ Flexible shifts – perfect for students!
- ✓ Work in the sun at California's most thrilling waterpark!

No experience? No problem! We provide on-the-job training.
Apply in person at Breakneck Bay or call 555-5581 for more info.

☀ Make a splash this summer – join the Breakneck Bay crew! ☀

1

It isn't even noon yet, but it's sweltering in the Ouch Shack, where the air ever-stinks like chlorine, teenage sweat, and anti-septic. I spray iodine on a man's raw, scraped skin. Despite the flaming skull tattoo on his back, he's sobbing like a baby and begging me to stop. And to think I fought for this job—I must be crazy.

"We have to sanitize the area so it doesn't get infected," I say in my preschool teacher voice.

He tries to move away from me, but this is an eight-by-eight-foot room. There's nowhere to go and I'm blocking the door. This shirtless guy could pass for a Hell's Angel—ZZ Top beard and probably two hundred pounds heavier than I am. But right now, I've got the spray bottle full of stinging disinfectant.

"Come on," he says. "Ain't that enough?"

"Let me just get the back of your knees and you'll be on your way."

He wails to the plywood ceiling, "Lord help me!"

I reach an arm around him and do two quick squirts—*spritz, spritz.* He flinches. "It stings like a motherfu—"

"It's over," I say, my hand on his hairy shoulder. "You're going to be okay. Just keep it clean."

Sniffling, he wipes his eyes. "Thanks."

"Here's your shirt." I hand him his Judas Priest tee and he reties his board shorts. "Next time read the warning signs and don't go down Scream River headfirst, okay?"

"'Preciate it, nurse," he mumbles as he brushes past me, pushing open the squeaky door and letting a burst of sunshine inside.

"I'm not a nurse," I call after him, but I can already hear his feet thumping the path, returning to the sounds of splashes and screams. I hang up my spray bottle, check my watch, scribble notes on my clipboard, and sit back on the stool where I fan myself with an issue of *MAD Magazine* someone left in here.

The Ouch Shack, from the outside, resembles a medical station: a square, white building with a hand-painted sign that says MEDIC in red. Or *said* it, anyway—some clown snuck in a tiny hyphen and added a letter to the end, so now it reads ME-DICK if you squint closely. Inside, it's a jumble of first-aid supplies and employee lockers. Workers sneak in here and party after the park closes. I know this because since even though I started this job just two weeks ago, I've cleaned up everything from crumpled Budweiser cans to used rubbers in the mornings when I open shop.

I try my best to keep it clean and take pride in my tiny domain. I exercise patience with the goon squad of teenagers who run this park, reminding myself it was only a decade ago that I was their age. I do a pretty damn good job of running this shack, though no one around here's about to praise me.

It's times like these—the lulls between injuries, the uninvited downtimes—that are the hardest. My husband, Mitch, the park manager, says I've got an itchy soul. He's not wrong. Something about stillness and stagnant air and silence sends me free-falling. I've got to keep busy, find something to clean, hum or sing or whisper to myself to fill the Big Empty. That's what I call the inexplicable horror of being alone.

Luckily, this job keeps me on my toes. Quiet is rare. Like right now—just as I put the magazine down and get up to grab a broom, there's my co-worker Rhonda opening the door with a parkgoer: a sunburned woman wearing a giant airbrushed shirt with a bikinied body on it. On closer inspection, "woman" might be too generous a description. She's still got baby fat on her sunburned cheeks and wears a neon fanny pack. I wrinkle my brow and rest my hands on my hips.

"There you are, Mrs. Blue," Rhonda says in her clipped tone. "We've got a wet one."

A "wet one" is park code for someone who drank one too many at the Wet and Wild Bar and can't be trusted to swim. Staff walks them up here so they can sit and sober up before letting them loose in the park again.

"Go to hell," the wet one slurs.

"Too late, ma'am." Rhonda leads her to a bench against the back wall. "I already work here."

"Breakneck Bay, my ass," the wet one says as she plops down with the elegance of a sack of potatoes. "This place is for goobs."

"Are you even old enough to drink alcohol?" I ask her.

"What are you, my mom?" she challenges, so wobbly she can barely sit still.

"My educated guess is that she snuck it in the park," Rhonda says to me. "I certainly hope they didn't serve her at the Wet and Wild."

"Well, they did," the girl says, lying down on the bench. "They made me a penis colada."

She giggles uncontrollably and closes her eyes. I exchange a look with Rhonda, who regards the girl with something between pity and disdain.

"It's not my business who they serve," Rhonda mutters. "I control nothing around here. What happens here is beyond my capabilities."

She repeats this as if she's reminding herself more than anyone else. Rhonda Wegman is the most responsible seventeen-year-old girl I've ever met in my life. Maybe *too* responsible. She speaks like a sixty-year-old librarian and dresses like a forty-year-old mom, sporting a tight ponytail and granny glasses that make her brown eyes appear extra-large. Rhonda is not one of the workers sneaking in here after hours for a party; Rhonda is the one who snitches on them. It's yet to be confirmed if Rhonda has any teeth, because she never smiles. Sometimes I want to shake her and tell her to lighten up a little.

Rhonda glances at my clipboard and points. "What is this?"

"Oh." I peer over her shoulder. "Sign-in sheet. I'm logging injuries, just in case it's needed later."

"Mr. Marrs will not like that." She shakes her head. "You know how he feels about paper trails."

"But—"

Rhonda pushes the clipboard into my hands. "It's not my job to tell you what to do, of course, but I'd get rid of it."

"He told me we need to tally injuries for the daily report."

"Right. Tally. Meaning count them, keep a score, and report. No details."

"I don't see how more information could hurt—"

"Mrs. Blue, I know Mr. Marrs. Trust me on this."

She knows Mr. Marrs? I bite my tongue to not tell her that, honey, Creighton Marrs is the sun to Mitch's earth. They're best friends from way back when. Last summer, before I moved up here, I stayed in Creighton's guest cottage when I visited. Two years ago, I went to his destination wedding in Jamaica. I didn't fill out an application or have an interview for this job that I am not qualified to be working—all thanks to nepotism. On top of that, Rhonda seems sometimes to forget that she's ten years younger than me, and she is certainly not my boss. Creighton is. We both report to Creighton.

But before I set the record straight, the rumble of the wet one's snoring interrupts the conversation. We view her with curiosity, then turn back to one another.

"So, do you mind?" Rhonda asks, pointing to my sign-in sheet. "I think we should dispose of this. I admire your push for transparency, but I don't think it will be well-received."

Rhonda is pushy, uptight, and nobody likes her much, but I have a soft spot for her. While other people might think she comes across as arrogant, the fact is she's pretty much always right. So I nod and rip the papers up, scattering them in the garbage bin along with today's bloody bandages, used cotton swabs, and Doritos bags.

"Mr. Marrs will never know this happened," she says solemnly.

"It's fine," I say, trying to hide my annoyance. "I'm not looking to hide anything from Creighton. I'm not scared of him the way you seem to—"

The door swings open again, cutting me off. When I see who it is, a grin spreads across my face and lights me up from my tiptoes to my earlobes.

My husband. My other half. Mitch. He hands me a bouquet of dandelions he must have picked for me on his way up here.

"Awww." I throw my arms around him. "What are you doing all the way up here?"

His hug smells like pine and shaving soap. When he pulls back, the faraway look in his green eyes hints that he's worried about something.

"Hey, babe. Is your radio working?" he asks.

My grin melts. "My …" I touch my belt, pull out my walkie-talkie, and press the side button. "Oops. Battery must have run out."

"I'll be on my way, Mr. and Mrs. Blue." Rhonda nods at us and heads out the door.

Mitch watches as it slams shut behind her.

"I wish she'd call people by their first names," Mitch says. "Makes me feel like a schoolteacher."

"Everything okay?" I ask, brushing a curl out of his eyes, trying to attract his full attention.

Mitch gazes past me at the snoring girl on the bench.

"Wet one," I say.

"Have you seen Gloria today?" he asks quietly, concern wrinkling his brow. "A housemate called and said she never came home last night."

I cross my arms. "No, not today. I saw her yesterday morning."

"Okay." He glances around the room, as if she might be hiding somewhere. "If you see her, would you let me know?"

"Of course." I bite my lip, thinking about the conversation Gloria and I had just a few nights ago. Her shaking hands, dotted with cigarette burns. The bruise. The smell of vodka on her breath. I try to not poke my nose into other people's business, but sometimes I can't help it. "I hope she's okay."

"I'm sure it's nothing to worry about." He chews the inside of his cheek. "Weird day. First, my truck wouldn't start. Then, when I got here, I was locked out of my office. Still can't find the keys. Then the Tsunami motor stopped working, and we're draining the pool so maintenance can check it out. And now, this Gloria thing."

"I thought you just said there was nothing to worry about?" I say, trying to catch his eye.

Stop thinking about Gloria. I'm right here! a little voice in me screams. My stomach flips like Mitch isn't telling me something. I blame Tiny Kit, my petulant inner child who lives in fear Mitch is going to screw things up. She's a part of myself I wish I could leave behind, but some scars run too deep. The best I can do is acknowledge her. That usually quiets her for a while.

"Yeah." Mitch kisses my temple. "These pipsqueak rec attendants are going to give me gray hair by the end of the summer."

"It's June," I remind him, putting a hand on his cheek. "Breathe."

He offers a tight-lipped smile.

"Want me to open the lockers?" I jiggle the keys clipped to my belt. Employee lockers are located here in the Ouch Shack and therefore, they're my responsibility. "I don't know, see if anything of Gloria's is in there?"

"Eh, I wouldn't want you searching employee lockers until I check with Creighton." Mitch rakes a hand through his hair. "Don't worry about it."

I almost say, *Aren't you the park manager? Can't you make these decisions without checking in with Creighton about every miniscule thing?* But the splashing sound of vomit interrupts the moment. The smell of it hits next.

"I think I just ralphed," the wet one moans from the bench.

"Another day in paradise," Mitch mutters, shaking his head. He gives me a look. "You wanted this, Kit. You *wanted* this."

"Thanks for the reminder." I hold my nose, open a cabinet for the mop and bucket, and flash him a smile. "I still do."

He blows me a kiss on his way out the door. "Unbreakable Kitty."

I love it when he calls me that.

I clean up the mess and give the girl a Dixie cup of water. An hour later, she's perked up. After a brief chat about the dangers of underage drinking, I let her go. When I'm alone again and the silence spreads throughout the room, I sing to myself—that melody that I've been chewing on since we moved.

But the restlessness is too much. I change the batteries on the walkie-talkies and listen to Mitch trying to get someone to find a key so he can open his office.

"How in heckfire are there no backup keys?" he asks. "Roger? Anyone?"

"Sorry Mr. B, dude," says Dwayne. "Maybe Gloria stole them."

Sounds of girls giggling. I'm guessing it's the twins who work in the admin building, who Dwayne's always finding excuses to hang around.

"Not funny, Dwayne," Mitch says.

"Code brown," a frantic voice says. "Code brown in the kiddie pool."

I wrinkle my nose. Code brown means exactly what you think it means.

"Go clean the kiddie pool, Dwayne," Mitch says tiredly.

Poor Mitch. This job is too much. Is this chaos why he didn't want me working here? Was he protecting me from it? If not, then here comes that same buzzing question I've had for the past two weeks since I started this job: why was he so dead set against me being here?

Gloria flashes to mind, the cropped-haired teen with raccoon eyeliner who apparently didn't come home last night. Mitch seemed worried. Last I saw her, she acted like it was any other day, slinging her purse into the locker, stuffing her jean jacket in before heading out to the park for her shift at the Rapid Danger ride. She's a partier. The girl is eighteen or nineteen; she probably left work last night and had a fun night out somewhere. Once upon a time, I had some of those.

I'm telling myself these things, but my stomach is full of bees. I replay the one real conversation I've had with Gloria, a few nights ago, and how upset she seemed.

Mitch told me he wanted to talk to Creighton before searching her locker, but I wish he'd think for himself sometimes. I've been trying to encourage him to step up a bit and act like the boss he is instead of always deferring to Creighton. And why not? I have the keys.

Well, I'm not afraid. If Mitch won't do it, I will.

I open Gloria's locker with a click. What I expect is emptiness, so my heart drops along with my jaw when I realize what I'm looking at.

Her purse and jean jacket are still here, right where she left them the last time I saw her.

2

The drive home from Breakneck Bay is breathtaking: a winding highway that hugs the Full Moon River as it flows through Hill Valley.

Founded during the Gold Rush in the mighty Sierra Nevadas, Hill Valley peaked in the nineteenth century and then dwindled into a ghost town—until 1977, when Creighton Marrs opened Breakneck Bay Waterpark. Since then, growth has skyrocketed. Tract housing sprouted in the outskirts. Forests were razed, and gas stations, grocery stores, and even a couple fast-food restaurants popped up like mushrooms after a rainstorm. Despite the economic boom the town has seen since Breakneck Bay opened, the citizens don't like us park employees much. So, when we moved here in March, Mitch insisted we live in the boonies twenty minutes away.

Somehow, Mitch and I are not locals, but not tourists either. Mitch moved out here when Breakneck Bay opened and has basically called Hill Valley home ever since, but he lived in Creighton's guest cottage until I arrived. The last few months have been us trying to plant roots here and make a go of it, although I still can't imagine living here when winter balds the trees and freezes the lakes, and the park is closed for an entire season.

But today, you'd never know snow had ever fluttered in the air. The valley and the mountains beyond it sparkle green. The speckled shadows from the canopies dance along the road like disco lights as I drive, singing along with the B-52s. I belt it out and bop my head, ignoring the fact that my heart beats faster and faster as the forest thickens.

"I'm so glad I'm alone," I tell myself, exclaiming over the music. "If Mitch were here we'd be listening to Steely Dan."

Still, I can feel it: a ratchet inside me turning tighter and tighter.

Gloria's face flashes in my mind. Her things left behind in her locker, everyone scratching their heads about where she is. A chill runs through me, but I shake it off. I'm not at work anymore. There's nothing I can do.

"So beautiful," I say softer, noticing the details of the lush woods: neon moss, blackbirds, that special gold shimmer on the sugar pines that happens in the late afternoon sunshine.

Beautiful. Big. Empty.

When I pull up into the driveway to our cabin, hidden at the end of a private road, I pull the emergency brake and turn the engine off. Bowie barks his hellos to me, and I love the sound so much it might as well be music.

Life in Hill Valley is no Santa Monica—no sidewalk cafés, no ocean breeze, no steady stream of passing strangers. It's taken getting used to. But one of the overwhelming pluses to country living is how much happier Bowie is in this house than he was in a tiny apartment. And my sweet mutt with pointy ears and short, funny legs deserves only the best. I come inside and squat for hugs and kisses.

"Hey buddy," I say with a laugh. "I missed you, too."

I hum to fill the silence and open windows to invite the breeze in. We decorated our cabin with an array of secondhand furniture—a leather sofa, a braided rug, a wall-sized shelf full of records, a wooden record console. It doesn't quite know who it is yet, but it has potential. I know the feeling.

I cross to the yellow Formica kitchen counter. Beneath the red trim line phone hanging on the wall, our answering machine blinks.

"Let me guess, Mitch," I say with a sigh. "You will not be home for dinner. Again."

Since moving out here, I've learned the hard way that my definition of working full time is not Mitch's definition of working full time. He practically lives at the park. He comes home after bedtime and sometimes leaves for work before the sun comes up. On his days off, he's often taking care of special projects or ridiculous emergencies. Last weekend, we canceled a dinner date because the underwater Ferris wheel got stuck, and he had to jerry-rig an emergency rescue operation.

I press *play*. It's a robotic female voice in mid-sentence. "... inmate at Los Angeles County Jail. Do you accept the charges?" A pause and a *click* end the message.

Worry knots my stomach. My body slackens with disappointment. Ah, that familiar, ghostly gut-punch only my brother can give me.

"Freddie, what on earth have you done now?" I say to myself.

I listen to the message again to double-check that I didn't miss anything. I'm sure he'll be calling back soon. I'm sure the call will end with an ask for money. I'm sure I'll be wiring it to him in the next few days. And round and round the carousel goes.

As much as I wanted my schedule to align with Mitch's, it never does. Once again, a blank evening awaits me. I fill it with records, tidying, phoning friends back home, and getting nothing but answering machines. In the silence, I stand with my hands on my hips, the thought of Gloria still banging around in my head. That conversation we had just this past weekend—it only lasted a few minutes, but I keep combing over it. The way she flinched when I confronted her.

"You okay?" I asked.

She turned to me, eyes brimming, hot-pink mouth twitching. She looked like a girl on the edge of losing it as she shoved her purse in her locker and slammed it shut. "What do you care?"

I tried not to ogle the scars on her hand or let my gaze linger on the bruise on her face. But she noticed. She covered the asterisk-shaped cigarette burns with her other hand.

"Nobody's hurting me, but even if they were, guess what?" Gloria cocked her head at me. I smelled booze on her breath—leftover from a late night? Or was she drinking before her shift? "No one would give a shit."

My heart twisted at the hurt in her eyes. I wanted to help her, but didn't know how. "You sure you're okay to work?"

"Of course. I'm fine."

"Listen," I said, touching her arm. "I'm here if you ever want to talk."

She scoffed and pulled away from me. "You are the *last* person who would understand. No offense."

Well, it was hard not to take offense. Because, what the hell? I was trying to be kind. She eyed me with disdain, as if I were some out-of-touch old person who wouldn't understand her.

I cleared my throat and tried again.

"Actually," I said, throat tightening. "My parents died in a murder-suicide. I think I understand a thing or two about abuse."

The way her jaw dropped and her face paled—all expression

washed away for just a flicker. It wasn't information I usually drop into casual conversation. But I sensed something off, and I wanted Gloria to know I was someone she could trust.

"Oh my God," she finally said, her voice softer. "That is so fucked up. Why are you ..." She shook her head. "That is so fucked up."

She slammed her locker shut. In the silence, my blood thrummed in my ears. Maybe I'd gone too far by blurting out my childhood trauma. But as she left, it seemed something I'd said had rattled her, turning her prickly anger to sadness.

"You're married to Mitch," she said.

I nodded.

She moved her eyes up and down my body, as if I'd just transformed. Something flashed in her wild eyes—jealousy? Judgment? I couldn't tell.

"You could do so much better," she mumbled.

My brow wrinkled. "What does *that* mean?"

Instead of answering me, she spun on her heel and said, "Have a nice day."

I let it go. Gloria seemed like she enjoyed shocking people, whether it was the black fingernail polish she wore, the safety pins in her ears, or the spiky hair on her head. I wasn't about to let some teenager get to me.

Now, though—alone in my house, knowing that she may have disappeared—the conversation sours in my memory. Was some man abusing her? Hurting her? Threatening her? Why would she hurl an insult about Mitch?

I wish he'd come home so I could talk to him about it.

I kill time hanging our wedding photos in the wood-paneled hallway outside our bedroom, lingering a moment on the sepia-toned beach wedding that was both only months ago and a lifetime ago. The twinkle in Mitch's eyes, like I was his entire world, our foreheads pressed together, my hair in the wind. It was the best day of my life, and sometimes that makes me unspeakably sad. Because I'm afraid it was and always will be.

I head into the bedroom to play my electric guitar, unplugged. Bowie is the best audience, watching with deep interest and howling when I sing a high note. I make a stew from last night's chicken, repeating the chorus to an imaginary song. But as the sun goes down and I sit to eat dinner alone, I can't deny it. The Big Empty is breathing down my neck.

It's bedtime by the time Mitch walks through the door and finds me in a dark house, doing dishes in the kitchen.

"For Pete's sake, what are we, vampires?" Mitch laughs. "What's with the lights being off?"

"I don't know," I say, staring down at the pot I've been scrubbing mindlessly for ten minutes now.

He gives me a juicy smooch on the cheek. "Reach in my pocket."

I narrow my eyes at him, deadpan.

"Not like that." He rolls his eyes. "I got you something."

I wipe my hands on my cutoff shorts and then reach into his front pocket. It's candy I used to buy in the market near my apartment back in LA. I smile.

"Awww, my weird cinnamon gummy bears," I say.

"They sell them at the gas station off the highway." He takes a hand to my cheek. "Hey. Something wrong?"

I point to the clock.

"What?" He waits for me to elaborate. "Did I do something?"

"Maybe next time you could call if you're going to be this late?"

"Kit." He massages my neck. "You know what kind of day I was having."

"It's almost ten o'clock."

"Sorry. It was bonkers—the Tsunami repair took almost the entire afternoon, and then Creighton showed up with blueprints and ideas and ... you know how it is when he comes around. I lost track of time. But hey, the important thing is—" He shakes the cinnamon gummy bears in the air.

"That is important. The *most* important thing, actually."

"Thank you for acknowledging my sacrifice."

"Any word on Gloria?"

"No one answered at the number we have for her." Mitch opens the fridge and studies its innards. "Creighton said it's not an emergency if we've heard nothing else about it. So I'm dropping it."

"Did she punch out yesterday?"

"No. But Creighton pointed out those kids forget to punch out half the time, anyway. That means nothing."

"She seemed upset when she was working this weekend. I had a weird conversation with her in the Ouch Shack when she was locking up her stuff."

"Yeah, she's kind of a loose cannon."

I wait a beat before deciding to tell him more. "She sure doesn't like you."

He widens his eyes. "That's news to me. Why?"

"Because you're her boss? I don't know." I point to a shelf in the fridge. "Stew's on the left."

"Groovy, thanks."

Mitch is a catch: golden-brown curls, sun-toasted skin, muscular, and hard not to stare at in his short shorts and crop top. But every time he says "groovy," I'm reminded that he's almost ten years older than me. That, and his musical taste— give me DEVO or Echo and the Bunnymen over Willie Nelson and the Moody Blues any day.

I sit with Mitch at our wooden dining room table while he

eats cold stew from a jar. I'll never understand how someone can care so little about food—cold, heated, bland, spicy. Mitch approaches food like someone who's swallowing a necessary pill.

"Pretty sure Freddie's in jail again," I tell him.

He stops eating and just swirls his spoon in the jar. "You're kidding."

"If only."

"What now?"

I shrug. "Not sure yet. Just heard a message from LA County on the answering machine. I'm sure he'll call back."

"I'm sure he will," he says unhappily.

In the silence, I can hear Bowie's tail thumping from the living room floor.

"Did you spend any time in your studio?" Mitch asks.

I shake my head.

"Why'd I go to all that trouble to fix that place up if you won't use it?"

"I'll use it," I say. "I played guitar today, just not out there."

"In LA, remember how badly you wanted a recording studio? Well, now you're living the dream!"

"I know. You're right." I swallow, not wanting to tell him that every time I go into that dark, soundproofed room, I feel like I'm suffocating. "I'll try tomorrow."

"Speaking of trying," he says, sipping the last of the stew from the jar.

My lips twitch with a smile. "Yes?"

He grins at me and raises his eyebrows. "I mean, full moon, right?"

Now I can't help but beam a grin right back at him. He's memorized my ovulation schedule. Which means he wants a baby, too, even if he doesn't show it all the time.

"Indeed, it is," I say, reaching under the table and squeezing his thigh.

He puts a hand on the back of my head and gently pulls my mouth to his. I lose myself for a little while in the kiss. The kiss is the opposite of the Big Empty. The kiss is warmth and safety. We go back to the bedroom together, and I forget the entire world for about twenty heart-racing minutes. Then I go to sleep and forget some more.

3

The next morning, I'm surprised that Mitch gets up with me when my alarm clock rings. Usually, he keeps sleeping, since my shift starts early and his starts mid-day.

"Thinking I might need to get a locksmith if we can't figure out a way to bust into my office," he says, getting dressed. "I'm heading in early today. Want a ride?"

I give him a playful smile. "Only if I get to play DJ. I'm not about to start my day with Bob Dylan."

"You drive a hard bargain, Kitty."

We drink coffee together and read the funnies and play footsie under the table like our best mornings back in LA. After a short walk with Bowie, Mitch and I hop into his truck to drive to work. I smile out the window. The forest that overwhelmed me yesterday is bright and full of wonder this morning, now that Mitch is beside me.

You could do so much better than him, Gloria's voice echoes in my ears.

My smile falters. She doesn't know how hard this man's

worked on himself. How much he's stepped up as a husband since we moved out here. It bothers me that a troubled teenager said such a thing to me, and I know exactly why: because there was a time in my life when I agreed with her.

The truth stings the most.

"I keep thinking about Gloria," I say. "You know what she said to me? She—"

"Babe. Don't worry about her," Mitch says, putting a hand on my knee. "Like Creighton says, you can't expect much from the yahoos willing to work at Breakneck Bay for minimum wage. We're lucky if they last a whole summer. Believe me."

He parks in the employee lot, above the back admin building of Breakneck Bay. At this hour, the park isn't open yet. It's eerily quiet—nothing but the soft churn of artificial water-falls and motors warming up. Food stands are empty; the rides are dark. But there are a handful of employees making the rounds in their Breakneck Bay shirts, picking up trash, heading to their stations to be the first ones in. I follow Mitch to the admin building.

Inside, there's an employee lounge: a bunch of mismatched sofas and teenagers smoking cigarettes and drinking coffee. Several of them look hungover, and I have to wonder if anyone spent the night in the Ouch Shack last night.

"Good morning, Mr. and Mrs. Blue," Rhonda says, waving smoke out of her face as she punches her timecard.

"It's the Bluebirds," Dwayne says, shaking a hang-ten sign at us from the couch, where he drinks a Tab. His acid-washed jeans are so tight they might as well be painted on, and he has something growing above his lip that I think is supposed to be a mustache. Mitch is Creighton's right-hand man, and Dwayne is Mitch's right-hand man-boy. "Captain Bluebeard. The Blues Brothers. Blue Oyster Cult."

Rhonda shakes her head and regards Dwayne with disgust. "You're stoned already, aren't you, Dwayne?"

"I can neither confirm nor deny," says Dwayne.

"Why are you sitting around, Dwayne?" Mitch asks. "On the phone, you said you were going to look for a screwdriver."

"I knew there was something I was supposed to be doing," Dwayne says, standing up and stretching.

"Wastoid," teases Valerie ... or Mallory? I always get the twins mixed up. They sit together at the large desk outside Creighton's office, which is dark. Creighton has the biggest office in the building, but it's usually the last place you'll find him.

I can tell Mitch hasn't had enough caffeine to deal with his pubescent employees, so he goes straight to the coffee pot and ignores them all. I go with him and am about to ask how I can help when the front door opens with a bang, and the human hurricane known as Billford comes in.

Billford's proper name is Bill Ford, but his strong Mississippi accent and lazy, slurred speech make him pronounce it like a single word: *Billford.* He's the largest man I've ever seen in my life—a lumberjack with a Neanderthal brow. He's got a booming laugh and a temper that flares up so frighteningly fast. I've seen him screaming at people before the toothless grin leaves his face. He's an eccentric, grumpy, middle-aged man with Einstein hair and a genius ability to build, jerry-rig, or fix everything and anything in the park—which is why he's been Creighton's Head of Maintenance since it opened.

"Heard you got yourself a dilly of a pickle there, Mitch, my boy," Billford says, coming over and smacking Mitch on the back.

"Might be time to call a locksmith."

"Now, why'd we do that? I *was* a locksmith. Dropped out of

high school to learn the trade—'course I ended up learning how to hotwire cars instead, but I digress."

Mitch sips his coffee and raises an eyebrow at Billford. "Can you pick a lock?"

"Pour me a cup of joe and let me work my meticulous magic," Billford says, cracking the knuckles on his sun-spotted, chapped hands.

Billford has a great vocabulary, but half the time I'm pretty sure he doesn't know what he's even saying.

"Hey, pretty lady," Billford murmurs to me.

I dislike it when anyone but Mitch calls me that, but I say a friendly *good morning* anyway.

Everyone gathers around as Billford works his "meticulous magic," which involves a safety pin, one of the twins' bobby pins, and a chewed wad of gum. We're all stifling giggles as we point silently at Billford's plumber crack. I wink at Mitch, who rolls his eyes as he drinks his black coffee. I'm telling him silently, *See? This job is fun!* Yes, it takes a lot to keep the teen employees in line. The rides in this park are janky and dangerous, and many Hill Valley citizens would love to see the place shut down. Creighton Marrs is part business tycoon, part mad scientist. But it's *fun*.

Then the door opens with a creak, and the giggling dies in the air—as if sucked out with a vacuum.

Inside Mitch's office, spattered over the light blue carpet, are gallons of blood. Actual blood. Puddles of it, crusted around the edges, darkening to a rusty brown.

The twins put their hands to their mouths.

Rhonda stiffens like a deer that sees a hunter.

The pause swells and suffocates the room.

A smell hits us all: metallic, musty, and sweet with rot. It's sickening.

Dwayne says uncertainly, "Is this a joke, dude?"

"What in tar*nation* happened here?" Billford says, turning to Mitch with an expression I've never seen on his weathered face.

I nearly dry heave. It's a horror movie, a crime scene—wads of flesh scattered, torn, bloodied clothes, and broken teeth catching the light. My knees buckle. I look away as fast as I can.

"Mitch?" I whisper, clutching his arm, whose face has turned white. "Is this real?"

HILL VALLEY POLICE DEPARTMENT
PRELIMINARY INCIDENT REPORT

Case No.: HVPD-82-640

Date of Report: 6/23/1982

Reporting Officer: Detective Gomez

Incident Type: Suspicious Circumstances / Possible Crime Scene

Location: Breakneck Bay Waterpark – Administrative Office

Date/Time of Incident: 6/23/1982

Reporting Party: Rhonda Wegman

SUMMARY OF INCIDENT:

On 6/23/82 at approximately 9:43 AM, officers were dispatched to Breakneck Bay Waterpark's administrative office following a report of possible criminal activity. Upon arrival, responding officers made contact with employee Rhonda Wegman who expressed concern about a suspicious discovery in Mitchell Blue's office.

Initial observations of the office revealed:

Bloodstains
    Teeth
    Ransacked office

Further investigation uncovered a ripped Breakneck Bay employee shirt with the initials GW on the tag beneath the desk. No forced entry was observed on the office door, and there were no immediate witnesses to any disturbance.

The scene was processed for evidence. A presumptive test for blood was conducted, results pending lab confirmation.

ACTION TAKEN:

Officers secured the scene for forensic examination.
Mitchell Blue was brought in for questioning.
Investigation remains ongoing.

4

Mitch and I sit alone in a colorless room in the Hill Valley Sheriff's Department, a building about the size of our house that they clearly haven't renovated in fifty years. The setting reeks of neglect: nicotine-stained walls, a low corkboard ceiling with a single light bulb hanging. On the table in front of us, some poor, interrogated soul scratched the word HELP. I trace it with my fingertip as Mitch mumbles to himself.

"I don't understand," he says, not for the first time.

It's hard for me to find the right response, because neither do I. I'm still trying to process what we saw earlier, trying to make sense of it, sickened by the red-splattered memory that won't fade. Were we looking at a crime scene? A prank? Everyone in the office seemed divided. Billford said it looked like a practical joke. The teens seemed shaken, as if they believed someone had been murdered. There was blood, but no body. I have no idea how seriously to take this, but either way, I'm shaken up.

All at once, it hits me that the last time I was interviewed by police, it was almost twenty years ago—and it was because of the murder-suicide that ended my parents' lives. No wonder I'm sweating so much.

I swallow the lump in my throat and force the thought from my mind. "Hopefully, the police will give us some answers."

He shakes his head. "I'm not saying a word to them until I talk to Creighton."

My brow wrinkles. "Why?"

"Because it's his park."

"But, your office."

"In his building. At his park." Mitch speaks out of the corner of his mouth, almost as if he's afraid of being watched by unseen eyes. "Someone spattered Creighton's office with red paint all over it at the end of last summer. Can't help but think this feels similar."

"You never told me that. Why?"

Mitch picks at a hangnail as if it's the most fascinating thing in the world.

"Mitch," I say, putting my hand on his.

"I don't know." Finally, he looks up, the lagoon color of his eyes quivering in the fluorescent light. "Because he's Hill Valley's boogeyman, I guess."

Just for a second, the intensity of his gaze is too much. The divide between us twinkles—how dedicated Mitch has been to Hill Valley, while I was living a separate life in LA. He's used to chaos. This isn't rattling him the way it is me. If this is par for the course in a Breakneck Bay summer, I'm understanding why he wasn't gung-ho about me joining staff.

I focus on a water stain shaped like South America on the wall. It's all too much. I need time to process.

"Kit, you don't—you don't think I actually had anything to do with that, do you?" he asks softly, squeezing my hand under the table.

"Of course not!"

"It's some kind of sick joke. It's going to blow over."

My stomach turns. It all feels like a bad dream, one I've had before.

I swallow. "And it has nothing to do with Gloria going missing, right?"

He doesn't blink. It's his thinking face—he stares right through me.

I can tell this thought is hitting him at the same time as me. The fact he isn't answering is only making me more uneasy.

"I don't think so," he says decidedly.

"Who else has keys?" I try, wanting to figure this out, wanting it to be over with. Wake us up from this nightmare.

"No one." He rakes a hand through his hair. "Mine are missing, spare's missing. Which is why Billford broke in this morning."

"They'll figure this out soon."

"Yeah," he says. "I'm thinking I should ask Creighton's advice before I say anything—"

We're interrupted by the door swinging open. A detective nods at us from the doorway. He's a short, stocky man in a cowboy hat, aviator glasses, and a bolo tie. He belongs in Texas, not California. Detective Plough is his name. He drove us here earlier in a long, awkward silence. "Mrs. Blue, time to skedaddle. Detective Gomez is about to interview your husband alone. I'll drive you home."

"Oh." I look at Mitch, whose mouth has hardened into a frown. "It's okay. I can wait outside the room."

"Gonna be a while," Plough says, holding the door open for me and waiting expectantly.

I exchange a look with Mitch, whose brow has furrowed.

"Am I under arrest?" Mitch asks. Though his tone is amiable, there's an edge to it. He has a distrust of the police, the law, rules, and the people who follow them. "Because if not, I'd like to head on my way. I've already told you, I know nothing about that mess in my office."

"You really want that, brother?" Plough asks him in a friendly tone. "Refuse to cooperate with local police right off the bat? Would look pretty bad for you. And things are already looking *pret-ty* bad for you as it is."

Mitch's face reddens. "I didn't do anything."

"If you didn't do anything, swell. Cooperate with Detective Gomez, and you'll get home in time for dinner." The officer nods at me. "Come on, Mrs. Blue."

I squeeze Mitch's hand and pick up my purse. "See you soon."

"Don't let them in our house, okay?" he says softly. "They need a warrant for that. Fourth Amendment."

I sling my purse on my shoulder. "Right, Fourth Amendment."

Mitch is an armchair constitutionalist. He's a man of many armchairs, really: a reader, a hiker, a traveler, a man who's worked an eclectic mix of jobs. It's one reason I fell in love with him. His interests are unpredictable and bountiful, and when he goes in, he's all in. Our house is filled with evidence of his many hobbies that have come and gone over the years: the handmade instruments, the figures he whittled, the stained-glass bunny pendant that hangs above our kitchen sink.

My gaze lingers on him. "I love you."

"This is a misunderstanding. We're going to figure it out."

I nod.

"Tick tock, tick tock," Plough says, tapping his boot on the floor.

I turn to follow him and glance back at Mitch one last time as the door closes. He looks so stunned and sad there at the table, a man-sized little boy. And I can't help the relief I feel as I walk away from him, alone with my thoughts for the first time since all that red.

5

I follow Plough into the late afternoon sunshine, where a smear of sunset is forming in the clouds. I slow my steps in the parking lot to appreciate it.

Plough stops in front of his unmarked vehicle and opens the passenger door for me. "Yep, check out that Hill Valley sunset. Not used to that back in Frisco, or wherever it was you came from."

"We're from Los Angeles."

"My condolences."

I climb into the passenger's seat, close the door, and focus my gaze out the window. I'm still stuck in a weird state of shock, not knowing how to feel or what any of this means. I get we need to figure out what happened in Mitch's office. It was beyond disturbing. But I also don't appreciate how the police have treated us since they arrived on the scene earlier. They swaggered into the Breakneck Bay admin building and threatened to shut the whole park down, then detained us in that room in their cruddy headquarters for what felt like hours. Meanwhile, whoever is responsible for that horror show back in the office is getting away. They could have crossed state lines by now. I'm understanding why Mitch distrusts the police.

"Smoke?" Plough asks after buckling in. He offers his open pack of Marlboros.

I shake my head. He puts one in his mouth and pulls out of the parking lot and onto Main Street, a long, Anywhere, USA strip with shops, restaurants, a drugstore, and a steepled church.

"How long you two been married?" he asks.

"Almost eight months."

"He a good guy?"

"Of course he is."

I stare out the window and cross my arms. He *is* a good guy. Aside from a bar fight or two, I've never seen him hurt anyone. Sure, he can be unpredictable—like the night he proposed to me after swearing off marriage for years. He's not perfect. But he's good. Through and through.

He lights his cigarette. "You know Gloria Wilson?"

I'm surprised by the question. "Not well. But yes."

"You were the one who found her clothing in the locker, am I right?"

"Yes." I give him the side-eye. "Why? Did something happen to Gloria?"

"Do you think it did?"

As he turns onto the highway that leads home, the tunnel of trees swallows us in shadows. I'm dizzy from his questions, and that familiar dread squeezes me from all angles—the dread of soon getting home and being alone.

"Listen, I have no idea what's going on," I tell him. "I just started working at Breakneck Bay a couple of weeks ago."

"Funny how the girls who go missing around the cesspool are always young and pretty, don't you think?"

I turn to him. "Cesspool?"

He blows a smoke ring. "What me and the boys call the park you work at."

"Nobody's gone missing before, as far as I know?"

"As far as you know."

I'm so aggravated, I imagine telling him to pull over and I'll just walk home from here.

"Was that ... Gloria?" I ask, feeling a little sick as I ask it. Somehow, I hadn't put it all together in my mind yet—or maybe I just didn't want to. They asked me about her, and I showed them where her belongings were in the Ouch Shack, but that was it. "If there wasn't a body in Mitch's office, how do you know?"

"There wasn't a body, but there were teeth and there was blood." He leans in, lowering his voice. "And a torn-up uniform shirt. Women's size small. Initials GW in the tag. Ain't that something?"

The information is smothering. Also, why is he telling me this? It's as if he thinks I know something about it, as if I'm not being taken home, but am still sitting in that interrogation room. Mitch would tell me not to open my mouth, not to say anything. So I don't.

The forest thickens, and the Big Empty presses in from all sides. I tune the detective out like the static that keeps blurting through his radio. When he pulls up to my house, I almost thank him, but then stop myself. They're holding my husband at the station right now. This detective has been nothing but suspicious and rude ever since he got me alone. I climb out of the car without a word and hurry toward the house.

Bowie isn't barking a greeting—he just wags his tail and pants joyfully when he sees me, which is unusual. Inside the house, I hang up my purse and kick off my shoes. I test a trembling hand in the air and exhale a long breath. Everything is so still, I can see the dust sparkling in the twilight air.

"Hey, Bow," I say, sitting next to him on the couch.

I pet him, and emotion rockets through me. The stress of that car ride and the wait at the station, the confusing questioning, the pandemonium at the park, the gore, and Gloria. That it could be her—that someone could have hurt or even killed a girl in my husband's office—it's sickening. Why would anyone do such a horrid thing? Why would they do it *there*, of all places? I'm spiraling and overwhelmed with that ancient, hopeless panic I've carried since childhood. Like the sky is falling, and there's no one I can trust and nowhere I can land my feet. Tiny Kit is sobbing. And then, before I know it, Not-So-Tiny Kit joins her.

Bowie licks my face as I cry into my hands, letting all the pressure go. Just let it all out. All the feelings that are too big to name, all the answers I don't have but so desperately want.

"He's going to be okay," I say aloud, feeling better just hearing my voice. "We're going to be okay. Not every day is a good day. Not every—"

I stop, holding my breath, suddenly aware of a mechanical humming sound I hadn't noticed before. A whirring that tickles my eardrums. It's the sound of water in the pipes of the house, coursing through the walls like blood pumping through arteries.

My hand goes still on Bowie's head. Why is the water on?

A chill infects me—little spider feet trotting on my neck.

I stand up and listen. Yes, it's definitely there: a faucet. Coming from the back of the house. Our bathroom sink? I step into the hall, and the sound mounts, louder, splashier.

Someone is in the shower.

I press my fingers to my lips and stand, frozen in the hall, staring at those sepia wedding pictures I just hung. Mitch's wide grin, his hair blowing. *Help me, Mitch!* I yell internally. But he can't.

There's something worse than being alone. This.

Who on earth is in my shower?

With a jolt, I consider running. Getting in my car and burning rubber to get the hell out of here. But I remain in place. This is my house. And what kind of a murderer breaks in and uses the shower?

Carefully, I remove the framed picture and keep it poised above my head, ready to strike. Mitch has a hunting rifle somewhere, but I don't even know how to operate it. I swallow and tiptoe into my bedroom, past the made bed and the alarm clock with digital red numbers. Hearing the water lapping makes me wonder if Mitch got out and made it home before me—but that's physically impossible. Or maybe one of us left the shower running? It was a hectic morning, who knows.

But then the sound of a man's cough echoes in the shower.

Deep, wet. Not Mitch's.

Holy crap. Someone's definitely in there.

I step closer. The picture trembles in my hands, and I lose my nerve. Then, a hairy hand reaches out, grasping to pull back the shower curtain.

I do not know to whom it belongs.

With a gasp, I drop the frame, glass shattering on the tiles.

And I sprint out of the room, screaming.

6

"Kit!" a voice yells as I dash into the living room.

I stop, hand to heart as I stand frozen, listening.

"Kit, Jesus *Christ*. You could have killed me!"

That voice—I know it immediately. Wrinkling my brow, I call out, "Freddie?"

I wait a moment as relief settles in, followed by disbelief. Sure enough, Freddie comes walking out of the hallway with one of my pink towels wrapped around his waist. He's gaunt, with long, dripping hair and a dewy goatee. His dark eyes flash.

"What the fuck?" he yells at me angrily.

"Are you serious? Fuck you!"

"Fuck *me*? You could have hurt me."

"What are you doing in my house?"

"What does it look like I'm doing?" he asks, gesturing toward the towel.

"How did you get my address?"

"You sent me a birthday card, genius."

"And so you ... what? Just let yourself in?"

"You didn't answer when I called. You left your door unlocked."

I'm still catching my breath. "I thought you were in jail. There was a message—"

"They let me out. It was a mix-up."

It's always a mix-up with Freddie, always some mistake or temporary setback, as if he hasn't accepted his fate yet. The rest of us accepted Freddie's fate a long time ago. Mitch calls him a delinquent who can't even spell the word.

But he's still my brother.

"Freddie," I say, my voice cracking. "Don't do stuff like this."

"What, I can't use your shower?"

I blow out a sigh and take a few steps to where he stands in the hallway.

"I can't see my baby sister now?" he asks sadly. "Is that why you haven't been answering when I call? Does Big Man Mitch not allow visitors out here?"

"Hello, I've been busy. I have a job."

He chews his cheek, looking just as hurt and lost as he did when he was a boy. I put my arms around him. He's wet. And too thin. And I will always think the skull tattoo on his chest was a poor choice in a series of many poor choices. Even so, I soak up the hug like I always do, because with Freddie, I'm never sure if it will be our last.

I pull back, my shoulders and cheeks wet. "You picked a hell of a day to show up."

"Have you been crying?" he asks, examining my face.

I'm suddenly so relieved he's here. Emotion wells up in me. I want to tell him everything. "Go get dressed, and I'll explain. You're dripping all over the hardwood floor."

I can tell Freddie doesn't want to go until I've explained my tears—he can't stand the sight of them—but he nods and does as I ask.

Same as it ever was.

———

I sit Freddie at the kitchen table and fix him a turkey sandwich. He wolfs it down like he hasn't eaten in days, which is a good sign. When he's been using, he rarely eats. I take a seat across from him and tell him about everything that happened today: the horrible crime scene, the police station, the weird ride home with the cowboy detective.

The thing I love about Freddie is that he's a hard man to shock. He's lived a life colorful enough to fill a memoir, and he's only thirty-three. He's hitchhiked across the country to see Black Sabbath. He played bass in a band in front of a thousand people and was an extra in a few movies, and he's had his ass kicked by gang members when he wandered into the wrong neighborhood. He's had an affair with a married suburbanite, been strung out on Skid Row, and robbed a convenience store. This is nothing.

He licks mayo from his fingers. "Did he lawyer up?"

"No," I say, folding my hands on the table. "Should he?"

Freddie shrugs. "Did he hurt someone?"

"Of course not!"

"You know that for sure?"

My voice sharpens. "He's my husband."

Freddie raises a single eyebrow. To someone else, it would be nothing, but the sight of it gets under my skin. I know every twitch of Freddie's expressions. I'm fluent in Freddie.

Growing up, we were inseparable. My aunt referred to us as one name, almost, mashing us together into a phrase that sounded like "Fraidy Cat."

FreddieKit! Clean up this mess!

FreddieKit! Answer the phone!

FreddieKit! One of y'all microwave some TV dinners!

Aunt Heidi was neither kind nor unkind, a six-foot-tall woman with a permanent frown on her face and a beer in hand. She didn't love us much, but she gave us a house to live in and she didn't yell or hit. I'm pretty sure she provided for us out of some warped guilt and obligation, since her brother, our father, was the reason we were orphans.

One summer, when Freddie and I were at sleepaway camp, my dad killed my mother and then himself. That sad story has loomed large over us, the glue that sticks us together, the sculptor that molded our personalities. The Tragedy, as we refer to it (which we don't often), is probably responsible for my neurosis and Freddie's delinquency.

So, my patience with Freddie runs deep. Life dealt him a hand of unplayable cards from the get-go. But Mitch and Freddie have crossed paths as drifters over the years, working a few jobs together before I ever met Mitch. Freddie even worked at Breakneck Bay a few years ago and got fired for stealing cash out of the Bahama Burger till—according to Mitch. Freddie never owned up to it. When we moved out here, Mitch made us rent a one-bedroom cabin specifically so there was no spare bedroom for Freddie to sleep in.

"He's going to be so pissed when he gets home and sees you here," I say, picking up Freddie's crumb-scattered plate and bringing it to the sink.

"I'm trembling with fear," Freddie says sarcastically.

"Do you want something to drink?" I open the fridge.

"Got any beer?"

I give him a long, knowing look. "We don't have alcohol in this house. I have water and Coke."

"Dr. Pepper?"

"No." I lean against the counter. "You know you can't stay here, right?"

Freddie's goofy, crooked-toothed grin melts. "Why?"

"This is a one-bedroom cabin."

"What about the couch?"

"Mitch will not be cool with that."

"Your husband's detained right now, and you're worried about what the fuck he thinks? Come on."

"He's not *detained*. He didn't do anything."

"Yeah, yeah. 'Course he didn't. Neither did I." Freddie winks at me and I debate poking him in the eye. Then, he straightens his posture. "Uh—speaking of which. If anyone reaches out to you from LAPD, I'm not here."

I stare at him, waiting for him to elaborate, but he doesn't. And I don't like the way he's suddenly avoiding eye contact. "What?"

The phone rings. I put a finger in the air and answer it.

"Hello?" I ask quietly, turning to the wood-paneled wall.

Silence.

"Mitch, is that you?" I try.

There's a faint sound on the other end, like someone's there.

"Hello?" I say.

I'm met with a static silence. Someone's breathing heavily, and it gives me the creeps.

"Hello?" I ask.

"Tell him it's time to tell the truth," the person says. "If he doesn't, it's going to get even uglier."

I can't tell if this is a man or a woman, young or old. They sound more like a monster in a movie than a person.

"Who is this?" I demand.

"Tell him, Medford, 1970. He'll know what I'm talking about."

Then a click. A dial tone.

My skin goosebumps.

Who *was* that? What did that mean?

I place the phone back in its cradle. The windows above the sink are pitch-black with night. Then, suddenly, they light up. I hear the crunch of tires on pine needles outside and the familiar rumble of Mitch's truck engine.

"Stay in here," I order Freddie.

I jog outside to meet Mitch in the dark, relief washing over me. A faint wind whispers in the trees, along with the thrumming creek water and croaking frogs. I run to Mitch, who looks exhausted, throwing my arms around him and not wanting to let go.

"What happened?" I ask. "What is going *on*?"

"I don't know. I'm so confused."

I pull back to look at him and place a hand on his face. "But they let you go."

"Yeah, I mean ... they got nothing because I *did* nothing. They kept running me around in circles, asking the same questions."

The red-spattered scene flashes once in my mind, like I flipped the lights on for a single second before flipping them right off again.

"What about Gloria?" I ask. "I don't understand. Is this all related?"

"How am I supposed to know?" He has a faraway look in his eyes. "It's like I'm being framed for something and I cannot, for the life of me, figure out why."

"Mitch, I just got the weirdest call."

He squints at the front window, where a shadow passes. "Is someone here?"

"Freddie's inside."

His face slackens with dread. "You're kidding me."

I grimace an apology.

Mitch looks up at the stars and sighs.

"I'm sorry," I say. "He just showed up."

"He's not staying here."

"Where's he supposed to stay?"

"There's no *room*."

"He seems clean."

"I thought he was in county jail? How'd he ... no, Kit, we're not doing this. Not tonight."

"He can stay in the studio, just for a night," I say quietly. "He won't come into the house."

"You really trust him out there with your musical equipment?"

I let that one slide. My brother's done a lot of nasty shit to people over the years, but rarely to me. "Please."

"Dang it, Kit," is all he says.

We head inside, the door banging shut behind us.

"Hey, Big Man," Freddie says to Mitch from the couch. He cheerses an invisible glass. Bowie's head is in his lap.

Mitch makes a beeline for our room, not even answering.

"Freddie," I say, my hands on my hips.

"What?"

I shake my head, not even knowing where to start.

"I'll get you a sleeping bag and a pillow," I say softly, heading to the linen closet. "You can crash in my studio tonight, but stay away from Mitch. He's stressed." I grab the bedding. "Come on."

I lead Freddie outside, walking around Mitch's truck to the standalone studio that used to be a shed. It's a red-painted building with a door and no windows that is so soundproofed inside, it resembles a padded room. There's an electric guitar hanging on the wall, a keyboard, some mics and cables, and a card table with my eight-track cassette recorder. The manufactured smell of new carpet and glue reveals just how little I've used this place. Mitch fixed this place up for me, turning it into a recording space. I haven't had the heart to tell him when I spend time in here, it's so quiet I can hear my blood in my ears. It reminds me of being buried alive.

"Look at this shit," Freddie says with a whistle. "This is perfect, actually. Anyone who comes knocking on your front door looking for me, they're not going to think I'm out here."

"Who would come looking for you?"

He ignores my question, gently strumming the strings of my electric guitar hanging on the wall. "Have you been playing much?"

I tuck his sleeping bag and pillow in the corner. "Not really. I've written one song since we moved out here."

He sits on the keyboard bench. "You wanna show it to me, or what?"

I can't help but smile. My brother has always been my biggest fan.

"Come on, if you're gonna cast me out of the house, might as well give me a little entertainment first," he says.

Secretly, I'm delighted he wants to hear me play. But I'm tired, and I want to get back to Mitch.

"Are you in trouble or something?" I ask. "Freddie, be honest with me."

"I'm always in trouble. Nothing I can't handle." He reaches out and tousles my hair. "Seems like *Mitch* is the one in trouble. Worry about him, not me."

I sigh. "You can stay here tonight. But don't touch my stuff, okay?"

He rolls his eyes and unfurls the sleeping bag.

"Do you need to use the bathroom before I hit the hay?" I ask.

"I'll piss in the woods. Hey, is there anywhere nearby where I can get some beer?"

"No. I'm serious, I will kick you out if you drink around

Mitch." I open the door. "I'll wake you in the morning. I'm up at seven for work."

"Seven?" he nearly screams.

"Yes. And you'll be getting up early to help. Our yard needs cleaning up, and you can walk the dog as long as you're staying here."

"Give me a—"

I shut the door behind me and head into the house. Bowie follows me as I make my way to the bedroom, turning off lights along the way. I kick my shoes off and Mitch pops in from the bathroom doorway with a blank look on his face, holding our broken wedding picture up in the air.

"What happened?" he asks.

"Oh ..." I press fingers to my mouth, not even sure where to start. "It was an accident. Freddie scared the hell out of me, and I dropped it. I'm sorry."

"It's okay. I'll find another frame." Mitch grabs his toothbrush and squirts toothpaste on it. "Funny, though, how things get ruined right when Freddie comes around again."

I watch him brushing his teeth in the mirror. Suddenly, I get a sickening image in my head of those teeth scattered along the carpet of his office this morning.

"Why are you staring at me like that?" Mitch asks me in the mirror.

"Nothing," I say. "Just exhausted."

I turn into our room, dress for bed quickly, and slip beneath the covers. Mitch gets in beside me and switches the lamp off. We cuddle, and finally, my pulse slows down and settles.

It isn't until Mitch is snoring that I remember the phone call—the rasping monster voice. I inhale sharply, holding Mitch tighter.

It's going to get even uglier.

7

The next morning, everyone is called in early for an "emergency FUBAR meeting" at Breakneck Bay. FUBAR is one of Creighton Marrs' favorite acronyms: Fucked Up Beyond All Recognition.

Dozens of employees, from food stand vendors to ride operators, cram into the admin building. It feels less like a work meeting and more like a pep rally. Teens sprawl cross-legged on the floor with sunglasses on, drinking neon sodas, smoking cigarettes, and Dwayne's boombox is blasting Prince. Creighton Marrs stands on top of a desk in the middle of the chaos, screaming into his megaphone. Ten years ago, you'd look at a picture of Creighton and Mitch and swear they were the same guy—shaggy-haired and bearded as Cat Stevens. But while Mitch is still handsome as ever, Creighton hasn't aged well. He's sweaty, balding, and dressed like he ran straight here from a tennis game at the country club.

"All right, people, grab a seat and shut the fuck up," he yells.

Rhonda rips Dwayne's boombox cord out of the electrical socket, and "Dirty Mind" stops mid-track. The room is humming with conversation, everyone pointing and talking about the fact that Mitch's office remains cordoned off with yellow police tape. I scan the room, hoping to glimpse Gloria, but I don't see her. I run my tongue over my teeth and wince, thinking about the smell that hit when we all opened Mitch's office. Thinking about the bruise on her face. So much violence and confusion; I'm not sure how it's connected—or if it is at all.

"What happened yesterday was unacceptable," barks Creighton.

A hush fills the room.

"I want to know who decided it was best to call the wiener patrol down at the sheriff's department before calling me. Because whoever it was, you owe me the ten grand I lost having to shut the whole goddamn park down yesterday. Who was it? 'Fess up. Now."

There are some whistles and tittering as everyone glances nervously around the room.

"It was I, sir," speaks up Rhonda, raising her hand. "Though, in my defense, I tried to call you first."

"Judas!" Creighton yells, half-jokingly, pointing a finger at her.

Rhonda doesn't blink. She's used to being yelled at by Creighton. It's probably written in her job description.

"But seriously," Creighton says, more soberly to the room. "Next time—though I hope to hell there *is* no next time—n*ever* call the police unless you talk to me first. Understand?"

A punk with a mohawk raises his hand. "What if, like, someone gets hurt?"

"Send them to the Ouch Shack," Creighton says. "Next."

"No, but like, *really* hurt," the punk says. "Like that Bronson chick."

An uncomfortable hush spreads throughout the room. No one likes to talk about Pamela Bronson, the employee who fell off Scream River and impaled her skull on a rock. In an unfortunate it's-a-small-world coincidence, she was a classmate of Dwayne's. The poor girl died after three weeks on life support last summer. Creighton Marrs' solution? To put up signs that say *All rides ridden at your own risk!* and to have everyone sign waivers when they buy tickets. He's still fighting a civil suit with the Bronson family.

Creighton's eyes narrow at the punk, and he goes still, as if everyone in the room ceased to exist except for the two of them. "What's your name?"

The punk slouches under the attention. "Charles, sir."

"Charles, which station?"

"Uh, Jungle Swing?"

Creighton snaps. "Not anymore. You're working The Riptide now."

Laughter sputters out of different corners of the room, along with a few ominous *oooh*s. Everyone knows The Riptide is the worst station to work in the park. It's a whirlpool with a current so strong that patrons are constantly being rescued from it. I've treated quite a few bumps and bruises from people who got so disoriented that they hurled into the concrete edges. The punk is muttering something to himself in anger, clearly mad that he spoke up.

"Anyone else?" Creighton asks the room, with a grin exposing his gold crowns. "No? Good. Listen. We're here for one thing and one thing only: to give people the time of their fucking lives. Professionals designed and built every ride here."

A silent fact check: Mitch has reported that almost all the rides here were designed on stray papers, receipt backs, or cocktail napkins by Creighton himself in a manic moment of inspiration and later built by Billford.

"Every ride is safety-tested," Creighton says.

Another fact check: They send dummies into the rides first.

Next, they send the newest teen employees in by promising them a hundred-dollar bill. Mitch describes this as a "paid hazing ritual."

"And we've never—not once—had anyone die here in the park."

I guess Pamela Bronson dying in the hospital weeks later from an injury she sustained here doesn't count in his mind.

"This is a safe place," Creighton says, voice softening to a soothing baritone, the mood seeming to settle as he says it. "And just to clear up any bullshit you might hear, Gloria Wilson left work on her own accord three days ago. Yes, she left her items in the locker. No, she didn't punch out. *That's* true. But one of our employees spotted her the next day, using the payphone by the highway."

Relief floods through me. That means the mess in Mitch's office wasn't Gloria. It was probably a sick joke. I hear a few sighs and *ohhh*s, as if I'm not alone.

"Get that through your heads," Creighton says. "An irresponsible teen skipping town and being a no-show at work has got nothing to do with yesterday's clusterfuck. And this guy?" Creighton points to Mitch, who stands next to the desk with his arms crossed. "He had nothing to do with whatever the fuck happened to his office. Here's my take: Someone is trying to sabotage Breakneck Bay. Someone's not after him; they're after *me*. They couldn't get my fuckin' keys, so they did the next best thing and trashed his office to send me a message. Maybe even someone sitting in this room right now." He lets his eyes drift from person to person, as if sizing everyone up one by one. "There are a lot of locals who want to see this place destroyed. I have a suspect in mind I'm trying to get local PD to look at right now." He narrows his eyes at the room. "Call it a hunch."

A suspect? I perk up. I don't doubt Creighton's theory. He's collected a lot of enemies over the years. Even my brother would love to drag him through the mud—years ago, Creighton was the one who accused Freddie of stealing from the cash register and firing him.

"But if I find out that someone on the inside has something to do with this?" Creighton stops and pans the room with a ferociously blank expression. "I'll ruin your life before it's even started. You won't be able to get hired to flip burgers south of the Oregon border when I'm through with you."

The room is still for a moment, a thick discomfort pervading the air as everyone exchanges wide-eyed looks.

"Now," Creighton says with a grin, his tone rising like a coach about to rally his team. "We're going to clean up this mess. We're going to put the bullshit behind us. And we're going to get back to the reason we're all here: to give our guests the time of their fucking lives, am I right? Meeting adjourned, and everyone get the hell out of here."

He switches the megaphone off and climbs off the desk. The employees stand, stretching, conversations breaking out everywhere. Laughter mixes with the sound of the coffee grinder, and soon Dwayne's boombox goes back on and Prince picks right back up where he left off. As the crowd disperses and pours out the front doors, I cross to the corner near the timecards and punch in. About ten feet away, Mitch is already ripping the police tape from his doorway. I sidestep to him and glance over his shoulder at his office, afraid of what I'm going to see in there.

"What a mess, right?" Mitch mutters.

I nod. Cops pushed the furniture against the wall, the desk on its side. They ripped the carpeting out and took it away for forensic testing, exposing the ugly concrete flooring. The many newspaper clippings and framed pictures that Mitch hung are askew, and some appear to be missing altogether—nothing but rectangles of dust.

"You know what? I'm glad," Mitch says, as if he's convincing himself. "Great. Take it all. Treat it as evidence. Test the blood and figure it all out. Because whatever happened in here, I had nothing to do with it."

"I know," I say, putting my hand on his arm.

His face is beet-red. He's humiliated. I don't see him shaken often, and when I do, he usually gets in his truck and disappears for a while to "blow off steam" and go hiking or fishing. Obviously, that's not an option today.

He sighs. "This just looks so bad."

"What was it that Creighton said about Gloria being spotted?"

"Dwayne saw her when he was driving home yesterday. Swore it was her."

This sighting loses a touch of credibility in my mind. Dwayne claimed he saw Bigfoot once, too. But I don't let on. I can see how people are looking at Mitch—like they're not sure about whether they can trust him. I feel so bad for him, stuck in the middle of all this.

"He said there was a suspect," I ask. "Who is it?"

"Oh, just one of Creighton's hunches. I'll tell you about it later. I don't want to fuel gossip. I just want to focus on work."

"Was the—was the blood we saw real? I don't understand."

"Kitty, I don't understand it either. But I promise I'll tell you if I do."

"Well, I'm sure they'll figure it out soon." I give him a smooch. "Gotta go. Duty calls."

"See you later," Mitch says to me, then speaks into his walkie-talkie. "I'm going to need a cleanup crew at HQ here, stat ..."

I head outside, grateful for the warm kiss of sunshine on my bare arms and the breeze that tickles my neck. For the peace of the park before opening, when I can still hear the birds chirping over the churn of mechanical rapids. Life is good. Hill Valley is heavenly. We're lucky to be here. This is all a mix-up, a hard week, but we can move on now. My legs burn as I start up the winding staircase to the Ouch Shack. A winding staircase for the injured—classic Breakneck Bay.

"Excuse me, Mrs. Blue?" a shrill, breathless voice calls from behind me. "Wait up!"

I stop and glance down the staircase, where Rhonda is running up toward me. Spotless sneakers, a high ponytail bobbing back and forth, clipboard in hand.

"Hi Rhonda," I say. "How are you?"

"Well," she says as she joins me mid-staircase, panting. "To be honest with you, not so well. I hardly slept last night. Insomnia. Maybe indigestion. Or hypochondria."

I don't think Rhonda knows that "how are you" doesn't need to be answered this literally.

"Sorry to hear that," I say, offering her a sympathetic smile. "What can I help you with?"

"Perhaps we could talk a little more privately?" she asks, in a hushed tone, as if the pine trees might be eavesdropping.

"Of course." I turn and continue up the stairs, hearing her footsteps behind me. My chest tightens, and I hope this has nothing to do with Gloria or Mitch's office or any of the other stress that has plagued me since yesterday. I'm sick of the negative energy and ready to put it behind me.

"Mrs. Blue, I have a new form that will become part of your daily protocol," Rhonda says when we're inside the Ouch Shack. She unclips papers that smell like fresh copier ink. "You're going to have to log names and personal information for injuries now."

I fight the urge to roll my eyes at the irony. Of course, it's not Rhonda's fault; she's just the one giving orders. But still.

"You mean like I was trying to do the other day, and then you told me to rip them up? Like that?"

"Exactly like that." She leans in. "After yesterday, I suggested it to Mr. Marrs. For legal reasons. It's quite probable inspectors will visit the park again soon, and they're going to want written reports this time."

"We're having another inspection?" I ask.

"Well, whenever any trouble here happens, an inspection will follow. Trust me, Mrs. Blue. This is my third summer working here."

People Creighton bribes usually run these so-called "inspections." Creighton surrounds himself with cronies, planting them everywhere he can.

I take the papers from her and nod.

"Also, um." Rhonda purses her lips. "There's something I'd like to ask you … privately. Woman to woman."

She can't look me in the eye as she says it and my first thought is, *My God, am I going to explain the birds and the bees to her right now?* But it's worse than that. Much worse.

"It's about Mr. Blue," she says quietly, "and Gloria."

My mouth goes dry. "What do you mean?"

"They seemed very … chummy." She straightens her posture. "But you're probably aware of this already, right?"

"Chummy," I repeat, the word itself seeming strange. A pulse jolts through me, as if someone has pushed me into an electric fence. *Not this!* Tiny Kit wails. I swallow a painful lump. "I'm not sure what you mean."

Rhonda takes a deep breath in and blows it out, her bangs ruffling in the air. "I was afraid of this. I went over and over it in my mind last night, in bed." The way she looks past me as she speaks—it almost feels like she's talking to herself. "I thought, of course, I would not go to the police, because that would be a betrayal of Mr. Marrs. But what about my duty as a woman? For instance, if I were married to Mitch, would I want to know?"

"Spit it out, Rhonda," I say, unable to keep my pitch from rising.

"Mitch and Gloria had been coming here after the park closed," she says to me. "Late-night ... chats. I saw them come up here together the night Gloria disappeared."

"Here?" I ask incredulously, pointing to the concrete floor.

"Indeed. In the Ouch Shack."

I'm trying to remain calm, but I'm dying inside. The pity on Rhonda's face ... this is so humiliating.

"Thank you for telling me," I say, trying to sound friendly, but aware there's an icy grip to my voice. "I'm sure Mitch had a good reason."

"Of course he did," Rhonda says. "I simply thought you should know. No harm in sharing factual information."

The silence is excruciating. She backs toward the door.

"Why don't you focus on your job, and I'll focus on mine?" I ask with a smile.

"Yes, Mrs. Blue," she says, and gives a nod before ducking out the door.

I wait until her footsteps fall out of earshot, and then I put my head in my hands and keep them there long enough to pretend the entire world disappears.

8

"Rhonda said *what*?" Mitch sits on his side of the bed in his tighty whiteys, facing the open window. Crickets chirp, and the fresh night wind tickles the air.

"That you and Gloria were—direct quote—'chummy.'"

"*Chummy?*"

The word *chummy* has echoed in my brain so many times today that the word now sounds absurd. *Chummy*.

"You tell me." I try to say it brightly, but it comes out sharper than I intended.

"I'm Gloria's supervisor." He turns to me. "What does that even mean?"

Mitch's confusion looks painful on his face. It's been a crap couple of days. We still don't know how seriously to take the scene at his office, whether to treat it like a dark prank or a serious crime. I'm also not in the mood to dive into making him feel better after what Rhonda told me earlier. Mitch has been on his best behavior; he's been amazing since I moved out here, but a tiny part of me is holding back, afraid. The years he's lived here before I arrived—they're a mystery to me.

"I try to do the right things, and somehow, it's never enough." He balls his fist and relaxes it again. "She comes to me for advice, and I try to help her out, and then ... then she disappears into thin air." He gives me a hurt look. "And apparently now my wife thinks I'm cheating."

"All I did was ask you." I speak softly, evenly, not wanting to get too emotional. "You never mentioned these conversations when we were talking about Gloria. Don't you think that's weird?"

"Why would I mention it? I have conversations with every person on staff."

"Private, 'chummy' chats." It comes out more bitter than I mean it.

"You know me, Kit. You know how I am. Some kid's in trouble—no questions asked, I'm there for them. I was a camp counselor, a youth group leader. Why do you think Creighton hired me for this job when he wanted to open the park? He knew I'd be good at managing teens. Heck, if I could sit still long enough to make it through college, I'd have been a teacher."

I nod because nothing he says is untrue. Mitch is easygoing and kind. There's something playful about him; it comes naturally. "Right."

"Gloria wanted to talk to me after work. We talked one, two times. That's it."

"What did you talk about?" I try to sound curious and not suspicious.

"She was interested in traveling, road trips." He holds his hands up. "Swear on my mother's life."

"You talked about road trips." I swallow. "Okay. Why did you talk about road trips?"

"She was a messed-up kid. I got the feeling she wanted start a new life or something. She told me she had been in foster homes and then a group home that kicked her out. I tried to offer advice, but she was all over the place. I'm not surprised she upped and disappeared."

"Well, why didn't you tell me about this when we first talked about Gloria going missing?"

His tone sharpens. "Don't know if you've noticed, Kitty, but I've had a lot on my mind."

"Yeah, I know you have, and I'm sorry," I murmur. "But this is bothering me."

He shakes his head as if this conversation saddens him.

I'm cross-legged on the bed, studying him, trying to make sense of him. Admiring his profile, the shape of his chin, his Adam's apple. That thoughtful look in his eye. There's a depth to him that makes me want to keep digging, always, and that's what keeps me so intrigued. I'd like to pour everything out of my heart right now—the burning ball of fear and jealousy and mistrust—but Mitch isn't in a place to hear it. This familiar dynamic is playing out between us, where the more I push, the more he pulls away. The dynamic has a momentum of its own. Once it starts, it spins out of control. And when he springs to his feet and starts pulling his jeans and shirt back on, I already know what's coming next.

"I've got to blow off some steam."

My stomach sinks. "Mitch, come on—"

But by the time I've scrambled to my feet, he's already slipping on his windbreaker and knitted cap. I follow him out to the living room, and desperation flutters inside of me like a bird trapped in a house.

"Don't do this, you said you wouldn't do this," I beg, but he won't meet my eyes. He grabs his keys and wallet from the mantel next to the door. "Don't throw it all away—"

"I'm not throwing anything away." He stops, closes his eyes for a meditative second. "I just need some space."

He opens the door, and I follow him outside. I don't want to follow him, but I can't help myself. I don't enjoy being this person, so scared of being alone. Then my chest tightens, and I'm watching him get in his truck. The headlights come on. The motor rumbles.

"Please don't drink!" I yell. "Stay here, we can get through this—"

The truck peels out with a roar of rubber meeting asphalt, and he drives into the night. The engine purrs quieter, quieter, quieter, until it blends into the hum of a nearby stream and then I can't hear it at all.

I look up. The trees, towering silhouettes against a black sky screaming with stars. People say it's quiet out here. It's anything but—it's the constant twitch of creatures in the brush and hooting owls, and the chittering buzz of insects. It's the swish of busy wind through creaky branches and pinecones dropping, and I try to be positive, I try to be grateful, but sometimes I can't stand it out here.

"It wasn't supposed to be like this," I tell the night.

A creak comes, a flickering sound in the brush. The hairs on my neck stand on end as I listen for creatures.

"Everything okay?" a voice says behind me, and I startle, adrenaline rushing for a single second before it registers that it's my brother. Freddie's cigarette glows orange in his hand. He steps out from the dark porch of the studio. I had, honestly, completely forgotten he was here. My mind has been a skipping record of worry all day long.

I turn around, blowing a steady breath out. "Do *not* sneak up on me. I'm on edge enough out here as it is."

"You two fighting?"

I shrug. "He took off."

"I thought things were better."

"They *are* better. This is just—it's been a terrible couple of days for him."

"And you, too, right?"

I nod. "And me, too." I scrounge my mind for optimism, some speck of sweetness to savor. "He hasn't had a drink in a long time. He's gotten a lot better."

"Good."

"He hasn't taken off like this since—I can't even remember when."

"Little Mitchie's growing up."

"Shut up, Freddie," I say sharply. "Don't you dare criticize him. He's trying his best."

"Well, then why's my little sister out here in the woods, all upset?"

I heave a sigh and shake my head at him. Freddie is so annoying: a troublemaker who can't pull himself together, yet still sits on a high horse and criticizes everyone around him.

"Is he two-timing you?" Freddie asks.

"Not your business. And no." I glance at the house, where a single window is gold and lit up and the rest is black. I have no idea when Mitch will come home. It could be hours; could be days. He has tomorrow off and I pray he doesn't slip. Maybe he's going to a meeting. He's finding a meeting somewhere.

"Sorry, sis, it's hard for me to trust the guy after all I've seen him do."

"What have you seen him do?" I snap.

Freddie opens his mouth, probably to tell me about one-night-stands and drunken nights years ago, when Freddie and Mitch worked together as roadies or farmhands or whatever it was the two of them did on their rambling adventures before I came along. Maybe even to tell me about wild nights back at Breakneck Bay the one summer Freddie worked there—but I don't want to hear it.

"Since I married him," I clarify. "What have you seen Mitch do that's so terrible? Why can't you just trust him?"

"Listen, I've got radar for deadbeats." He smiles to himself, throwing his cigarette on the ground and smooshing it with his shoe. "Takes one to know one."

"He's changed. Matured. You should try it sometime."

"I've tried it, believe me. But eventually, I accepted what I am."

"And what's that?"

His eyes glimmer in the dark. "An outlaw."

I roll my eyes. My brother talks big, and I know he's done some awful things—but to me, he'll never be anyone but the kid who acted tough all day long only to cry for his dead parents in the middle of the night.

"Sure," I mutter. "Okay. Jesse Fuckin' James over here." I blow out a sigh, suddenly exhausted. "I'm going inside."

"Want some company?" Freddie asks, in a softer voice.

He knows me so well. He probably recognizes the dread in my eyes as I look at my house and imagine a night alone.

I nod.

"Let's listen to some records," he says, following me through my front door and into the warmth.

An invisible fist that has been squeezing my heart relaxes. Sitting here next to Freddie and blasting the Wipers, nodding while he lays out his grand plan to refurbish motor homes. It's all pipe dreams with Freddie; it's always some shiny new thing, but just having him here is a distraction, and I'm grateful. I can't help but mirror his goofy grin with one of my own. And all at once, a gust of wistfulness—I want this version of Freddie all the time. Not the boastful "outlaw," or the mess, or the addict. The sweet guy who enjoys listening to records and hanging out with his little sister.

"Ever wonder where we'd be if ... " I stop a moment,

contemplating how to phrase it. "… if we had never gone to live with Aunt Heidi?"

"No," he says so quickly that I know it's a lie.

"Come on. Really?" I study him, his dark eyebrows just like our dad's. His wily hair, just like our mom's. "You think if none of that had ever happened—if Dad had gotten help or something—you'd still be the same?"

"Some people are beyond help. Dad was one of them." A shadow passes over his face. "No point in talking about what can't be undone, you know?"

I swallow and nod, trying to push the thought out of my head—the one where I try to picture the crime scene we were never there to witness. My parents dead in their bed together. I used to want to know details someday, but as I got older, I decided I didn't. I'd rather not know how it happened, or what weapon he used. All I know is this: Our father was a wonderful man ninety-five percent of the time. The other five percent, he was an unrecognizable monster.

"*I ams what I ams*," Freddie says in a Popeye voice.

The serious moment is over. He starts a tickle fight that almost ends in me peeing my leggings with laughter. My bracelet gets caught in his hair as I try to push him away, and then we have to walk together to the kitchen, conjoined twins, so I can get a knife and cut the bracelet out. We're doubled over in laughter as I saw through his knotted brunette locks.

"Geez, ever heard of a hairbrush?" I ask him.

"Har dee har dar."

My smile melts as I see his neck—a constellation of scabby scratches that looks like someone dug their fingernails into his skin. The knife makes it through, and his hair breaks free from my bracelet, but I'm still stunned.

"God, what *is* all that?" I ask.

He reaches up to feel his neck, and then his eyes go wide as he seems to remember.

"Long story," he says, laughing nervously. "Got into a fight."

"With who? A cheetah?"

His expression darkens, and his tone sharpens. "A crazy chick, that's who."

My jaw drops. "Jesus, Freddie."

The moment expands. The record ended, and now we're steeped in silence.

"I should get to bed," he says, clapping me on the back. "Night, sis."

He heads back out to the studio. What the hell was that? What "crazy chick" did my brother get in a fight with, and why is he acting so weird about it? On second thought, I don't even want to know. As I'm left in the house listening to Bowie's toenails clicking on the hardwood floors and the refrigerator whining in the kitchen, the dread comes back.

I lie awake in bed and watch the moon's slow crawl across my windowpane.

I keep the lights on for Mitch, even though I have the sinking feeling he won't come home tonight.

9

I wake up to an empty bed, flick the curtain, and glimpse an empty driveway. Empty heart to match.

Quiet throbs in my ears.

Springing out of bed, I tromp down the hall in my slippers to make some noise, fill the air. I'm overjoyed to see Bowie and stoop to give him a hug. I brew coffee and hum a cheerful song, trying to push the horrid, hypothetical images from my mind: Mitch dead, his truck wrecked. Mitch in the drunk tank. Mitch snoring in another woman's bed. When I remember Freddie's out there in the studio, I'm relieved. Maybe if I have his company, I'll be able to hold back the flood burning behind my eyes, just waiting for the dam to break.

Outside, it smells like fresh soil and sap. The birds singsong invisibly in the trees, and the sun warms the top of my head. *Please be a good day,* Tiny Kit says in her wee voice. I knock on the studio door with a mug of steaming coffee in my hand.

"Morning!" I say as I open the door.

Thick weed smoke escapes, hitting me with such intensity that I cough. I can barely see the room inside.

"Really, Freddie?" I ask, annoyed.

I wave my hand in front of my face. The skunky fog lifts, and there's Freddie, still in his sleeping bag on the floor with a fat, lit joint in his hand and wearing a Cheech and Chong expression.

"Put that out right now, or I'm going to scream," I tell him.

"C'mon." He shows off his gap-toothed grin. "Have a hit; it'll do you some good."

"I'm dead serious."

He snickers, dropping the joint in an old soda with a *hiss* sound.

"Why do you have to be like this?" I ask, handing him the coffee, no longer feeling generous. I plop down beside him on the end of his sleeping bag. "You're thirty-three years old."

"Age is just a number, man."

"If Mitch comes back and sees you smoking dope, he'll have a fit."

"So Mitch never came back, then."

Freddie says it with a resigned disappointment, like he knew it all along. Infuriating.

"Who are you to judge?" I ask. "You're sleeping in my music studio, stoned before eight o'clock in the morning."

"I'm not judging. I just ... it's a bummer seeing him stress you out like this."

Siblings hold entire worlds. I peer at his face and remember him as a child, remember myself, my mother, and father. Sometimes, gazing at Freddie is gazing into my personal funhouse mirror.

"I'm not stressed," I assure him, sitting up straighter. "It's fine. Mitch needs space sometimes."

"He storms off like a fucking baby."

I swallow the bitterness, take a deep breath, and say, as kindly as I can, "As soon as you find a job, sober up, and get an actual life, you can call other people 'fucking babies.' Until then, can it."

"How about you take me with you to Breakneck Bay? Help me get my old job back?"

I can't tell if he's kidding or not at first. Then I see his lips twitching, trying not to laugh.

I roll my eyes. "Remember? They banned you from the park when they fired your dumbass years ago."

"Oh, I've been back." He grins. "You think that greedy fuck Creighton Marrs can tell me what to do?"

"When?" I ask. "When have you been back?"

A cryptic look is all I get from him.

"Stay away from the park," I say, standing up. "Don't embarrass me, or I will make sure they kick you out."

"I'm just joshing. I'm not about to get up and follow you."

I turn toward the door.

"But—you haven't told anyone I'm here, right?" he asks.

My hand hovers on the doorknob.

"Because I'm kinda trying to lay low right now, if you know what I mean," he continues.

Lay low. A queasy jolt hits me as three things come to mind at once. One, that answering machine message from the LA County Jail. Two, those disturbing scratches on his neck and the accompanying comment about a "crazy chick" he got in a fight with. And three: now this. Is Freddie visiting me—or is he hiding from something?

Mitch was right. I never should have let my brother stay with us.

"Freddie," I say finally. "Figure your shit out."

I slam the door behind me as I leave.

———

There's a brick that won't budge off my chest. I drive to Breakneck Bay for my shift, fix my face into a smile. The park's not open yet. I scan every waterslide, pool, and rocky artificial river within eyesight for Mitch, each palm tree and shuttered snack bar. I do double-takes at every employee I pass in cutoff shorts and a neon shirt. Yes, it's his day off, but Mitch comes in here on his days off all the time. The man's a borderline workaholic.

I spot Dwayne flirting with a side-ponytailed girl working at the Cool Cone soft-serve stand outside the admin building, leaning over the countertop like he thinks he's some kind of Casanova. Dwayne's so fixated on the girl he doesn't see me. I'm sure of it, because I hear him saying, "What if I'm working for the next Ted Bundy?"

My gut crumples as if someone kicked it. I freeze, processing what I'm hearing. It's so ugly. So wrong. Dwayne must know it's wrong because when he turns and notices me standing here, his face goes from a goofy grin to slack self-consciousness.

He swallows. "Uh ... hey Kit. How's it hangin'?"

Not knowing how to respond to what I overheard, still in shock, I automatically switch to my default friendly smile. I give him a cheerful wave and pretend I didn't hear a thing. Def Leppard blasts from stereo speakers somewhere.

"Hey Dwayne, how are you?" I ask.

He straightens his posture. "Uh ... radical."

"Seen Mitch this morning?"

Dwayne cocks his head and nervously laughs. "Isn't he, like ... off today?"

"Oh—yeah." I wave a hand in the air. "He went out to run some errands and said he might stop by."

Even with mirrored sunglasses on, Dwayne's face conveys his disappointment with the news that his boss might show up today. "Haven't seen him, but, uh ... I'd better get going." He turns to the girl. "See you on the flip side, Stacey."

"Later, Dwayne," she says with a smile that shows off her retainer.

Gossip, I decide, as he hurries away. Just teenage gossip. Everyone's on edge and speculating. Nothing more. Watch, it's all going to blow over soon. Probably some ugly prank, like the time someone put soap bubbles in Whitewater Falls or red dye in the Tsunami pool.

The admin building is unusually quiet. The lounge is empty. Mallory and Valerie sit behind their desks, busy with paperwork. When I pop my head into Mitch's office, the door ajar, I see why.

Creighton Marrs is sitting at Mitch's desk, brows furrowed. He wears a fixed expression of sinister contemplation and a Yankees cap, his fat-fingered hands tented in front of his face.

"Know who was here today?" he booms.

Creighton is a man who does not believe in greetings, who has a volume knob permanently turned too high. He has energy that ratchets up your blood pressure just by being in the same room. Like right now.

"No. Who?" I ask from the doorway.

He curls a finger to summon me, and I step inside to come closer.

"The FB-fucking-I," he tells me.

"What? Were they here? Why?"

"Fuck do I know? They said they wanted to talk to your husband."

My stomach turns.

"After that, some putz from the Hill Valley Sheriff's Office came trying to take our employee files. I said, get a fuckin' warrant or get the hell out of here."

I grimace, not knowing what reaction he wants from me.

"Do me a favor. Close the door, sweetheart," he says, quieter, gentler. "I want to chitchat, just you and me."

Slowly, I close Mitch's office door with a click. Dread grips me as I turn around and approach the desk again. Creighton's intense stare and molasses-slow smile make me feel like a deer ready to sprint into the woods. I've known him peripherally for years—even went to his wedding, stayed in his guest house—but I've never been able to relax around him.

"How's Mitch?" he asks.

"He's ..." I make a shrugging gesture because that's about all I know. I can't help but glance at the floor, where the carpet is gone. The blood that was there—it's dizzying to think about. "What is even going on? Was someone actually hurt here, or was it a joke?"

"My opinion? Neither. Just some jackass trying to send me a message."

"Send you a message?" I ask incredulously. "In Mitch's office?"

"My office was fuckin' locked, and Rhonda and I are the only ones with the keys. Think about it. Mitch has the employee files in here, and there was a message in blood written on the wall above it." Creighton swivels on the chair and points to the wall, which someone has since scrubbed. "It said 'KILLER.'"

My heart skips an ugly beat.

"Killer," Creighton repeats. "Above the *employee* files. Who do you think they're talking about?"

I open my mouth, but don't know what to say. I didn't see the writing on the wall—literally—when we discovered the blood. I wasn't exactly in a place where I wanted to scrutinize the scene.

"Pamela Bronson's family has been crawling up my ass for

nearly a year now. They tried criminal charges. That didn't work. Now they're cooking up a civil suit. Her brother showed up at my house a month ago, and I had to call the police. Mitch tell you that? Fuckin' hippie hopped up on pills." Creighton grins, almost proudly. "This ain't my first rodeo. I know there are many people in this town who'd love to see this place shuttered. Not just this town. I've got enemies all over the fuckin' place."

I nod. "Right."

Relief blooms inside me. What Creighton's saying makes sense. He's probably the most hated man in town. Someone was trying to send a message to him via Mitch.

"But now the FBI's here asking questions. And that—" Creighton stabs a finger in the air. "—*that* I don't like."

My head is swimming. I can feel a hum just below the surface—a whisper that something's not right.

"Mitch wouldn't like it either," Creighton says, raising his thin eyebrows. "Because when shit gets pinned on me? He knows where the bodies are buried."

I swallow. What the hell is he talking about?

"I've got to get rid of all this," he mutters, as if to himself. He turns, chair squeaking, and contemplates the file cabinet. "The fuckin' paper trails so they get nothing, absolutely nothing."

"You're going to toss the files?" I ask, with a tinge of disbelief.

"Well, not me. That wouldn't look good. I'll let Rhonda do it."

Poor Rhonda. A seventeen-year-old girl being responsible for—what is this, anyway? Burying evidence? Doesn't seem right.

I wonder what's in those files.

Is there something in them that made someone trash this

office? That made them write *killer* on the wall? Why doesn't Creighton want anyone to see them?

God, I want to look in those files right now.

"I'll get rid of them for you," I say.

I say it before I even think it. My mouth moves before my brain does.

But if no one else is going to dig into those paper trails, I will.

"Hey, that'd be great. What a swell broad you are." Sarcasm? Sincerity? Who knows? Creighton blinks his lashless eyes at me. "Rhonda's great and all, but she's got an unfortunate infatuation with ethics. You and Mitch are the only people around here I trust."

Translation: The only people around here dodgy enough for Creighton's taste. I let the backhanded insult pass.

He stands and beckons me to a corner to retrieve a box of file folders from the cabinet. He picks it up and shoves it into my hands. I startle at how heavy it is. A woozy feeling bleeds over me as I glance down and notice the file that sits on top.

WILSON, GLORIA.

Two feelings fork within me: I can't believe I'm doing this, and I can't wait to look in that file.

"One thing, though ..." I swallow, faltering a little, edging on losing my nerve. "Are we absolutely sure that nothing happened in here? That no one was hurt? Because if there's a chance that something happened to Gloria—or anyone—it doesn't look good to throw this stuff away."

"What the fuck do I care about looking good? If I cared about looking good, I'd get a toupee and wear snakeskin boots."

Kit, what on earth are you getting yourself into?

I should put the files down and walk away. I don't understand what is going on here, but it's fishy. And I'm volunteering to become a part of it.

"Creighton," I try, using my soothing voice I reserve for the screamers and the criers in the Ouch Shack. "What if something actually happened to her?"

"Nothing happened to her, Christ Almighty!" he says with a scowl. "She's a little bimbo who took off one night, come on."

It's such an awful thing to say; I don't know how to respond.

"This isn't just going to cover *my* ass, Kit." He tilts his head and narrows his eyes in something resembling pity. "It's for Mitch as much as it is for me. Don't you want this shit to go away?"

I nod. He's right. I do. Whatever happened, it wasn't Mitch's fault, but it's unraveling him.

"Should I dump them now?" I ask. "Or after my shift—"

"Don't worry about your shift. Rhonda'll work your shift. This is your assignment." He smacks my back once, and it stuns like a slap across the face. "You're a great gal, Kit. I've always told Mitch." He laughs too loudly. "You're the only woman who can tame him."

I press my tongue to the roof of my mouth so I don't say something I might regret. "Thanks."

Creighton keeps his hand on my back. His touch makes me squirm. I shuffle forward, away from him. But he moves right alongside me, his hand there the whole time. "Do me a favor, go tell Rhonda she's working Ouch Shack today."

"Okay," I say as he opens the door.

He pushes me out into the lobby and points a finger at me. "I'm counting on you."

I nod. He shuts the door, and I hear the click of a lock. Stunned, as bewildered as someone hit by a one-minute tornado, I turn to the lobby. Across the chocolate carpets in the circular room, I spot Rhonda's ponytail bobbing in her corner of Creighton's office. Back and forth, back and forth, just like the roller in the typewriter she's *clack-clack-clack*ing away at.

Still in a daze, I glide across the carpet. I stop at Creighton's doorway and make a dramatic throat-clearing noise, jolting Rhonda's attention from her typing.

"Sorry to interrupt," I say. "Just spoke with Creighton and he gave me ... an urgent assignment. He wanted me to tell you that you're on Ouch Shack today."

Rhonda blinks, her eyes buggy behind her lenses. "Pardon?"

"You need to fill in for me today."

With a sigh, Rhonda accepts the news. She has a quick look up at the ceiling, as if God might be there somewhere in the popcorn asbestos to help her. Then she turns her moon-round face my way, her eyes grave.

"Safe to assume this is an order coming directly from Mr. Marrs?" she asks, with a slight frown.

"Safe to assume," I agree, my arms aching with the weight of the box.

"Let me walk you out, Mrs. Blue." She stands up and brushes off her plaid skirt, which reminds me of something a Catholic schoolgirl would wear. "Where are you headed?"

It's a good question. I meet Rhonda's eyes and notice they're a color I've never quite seen before—light green with gold.

"My car," I say. "But I'm fine, really—"

"I insist." She grabs a fanny pack hanging from her chair, slings it around her waist, and clicks its belt. She clips her walkie-talkie onto it. Then, with a nod, she says, "Ready."

I wish Rhonda weren't walking with me. I'm uncomfortable enough as it is, and apparently carrying what could be evidence. As we step onto the path alongside Rapid Danger, Scream River, and nearing the underwater Ferris wheel, the blaring sunshine gradually darkens. The trees thicken. We head toward the park perimeter, greeted by the sound of running water and the stink of chlorine.

"I wanted to say I'm sorry, Mrs. Blue," Rhonda says somberly.

"Kit," I tell her. "Just call me Kit."

"I didn't mean to interfere or overstep. My mother raised me to follow the Golden Rule. But, being the peculiar person I am, sometimes living by that advice gets me in a bit of trouble."

We walk the long staircase up the hill to the staff parking lot. The smell of garbage mounts as we approach, because staff parking is also where the Dumpsters are. I ignore that and breathe through my mouth, admiring the scratchy shapes of pine trees, like someone divine painted them with an invisible paintbrush.

"Another thing—you probably don't know this about me, Mrs. Blue—I'm a journalist. I've been editor-in-chief of the *Hill Valley High Beacon* now for two years. So I can be nosy and I don't mean to be. It's just how I'm wired. Did you know I won an award because my undercover story last year helped nail the local graffiti artist targeting a Baptist church—"

"Rhonda," I say, unable to help my annoyance, hurrying up the stairs faster as if I can outrun her. "I'm busy right now. What is it you need?"

"Sorry is all I'm trying to say," she says, slightly out of breath. We stop at the top of the staircase, taking in the park's view. From here, the pools shimmer like spills of jewels. The slides and tunnels are neon snakes. "About what I brought up yesterday. About—"

Silence spreads between us. Rhonda seems suddenly hypnotized as she stares down at the box in my arms. And with a zing like a toaster in a bathtub, I suddenly realize what she's seeing as soon as she says the words out loud.

"Gloria Wilson," she whispers.

We both look down at the file folder. Guilt writhes inside me as Rhonda's gaze slowly pans to me—confused, accusing.

"This is nothing," I say, my eyes widening. "Creighton—"

"You know, Mrs. Blue," Rhonda says, backing away with her hands up. "Honestly, I'd rather not know." She purses her lips. "I'll cover the Ouch Shack."

"Please do."

Rhonda lingers a moment, her hand on the railing at the top of the stairs. "I hope everything's fine," she says decisively, as if her saying it makes it so.

"Me too," I say.

Rhonda nods once and heads down the stairs with a skip in her step that reminds me she's still more child than woman. I look down at the all-caps file name, GLORIA WILSON, and back up at the trees, as if they hold answers. I'm positive they do—it's a shame I don't speak their language. Their branches roll with the wind, an emerald, upside-down sea. Guilt spreads throughout me. And I heave the box into my trunk, stunned, wondering what on earth possessed me to make myself a part of this mess.

But I know the answer. It's simple: curiosity.

I look around the lot. I'm alone up here, just me and parked cars. Quickly, I pick up Gloria's folder with shaking hands, ruffle through the pages numbly—tax forms, job application— but nothing stands out to me. I put it back and close the trunk with a thump that jolts me from the inside-out.

I need to know what Creighton is hiding about the girl my husband was apparently so *chummy* with.

Hill Valley Gazette
June 1982
Letter to the Editor

The Death of Hill Valley's Charm

By Martha Ellsworth

I was born in Hill Valley and have lived here my entire life. It used to be a peaceful town where summer meant children playing by the creek and neighbors gathering on their porches. Now, all I hear is screaming — not of joy, but of thrill-seekers hurling themselves down the water slides at Breakneck Bay Waterpark.

Since it opened, our quiet community has been overrun. Traffic clogs our streets, trash lines the riverbanks, and worst of all, ambulances race to the park every other day. We all know the stories — broken bones, near-drownings, reckless stunts encouraged by careless management. And that's not all. Just ask the Bronson family, who lost their daughter Pamela last summer under suspicious circumstances while the park continues to claim no fault. Creighton Marrs, how do you sleep at night?

Hill Valley was never meant to be a tourist trap. But thanks to Breakneck Bay, our town's charm is vanishing fast. How much more noise, chaos, and injuries are we willing to accept before we say enough?

10

As always, the drive home from Breakneck Bay is pretty as a postcard, but I want to puke.

I crank Heart's "Magic Man." My heartbeat thunders along with the song as my hands choke the steering wheel. Sunshine and shade speckle the forest. I drive slower than usual, my eyes peeled for some sign of Mitch. Maybe he's on this same road and I'll pass him, or he's pulled over on a shoulder, or, God forbid, he crashed his truck. The Big Empty is riding shotgun with me, so I'm relieved to see other human beings when I pull into downtown Hill Valley and cruise up and down Main, eyes peeled for the burnt orange of his truck.

Finally, I park in front of Al's, the only dive bar in town, my stomach a lump. I head inside and ask the lumberjack-looking bartender with bags under his eyes if he's seen Mitch, showing him the photo in my wallet of our wedding day.

"Nah, don't know him." The lumberjack glances at my shirt and sputters a bitter laugh. "Work at Break-Your-Neck Bay, huh?"

I look down. "Yeah."

He shakes his head, like I'm a real shame. "That place ain't safe. I'd never let my daughter go there, not after what happened to Pammy Bronson."

I thank him for absolutely nothing and continue on.

It's my first time doing these rounds in Hill Valley, but I remember the routine. I learned it in L.A., on the worst weekends of my life. I check the hospital for any ER visits from Mitchell Blue. The hospital is right next door to the police station, where I consider popping in just in case he's in the drunk tank, but I hesitate in front of the building. There's a foul taste in my mouth as I remember our interrogation there the other day—do the police see me as a concerned wife, or the wife of a suspect?

I hurry back to the car, get in the driver's seat, and put my head on the wheel to collect myself. I'm drowning in open air.

This déjà vu is killing me. It's like every time Mitch has left me over the years since we started seeing each other, all coming back—not as a string of memories, but a nameless, overwhelming feeling for our on-again, off-again relationship. The way he was before he quit drinking: his moodiness, his restlessness, his bursts of irritability that came from nowhere. He broke up with me numerous times before coming back, sorry. And then he finally quit drinking. He was ready to settle down and asked me to marry him. It was what I'd been holding out for—the man I knew was in there, the best version of himself. Things have been so promising since we got married. And now this. Now we're back to this.

I make one last stop: the town park at the end of Main. A playground, a tennis court, and a basketball court are near the creekside. There are ash trees huddled around the expansive lawn. I survey the benches for any sign of him, but no. He's not there. Just a mother pushing her little baby in a swing, the sight of which yanks at one of my heartstrings.

I glance in the rearview and imagine a baby back there, giggling in a car seat. The thought seems impossible.

Maybe it's better this way.

The imaginary baby vanishes, and then all I notice is that box of files I said I'd get rid of. Since I can't find Mitch, I might as well deal with that.

I park in a nearby lot, open the trunk, and stare at the box. My hand gravitates to the top folder: WILSON, GLORIA. I flip through it. But to my disappointment, there's hardly anything there: a blurry driver's license photocopy, a bare-bones application. She has a *fuck you* expression her face and looks like she could be a singer of a punk rock band. Her phone number ends in 5309 and I get that stupid "867-5309" song stuck in my head. Ugh.

I flip through the other files, which are in alphabetical order. AARONS, CHAD. ATKINSON, JOHN. BRONSON, PAMELA.

I freeze, index finger lingering on the name.

Pammy Bronson.

With the flick of my wrist, I pull the file and lay it on top of Gloria Wilson's. I flip a page and see a Xeroxed photo of Pamela's driver's license. She's soft and pretty. Wavy hair, parted in the middle.

And now she's dead.

Mitch's handwriting is there underneath it. *Date of hire: June 11, 1981. Station: Scream River.* And his bubbly *MB* signature. When I check Gloria's file, it's a different date of hire—*April 30, 1982*—but it's Mitch's handwriting and signature again.

I know he's got nothing to do with it, but I don't like my husband's proximity to dead and missing girls. But after checking the other files, I see his signature is on every single one of them. Apparently, being park manager means he's the final say in hiring.

Still.

MB, MB, MB. The files all blur together, all signed by Mitch. But one file stops me cold: FULLER, FREDERICK.

My brother.

I had totally forgotten he worked here.

I flip the file folder open. Freddie's eyes are so wide in his driver's license he resembles a madman. His hair is frizzy, and his grin is so wide you can see his missing molar. If I didn't know him, I'd steer clear of that guy. Mitch's handwriting is on this one, too, recording the hire date 5/31/79 and *Station: Scream River.*

My brow wrinkles. Scream River? I didn't know Freddie worked rides. I thought he was fired from stealing from the Bahama Burger?

His paperwork gets a special red stamp that says DO NOT ADMIT, along with *86'ed, 6/22/79* in Mitch's handwriting. Freddie couldn't even last a month without screwing up so badly that the park banned him. I wish I could say I was surprised.

I'm not seeing anything exciting. I shove the files into the box and drop it in the Dumpster. *You're welcome, Creighton.*

When I finally pull up to our driveway, I spot the familiar burnt orange of Mitch's truck and immediately breathe a sigh of relief. "Well, look who's back."

I jump out of the car and jog inside, keys jingling in my hand. I push the front door open and, immediately, there's Mitch, looking a mess—hair wild and curly, bloodshot eyes, scruffy-faced—but he's here. On the bed beside him is our wedding photo, newly framed in beautiful wood. He fixed it.

I go straight to him, plop next to him, and put my arms around him. My heart sinks at the smell of him: whiskey, sweat, and pine trees. He takes a moment, but he circles his arms around me, and then I feel the shudder of him sobbing into my shoulder.

I've never seen Mitch cry.

I've seen him punch a wall, I've heard him yell, but I have never seen him break down like this.

It's so startling I don't know how to respond at first.

"I didn't do it," he says wetly. "I didn't do it. I didn't do it. I didn't—"

"I know. I didn't think you did." I hug him closer and say into his ear, "It's okay, baby. It's okay."

This moment scares me more than anything else that has happened so far. More than the bloody scene, more than the suspicion that has passed over us like a storm, more than the file folders with the names of a missing girl and a dead one.

Because this version of Mitch?

I don't recognize him.

11

I'm in the Ouch Shack on Saturday afternoon, mopping up a puddle on the floor, when the door swings open and Detective Plough stares back at me from the doorway.

Forceps on my chest. Just the sight of his uniform makes me want to run away like a jackrabbit in the woods.

"Me-dick," he says in announcement.

I'm frozen, my hand still on the mop.

"Says 'Me-Dick' out there on the sign," he clarifies.

"I'm aware."

"Mind if I come in? Just got a few things on my mind."

He doesn't wait for my answer, just saunters in. His badge hangs from his belt, his gut protrudes over his blue jeans, and he's wearing a ten-gallon hat like some doofus you'd see at a rodeo. This place suddenly feels the size of a closet now that he's strutting around in it. He gazes at a corner we call the Goon Gallery, where Polaroids of parkgoers who've been kicked out are tacked to the wall. He stops and flips absentmindedly through the First Aid equipment, pulling the top off a jar of cotton balls. He smells the iodine spray and puts it back.

I push the mop and bucket to the corner of the room, crossing my arms. I don't like how he doesn't take his sunglasses off inside. And I really don't like the way he's eyeing me right now and tapping the badge on his belt. My pulse is fast as a hummingbird's.

"What can I help you with?" I ask as kindly as I can through my teeth. "Does Creighton Marrs know you're here?"

"Well, it might surprise you, but I don't give a shit about Creighton Marrs. You might think he runs this town. I know better."

I put my hands on my hips and recite the line Mitch drilled into me earlier this week. It's my first time getting to use it because, until today, we have had no one from the police contact us since the interview that first day. "Mitch and I aren't talking to anyone without consulting our lawyer."

"I'm not here about Mitch," Plough says. "What makes you think I'd be here about Mitch?"

I feel so cornered. I stare behind him at the door, hoping some injured person will burst in and interrupt us.

"I'm here about Gloria Wilson," he says, then points at me. "Unless—" He looks behind himself, then back at me, with mock surprise. "Why, do you think there's some connection there?"

I shrug. "I thought figuring this stuff out was your job."

He knocks on the lockers. "Heard you were the one who found her things in here, is that right?"

"Yes."

"Wallet, purse, jacket."

"The police took it. You all have it."

"How well do you know Gloria?"

"Not well. I barely ever spoke to her."

"Know where I might find her home address?"

I wrinkle my forehead. "Don't you have it?"

"If I had it, would I be asking you for it?"

"Why would I have it if you don't?"

I try to be patient with human beings, to believe they're mostly good, but this guy's a grade-A asshole. The boy who probably stole kids' lunch money in grade school and grew up to join the force so he could become a professional bully. I wish I could wipe that sneer off his face.

"Thought the waterpark would," he says. "We don't have her phone number. Have nothing on her except a name and people who work here saying she stopped showing up to work."

My head is swimming. What he says seems impossible. This is so confusing—is he lying to entrap me? "I thought she was reported missing?"

"No one filed an official report. We got an anonymous tip called in, the same day somebody called here and reported she never came home from work." He pops his neon gum. "But now there's no record of Gloria Wilson ever even having *worked* here."

Sweat threatens to break out all over me. Does he somehow know I got rid of the files? Am I about to get arrested for something I did for my boss? I can't find the words to respond, so I just shake my head.

"Did your husband spend much time with this mysterious, disappearing girl?" he asks.

The question feels like a dig. All I can imagine is Gloria and Mitch in this room late at night, murmuring to each other—and I stop there. The thought writhes.

"You'd have to ask his lawyer."

"Lawyered up already, huh? That was fast."

Plough takes his sunglasses off for the express purpose of eyeing me for a long, awkward moment. His gaze is sharp blue and strangely kind, out of place with the rest of him. My walkie-talkie chirps suddenly with banter.

"Dead possum near the bumper boats, over."

"Roger."

Plough snickers and shakes his head. "This fuckin' place." He heads toward the door. "Sure I'll be seeing you again soon, Ms. Blue."

"Mmm," I say, because he doesn't deserve a full word.

The door slams after him. I listen to his footsteps clomp down the steps, slow and steady. Then all I hear is happy squealing, rushing water, and the Go-Go's singing "We Got the Beat" out of a loudspeaker. It's summer out there, but in here? It's dark and dank, a sweltering dungeon perched on a hill.

I chew a fingernail. Gloria was never officially reported missing.

Maybe Dwayne was right; she just left. It was all a coincidence that it happened at the same time as the scene in Mitch's office. Somehow, none of this makes me feel better. Because all I can think is that now, thanks to me, there is no paper trail leading police to Gloria. Which is exactly what Creighton wanted.

I open the locker that used to hold her things. Empty. No trace of her.

All at once, I have the most terrible thought—the times I've opened up here in the mornings and cleaned up garbage that I assumed was kids partying. Cigarette butts. Beer cans. Condom wrappers. Did I clean those up the morning after I last saw her, after she had a "chummy" chat with Mitch?

I dry-heave at the thought.

My shaking hand slams the locker shut.

12

Ever since someone trashed Mitch's office and the Gloria mystery began nearly a week ago, it doesn't matter how sunny the weather is. A secret, dark cloud cloaks Breakneck Bay.

I can't tell if it's me—if it's my cloud—or if the air really has changed. Mitch wears a permanent, serious expression now, like he's perpetually lost in thought. The teenagers who usually joke with him are dead serious when he's around, as if they're afraid of saying the wrong thing. Dwayne suddenly started calling him "sir" out of nowhere. Creighton stomps around yelling about how great Mitch is, what a standup guy he is, and all it does is make Mitch seem more suspect.

The stress might give me an ulcer. Every time I look out my window at the gorgeous curtain of greenery, all I think is how badly I miss my loud apartment in Los Angeles.

"I'm thinking about quitting," I tell Mitch as we lie in bed tonight.

It's Saturday night. We ate pizza. We had make-up sex. It's not silent, exactly, because I can hear the crickets chirping and the wind whipping the trees through the open window. I can also hear Freddie wailing on my electric guitar out in the studio. Apparently, soundproofing the walls doesn't matter if you crank the amp that loud. I hope it didn't annoy Mitch. The only way we let Freddie stay here so long is by him staying completely out of Mitch's hair. I don't want to rock the boat. Luckily, he seems too exhausted by work to care about Freddie.

Mitch lies on his back, shirtless, staring at the ceiling. "Hey, that's an idea."

Even though he's just agreeing with me, I can't help the twinge of disappointment. I guess I had hoped he'd beg me to stay. That, despite the stress, he enjoyed working together.

He blows out a long breath and waits a beat before adding, "You're too good for that place."

I squint, trying to read his blank face. "How so?"

"I don't know. Is it really your scene? Like you keep bringing up the whole thing with Creighton, how paranoid it made you to throw some old files away. He plays by his own rules, it's how he is."

"I thought it would be nice to work together, considering that you're there almost twenty-four hours a day," I say. "And Creighton offered me a job. But I'm getting the feeling you don't want me there."

"Well, do you understand?" Concern quivers in his eyes. "I didn't think working in this kind of chaos makes you happy. And yeah, Creighton's got some shady practices."

I'm not even sure how to respond. "If it's so shady and stressful, why are *you* still there?"

"Creighton's like a cousin to me. I've known him since before we had hair on our chests."

"So shared history means you'll defend anything that goes on there? What happened to Pamela Bronson is A-OK with you?"

Mitch turns to me, his lips a line. "Why are you talking about her?"

My mouth hovers open. Honestly, I'm not sure. Since I snuck a look at her file, the name has been rattling around in my brain. I haven't told Mitch that I looked through the files—he thinks I tossed them all, no questions asked—and it's weighing heavy on me. It's the first secret I've ever kept from him. And I don't even know why I'm keeping it. I'm listening to my instincts, even if I don't understand them.

Maybe a tiny part of me doesn't trust him. Which is crazy. He's my husband.

"Why are you talking about her?" he repeats, louder, sitting up. "What does she have to do with anything?"

"Because." I straighten up and hug my pillow, as if it can buffer this tension thickening in the air. "It's an example of how dangerous the park is and the fact Creighton doesn't take any responsibility—"

"Her family's suing him," he reminds me. "For tens of thousands of dollars. He's going to end up paying through the nose for it."

"Tens of thousands of dollars doesn't give someone their life back."

He lies back down and faces the window. I'm left staring at his freckled back. I trace a heart on it and he turns back around, giving me a concerned look.

"I'm worried about you," he says. "Do you think you'd be happier back in LA?"

I'm so stunned I can't breathe for a second. "Are you being serious?"

"You seem unhappy since we moved here."

My eyes prickle. "What are you saying? Are you actually suggesting I go and you stay?"

"It's how we used to do it," he reminds me, taking my hand

and kissing it. "Every year I'd come work here, March through September, and then stay with you October through February when the park closes."

"We're *married* now."

"I'm not suggesting we get a divorce, babe. You'd be near your friends again. Maybe take some city college classes or something, play music with other people."

"Half the year. You want to be away from me half the year. Is your job that important to you?"

It hurts, the way heartbreak always does. I'm sitting next to the love of my life, and I've never felt so alone. Warm wind blows the curtains, and Freddie's guitar solo carries into the room from the studio, a high-pitched screech.

"You could take Freddie back to LA," Mitch adds with a touch of bitterness. "Since, apparently, he can't live without you."

I shake my head, overwhelmed with confusion. How did we get here? How are we having this conversation? I moved my whole life out here. I thought we were solid. I've been wanting to start a family and settle down. Now he's talking about living apart again, going back to the rocky road we were on before?

"Why are we fighting?" I ask.

"We're not," he says gently, squeezing my hand. "We're having a conversation."

"I don't want to quit. I don't want to move. I want to be here with you, full stop." I squeeze back. "I love you."

"I love you, too, babe. My love is never a question; you know that, right?" He puts a hand on my cheek, offers a tired smile. Then he switches his lamp off and settles into his pillow. "Let's just get some sleep."

"Night."

"Night."

What I want is his arms around me. What I want is to be

told he doesn't want to be apart. But I'm afraid to show him how much I need him, because it only seems to push him farther away.

I'll be patient and give him space. I close my aching eyes and will myself to sleep.

The next thing I know, it's morning. His side of the bed is empty. A distant but piercing sound jolts me upright. A man is screaming.

It's Mitch.

Mitch, cursing at the top of his lungs. Bowie is barking over his voice, adding to the chaos. It takes a second to become real. I'm conscious. This is happening.

I've woken to a nightmare.

13

In a flash, I'm out of bed, bleary-eyed but tearing through the house toward the sound.

It's coming from outside.

I sprint through the living room and through the open door, out to the front porch, nearly knocking my head on a hanging plant. In the honey light of morning, Mitch stands in the driveway, eyes bulging. He looks like a maniacal stranger. He's barefoot in the pine needles, still in his pajama bottoms.

"You see this?" He points at his truck. "*See?*"

My heart races out of control, hand pressed to my chest as if that might keep it contained. I see, now that he's pointing at it, and at first my stomach flip-flops. Blood is everywhere on his truck, oozing in thick rivers from the top down, streaked over the windows, and dripping down the sides into the dirt below. The first thing I think of is the disgusting scene in his office, and I can almost taste the metallic tang of blood, but then the smell hits me. Chemicals. Plastic.

It's not blood; it's paint.

The relief hits next.

I let out the world's biggest sigh. "Oh my God, I thought you were hurt."

"Why is this happening to me?" Mitch's shoulders sag as he stares at the mess in disbelief. "I just—I don't understand, Kit. I don't understand."

I put my arms around him, and it takes a stunned second before he hugs me back. My eyes follow the dripping red writing on the truck, the pattering of paint on the leaves. My gaze drifts across the leaves, where the trickle continues—dead-ending on the steps of the studio. There, an open can of paint sits on the steps, knocked on its side with a scarlet spill.

My heart twists at the sight of it.

"Mitch," I whisper.

I pull back from him and nod toward the studio. We stand side by side, taking it in, the disappointment settling deep into my bones.

"Oh," Mitch says, with a touch of surprise.

"Freddie wouldn't—"

"Kit."

"Why would he?"

The sigh Mitch exhales could blow down a house of cards. The doubt, the anger in his quivering expression—it's like someone pulled a thread, and I'm watching my husband unravel before my eyes.

"Freddie didn't do that," I say as gently as I can. "There has to be another explanation."

"Come on, we can put two and two together." He steps closer to his truck, as if seeing it in a new light. He studies it and then glances past me at the house. Then I see it: in identical red paint, the misspelled word GILTY on the front door and KILLER on the windowpane.

The message, the red paint—it's dizzying and disturbing.

KILLER was written in Mitch's office. The message

Creighton thought was meant for him. This has to be related, right?

Mitch steps closer, his palm soft on my back. "Notice anything?"

I remind myself to breathe. I'm at a loss. I truly don't know what he's trying to get me to admit, but it's dancing there in his eyes.

He says the next part in my ear, a low buzz that sends a shiver down my spine. "Who wouldn't know how to spell the word '*guilty*?'"

Inside my soul, an icy wind blows a door closed. I shake my head.

"Who else would it be?" he says.

"And what?" My brain scrambles to add all of this up. "Freddie trashed your office, too?"

He gives a performative shrug. "All I know is that where Freddie goes, trouble follows. You can't ignore the timing. Everything was fine until Freddie came along."

It's so absurd, I let out an uncomfortable laugh. "Ridiculous. Why would—"

"He's always hated me." Mitch paces in front of the truck, rubbing his chin as his words pick up momentum. "He doesn't have the guts to face me head-on, so he pulls crap like this to get under my skin."

"He—"

"He wants me out of your life," Mitch says. "He wants you all to himself."

"Mitch, come on."

He turns to me. I've never seen him so exhausted. It's like he's aged a year in the past week.

"He needs to go," Mitch says, blankly calm. "Before I do something that I can't undo."

I'm free-falling here. I have no idea if Freddie did this. It doesn't seem like something Freddie would do, but neither did stealing my stereo and selling it for heroin. His permanent record reads like a long, shocking litany of wrongs I wouldn't ever imagine he'd commit, that I still can't wrap my head around: assault, battery, robbery. And here we are. It's been building for years, but I've finally reached an impasse, a fork in the road where I have to choose between my love for my husband and my love for my brother.

"Fine," I say hoarsely. "I'll tell him he has to go."

"Now, please."

"I know." My eyes fill, but I hold the tears in. "I'm sorry."

I rub his back. He shakes his head at his red-spattered truck. It's such a jarring sight, as if the sick worry I've bottled up has exploded everywhere, and now we're forced to stare straight at it.

I wake Freddie with a gentle shake and a whisper, telling him about what happened to Mitch's truck and our front door. I tell him he has to leave.

"Where the fuck would I have gotten red paint?" he asks, lacing up his shoes, his hair wild and bedheaded. "I don't have a car, man."

"Same way you got up here. Hitchhiked? Walked to town while we were at work?"

"Why would I do that? He's lost his mind."

I pack and zip up his backpack. "I don't think you did it," I say, though it comes with less conviction than I want. Because a little part of me is whispering, *But who else would have done it?*

My mind can't defend this, but my heart just can't swallow the idea that Freddie would do something this screwed up.

Freddie appears shocked that I believe him. "Well, then, why are you kicking me out?"

"First off, this was supposed to be a temporary visit, anyway.

And Mitch is worn so thin from everything—I'm afraid of him taking it out on you."

"That worries me, 'cause I don't want him taking it out on *you*."

I shake my head. "I'll be fine. Come on, let's get going before he comes out here."

We go outside. Freddie stops to study the paint can on the steps. He takes a long, puzzled look at Mitch's truck.

"Why would I do that?" he asks me. "Give me one reason."

I pull his sleeve. Freddie shakes his head, slinging his camouflaged backpack over his shoulder. We get into my car in silence and drive down the hill. My head swims, and Freddie just keeps saying, "This is crazy. This is *nuts*."

He's not wrong, but I don't know what to do.

I take him to the motel next to the hospital.

"I'm not staying at a motel," he says. "I'd rather sleep under a fuckin' bridge."

"Why won't you just accept my help?"

"What part of 'laying low' do you not understand? I don't want a paper trail right now."

The déjà vu of that phrase—it occurs to me that, even though Creighton Marrs might be a business tycoon and my brother might be a professional loser, they apparently lack the same moral compass.

"Look." Freddie sighs. "On the level? Cops have a warrant for me in LA."

This is the first I've heard of it. "For *what?*"

"Nothing that matters. Wasn't my fault. But if I have a warrant, why would I call attention to myself right now by vandalizing Mitch's truck? Makes no sense."

I can't deal with my brother's legal woes right now. I give him every bit of cash I have from my meager savings. I fight tears when I hand it to him, because he looks just like he used to when he was a kid. As if he doesn't understand why the world keeps dealing him such shit hands. And I get it.

Freddie gapes at the money in his palm, expression darkening. "How much does it cost these days to pay your big brother to go away, huh?"

"It's not like that."

"How much am I worth?" He counts the twenties in his hand. "Sixty? Eighty? Wow, a hundred bucks. Is that all your loser brother costs?"

"I'm trying to help you out."

"I don't want your money," he says, glaring at the wad in his hand. "I want you to act like my sister."

"Take care of yourself." I pull him into a hug, a weight pressing on my chest as I hold him closer. I hate the fear wriggling deep inside me that this might be the last time. But this is the way it is with Freddie. *I'll see him again; this isn't the end.* I think the thought, but I don't feel the feeling.

The ride home is suffocating. I drive farther into the shadows of the forest, the song on the radio hitching with static. I'm numb. Lost. I don't know how I got here, or what comes next.

When I get home, Mitch has already wiped the red paint off our window. The front door smells like fresh paint, and a tarp covers Mitch's truck. I step inside and hear the shower.

It isn't even nine o'clock. It's been such a disaster of a morning. I totally forgot that, although Mitch has today off, I still have to work. The answering machine light blinks from the counter, and my first thought is that it's Freddie calling me, needing something from me already. I press the red play button.

"Olympia, Washington. June 1971," a voice hisses, the rasp of it instantly giving me goosebumps. Man, woman, old, young, I can't tell. It sounds witchy and evil. "It's time to come clean. If you don't, you'll be sorry."

Click.

I roll the tape back with a gulp and play it again, skin crawling. And suddenly, the memory snaps into place. That voice—it's called before. I completely forgot. What did it say?

Medford, Oregon. April 1970.

Olympia, Washington. June 1971.

"You okay?" Mitch's voice says, yanking me from my concentration. He stands in the doorway to the hall, a towel wrapped around his waist, his curls wet.

He shaved. He looks fresher. But he still has that exhausted look in his eyes.

Don't make him more upset, Tiny Kit says.

"Yeah," I answer, erasing the recording with a press of a button. "Just a wrong number."

He burns me with his gaze so long I feel like I might catch on fire.

"Well, Kitty," he says. "Time for you to get ready for work, right?"

I nod. But when he turns around and heads back to the bedroom, I walk to the notepad that hangs on the refrigerator and write *Medford, Oregon, 1970* and then *Olympia, Washington, 1971.*

I tear the paper off, fold it into a tiny square, and tuck it in my record shelf—right next to Heart's *Dreamboat Annie.*

1970

He's been watching her for days.

That's all he tells himself it is. Watching—nothing wrong with that. Taking in the human scenery. No rules broken. Just a man pulled off the interstate, VW camper bus with the engine killed, flower-power curtains shut with a slit between for him to peep out at the forest.

From the belly of the vehicle, it's dead quiet. He can see the wind fighting with the pine branches and bending the necks of wildflowers back, but not hear a whisper. He can feel the urge building, crawling up his neck, an itch in his palms. His muscles clench as his gaze sharpens on the target: the girl with the red backpack and the twin braids in her hair.

He imagines she smells like sugar and sweat.

His mouth waters. He squeezes his fists.

Every day at three p.m. the yellow bus stops along the interstate and drops her off, all by herself. He spotted her three days ago when he was driving by on his way to his new job at the hardware store. On a lark, he came back the next day and there she was again, that delicate thing, a baby bird with a bounce in her step. She didn't even peek over her shoulder, just hurried into the woods, talking to herself, singing off-key, kicking up dust with her cowgirl boots, swinging her Monkees lunchbox. She's the perfect age: twelve or thirteen, just budding, a rose about to bloom. Every day since then, he comes back to watch her. Every day she gets off the bus and disappears into the thicket while his heart skips and sinks at the same time.

She might not know it, but she's his now.

Hawk drinks from his flask and tries to numb the urge. But the more he drinks, the thirstier he gets. Angry, flask drained, he pulls onto the highway and drives to a roadside diner. In the parking lot, hippies panhandle with cardboard signs. Hawk flashes a peace sign and clinks a quarter in their tin cans. Then he heads inside and slides into a booth, studying the menu with shaking hands. The waitress is a busty redhead who chews a wad of gum. Hawk orders a burger politely as different shades of red explode in his mind. He imagines how satisfying it would be to smash her head with the ketchup bottle. It makes him feel better to imagine it. It almost makes him forget the girl. Almost.

When Hawk gets the urge, it goes away if he just keeps moving. Drink some coffee, booze, go hiking, dancing, find something to fix, journal. It'll fade. But today is different. Even when he's eating, he's still hungry. Still thinking about her. He parks up at a lookout spot and watches the sunset. He's still Hawk. For the first time in his life, he wonders if he might always be Hawk. He lets himself fall into the fantasy: her hair up close, the plaits soft against his calloused fingertips. Her fragile neck bones between his hands.

Hawk knows he has a problem. Maybe even a sickness. That's what people would say, wouldn't they? But the same folks would watch bobcats and owls and coyotes hunting prey and call it natural. Hawk wonders if he isn't entirely human. Because human comforts don't satisfy him. A soft bed, a warm meal, a smile from a beautiful woman, a fresh town, a business venture—he's had all those things. But the things he's never supposed to have … that's what he wants most of all.

Tonight, Hawk tosses and turns in his sleeping bag. He still has that nervous energy running through him like an electric current. It's excruciating. He throbs and aches with a vague, awful need. For the first time in his twenty-plus years on this planet, he considers what might happen if he follows the urge and doesn't deny it. If he did it, just once.

"The hawk rips into his screaming dinner with love in his heart," Hawk says in the darkness of his van, and he likes the sentence so much he says it again. "The hawk rips into his screaming dinner with love in his heart." And then he sits up, flicks on a flashlight, and writes it down in his notebook in all caps. He uses his left hand. It doesn't look like his handwriting.

THE HAWK RIPS INTO HIS SCREAMING DINNER WITH LOVE IN HIS HEART.

Here's what people get wrong about predators: They think predators do what they do out of hate, but that's backwards. Predators love their prey—an unrequited, one-sided love. They seek it. Dream of it. Their lives revolve around it, a deep-seated desire that transcends everything. The predator dies without its prey.

But it goes even deeper. You might think prey thrives without the predator—but only at first. Because without the predator there to keep the balance, the bunnies' population explodes. They eat all the grass, all the resources. They throw everything out of whack.

Here's the sad truth: bunnies are meant to be eaten.

The next day, Hawk pulls over in a hidden spot up the road. He gets out of his van and hurries through the meadow, his boots crushing wildflowers, the hiss of the wind in the trees. He waits behind an oak, picks up a jagged rock the size of his fist, and hides it in his jacket.

He hears the girl's footsteps before he sees her. The sight of the sunshine in her golden hair turns him to helium. This near her, he realizes with just the slightest twinge of disappointment that he was wrong. She's younger than he supposed; a tall, skinny child, nine tops. But it's too late now. Nature never asks permission. He steps out from the shadows and gives a smile. He whistles a tune through his lips: a dreamy, haunted version of Jackie DeShannon's "Take Me Away." The hairs on his neck stand on end, and the urge changes into a rush of pleasure that spreads throughout his body. She turns to him, hypnotized by the pretty sound.

"Hey there," he says.

The little girl stops. Up close, he sees her eyes are a deep blue. She doesn't detect danger, just beams a toothless smile. Pure, innocent, and unafraid.

"I just caught a bunny," Hawk says, clutching the rock as hard as he can under his jacket. "She's the softest thing I've ever caught. Want to feel her?"

He walks toward her, his hunger louder than ever.

BREAKNECK BAY WATERPARK LIABILITY WAIVER

By purchasing a ticket and entering Breakneck Bay Water-park, guests voluntarily assume all risks associated with water-based activities, including but not limited to slips, falls, collisions, drowning, heat exhaustion, equipment malfunctions, and unforeseen hazards. Breakneck Bay, its owners, and employees are not responsible for injuries, accidents, or loss of personal property, regardless of cause. Riders acknowledge that attractions may operate under extreme conditions and waive any claims against Breakneck Bay for bodily harm, temporary or permanent disability, or other damages. Ride at your own risk—**thrills aren't for wimps!**

14

The first weekend in July, a heat wave oppresses the valley.

Breakneck Bay's asphalt could fry an egg by noon. Humidity is inescapable, and sweat is eternal. Steam radiates off the paved paths as if we're in some sun-kissed version of hell, and no matter where you turn, it smells like a nasty combination of bodily fluids, pineapple ice cream, and chlorine. Miles of sunburnt skin. The man-made rivers and pools writhe with screaming people. Everyone is louder, drunker, and angrier when it's pushing a hundred degrees outside.

The crowds get bigger by the day as schools across the country empty and droves of tourists flock to the park. A vein in Mitch's forehead is permanently throbbing as he answers "one idiot emergency after the next" on the walkie-talkie all day long. Someone gets stuck in the Human Cannon and Billford lubes the whole thing up with lard from the Bahama Burger to get the kid out. There's a slip and fall in Sprinkler City. Some pre-teen joyriding one of the Go Karts ends up at a drive-thru five miles up the highway. I treat gashes, raspberries, bruised ribs, and call an ambulance for an elderly man in a Speedo who gets heatstroke. The EMTs who arrive mutter under their breath about "Break-your-neck Bay" and when Creighton berates them as they drive away, they flip him off.

"We don't need those cocksuckers up here in our park," Creighton yells at Mitch. "We're getting our *own* ambulance."

He must be joking. That's what I think, anyway, until I show up to work the next morning and behold the beat-up ambulance parked outside the admin building. Dwayne's behind the driver's seat, shirtless, a cigarette dangling from his lip.

"Hey baby, want a ride?" he asks as he leers out the window at the twins, who stand shaking their heads.

"Yeah, right," I hear one say to the other. "And end up dead in a ditch."

"Hey, fuck off," Dwayne says, his face darkening. "That's not funny."

They turn back to the admin building, and I'm left here wondering what on earth that was about. Dwayne chews his cheek for a moment before turning up Led Zeppelin and head-banging in the front seat.

"The ambulance thing seems like a bad idea," I tell Mitch over a very late dinner Saturday night.

He twirls his spaghetti with a yawn. "Like Creighton says, better than relying on townies to respond to emergencies."

I study Mitch, counting the silver hairs that have sprouted around his temples since summer started. He's sunburned and has a twitch in his left eye. He's had insomnia. Since his office and his truck got trashed, the stress settled into him and never left.

"May I ask how Dwayne is qualified to drive an ambulance?" I ask.

"Probably the same way you're qualified to be running a medic tent." Mitch offers a soft, crooked smile. "Same way I'm qualified to be park manager. If you're looking for a job where things make sense, this ain't it."

"Mitch." I wipe my mouth with a napkin. "What makes you want to stay at Breakneck Bay?"

He thinks for a minute, peering at the window, where the curtains rustle in the night breeze.

"It's not perfect," he finally says. "But I kind of feel like—I don't know. I've been there since it opened. It's my park too, you know?"

It's not, though. It's Creighton's park. Creighton's got the empire and the fancy house on the hill. But I don't tell Mitch this, because I don't want to belittle him.

"I helped Creighton build Scream River back when that was its only attraction. I hired Billford and the two of us traveled around picking up waterslides in a U-Haul," he says, grinning at the memory.

I try to imagine what it was like then—just one steep, fast waterslide between a golf course and the highway. Scream River.

I get a chill. "Scream River's the attraction where Pamela Bronson died, right?"

Mitch's grin disappears. "Yeah. What a tragedy."

I push my noodles around, the red sauce suddenly unappetizing. The mention of Pamela put a dimmer on the conversation. "Hey, when was it Freddie worked at the park again?"

"Wasn't it three summers ago? Because you and I had just started getting serious. You came up and visited for a week right when Freddie started."

"And then he got fired for stealing."

"Not only did he steal from the till, but he stole the entire *cash register* out of the Bahama Burger. I mean, that's a whole new level there—hawking a cash register." Mitch shakes his head and laughs.

"Oh, Freddie," I say.

My heart aches. I haven't heard from him since I dropped him off downtown. I don't know where he is now, but I'm sure he's up to no good.

"So, he never worked on Scream River?" I ask, thinking about his employee file. "He was at the Bahama Burger."

"He might have started on Scream River. Pretty sure something happened, maybe the ride got shut down for repairs, so he moved to the Bahama Burger." Mitch looks up. "Why?"

"I was just wondering if he knew Pamela Bronson."

"Nah, Pamela was last summer. They never worked together."

That name *Pamela* takes up space, grows wings, causes a hush to fall between us.

I think of all the injuries I've treated this week. The chaos has been nonstop, but one question won't leave me alone.

"Do you ever think the rides are too dangerous?" I ask.

Mitch seems to consider it but shakes his head. "People who come to Breakneck Bay come for the reputation the place has. It's the whole point of the park. This isn't Disneyland. There are signs everywhere reminding people. And waivers at the entrance."

The phone rings. I put my napkin down.

"I'll get it," I say, scooting my chair and grabbing the receiver. "Hello?"

The muffled sound of breathing tickles my eardrum.

"Hello?" I try again, nerves standing at attention.

"Omaha, 1972," the familiar, witchy voice says.

I curl the cord around my finger, heart racing, my patience thinning. First it was Medford. Then Olympia. Now Omaha. What the hell does it mean?

"What about it?" I ask, voice tight.

White noise.

"Why don't you just spill it already?" I say.

I don't expect the voice to answer, so it's a shock when I hear a hissing whisper. "Tell him to turn himself in. *Now.* Or he's going to suffer."

I glance at the dark window. A shiver wiggles down my spine.

"Who?" I ask. "What are you talking about?"

The line clicks in my ear. I don't even notice my hand is trembling until I put the phone back in its cradle.

"Kitty, everything okay?" Mitch asks. "Who was it?"

"Someone said, 'Omaha, 1972,'" I say.

The instant I say those words, his face goes blank. Like he's trying to comb his memory for meaning.

"They've called before," I say.

"What do you mean?"

"I didn't want to worry you."

"Wait, back up." He rubs the stubble on his chin. "Who's called before?"

I shake my head. "I don't know who it is. They keep dropping city names and years. Medford, 1970. Olympia."

"Medford. Olympia. Man? Woman?"

"Woman, I think. They said something like, 'Tell him to turn himself in.'"

"Who? Tell who to turn himself in?"

"They didn't say."

Mitch paces in the dark kitchen. Bowie gets up from his nap on the floor and starts following him back and forth. I'm about to comment on how cute it is, Bowie's tongue lolling out as he trots after Mitch's sneakers, when Mitch stops.

"Am I being tested?" he asks, his eyes bloodshot. "What is all this?"

I shake my head. "I wish I knew."

His eyes flash like he wants to run out the door, to hit the bottle, to explode. But Mitch takes a sleeping pill and heads to bed early. Me though? I can't sleep. That voice keeps rattling around in my head. Medford, Olympia, Omaha—it sounds less like a threat and more like a rock band tour.

As I stand in the dark kitchen, hands plunged in a warm sink full of dishes, it suddenly hits me for the first time—what if those calls have nothing to do with Mitch or me?

What if they've been for Freddie?

Freddie was a roadie for years. He's a lifelong drifter and an on-again, off-again drug addict. He apparently has a warrant out for his arrest. And, of course, those scratches on his neck, courtesy of some "crazy chick" he never explained.

Where Freddie goes, trouble follows.

I check on Mitch, who's snoring away. Honestly, thank God, the man needs a good night's rest. I spoon him, but he's so conked out it's like cuddling a warm corpse.

I toss and turn in the dark, resentful. I invited Freddie into our home, and next thing I know, someone's vandalized Mitch's truck and we're getting threatening calls.

Something's coming. And it's not just the heat.

15

Monday morning, when I pull into the employee parking lot above Breakneck Bay, there are only a few other vehicles. One of them is that beat-up ambulance I still can't believe is real. It's tranquil up here: birds chirping, a gentle breeze, nobody screaming yet. I walk across the lot, the thrum of music coming from somewhere. I get a shiver, peering around the trees and feeling almost ... watched. By the end of the day, the lot will be so full it's practically an employee tailgating party.

That's when the sound of coughing erupts, and I realize that Dwayne's right next to me in the driver's seat of the ambulance. I hadn't realized anyone was in there, but now that I step closer, I can hear the synthesizer-heavy march of Gary Numan's "Cars" and smell the unmistakable skunk cloud of pot smoke.

"Hey," I say, sneaking up and startling him.

He stashes the joint in his ashtray and tries to act casual, putting his hands behind his head. "'Sup, Mrs. Blue?"

"Why are you here so early?" I ask him.

"Well, Billford's supposed to be teaching me how to change the oil on this sexy beast." Dwayne pats the steering wheel.

"But then I pulled in and saw the fuzz was here and figured I'd wait it out."

"What?" I ask, seeing my own wrenched confusion in the reflection of his wayfarer sunglasses.

"Coppers." He looks at me over the lenses. "Five-O."

"At the park?"

He points his chin toward the park. "Check it out, dude."

I peer over the edge of the staircase leading down into the park. He's right. A single police car waits in the roundabout at the entrance.

My stomach drops. "What now?"

"Fuck do I know?"

A stoned teenager in a renegade ambulance—who approved this idea? Also, Dwayne's worried about the "fuzz," so he waits it out by smoking drugs nearby. Genius move. I fight the urge to shake him and tell him to get his act together. The joint he tried to ditch when I walked up is still smoldering in the ashtray. Covertly, he tries to close the lid.

"Dwayne, dare I ask why you're suddenly driving an ambulance?"

"Because Mitch told me to. Why else?" It sounds sharp, edging on bitter, but he sweetens it with a toothpaste-ad smile.

"Did Mitch tell you to smoke pot on the job?"

His goofy smile melts, and his posture straightens, as if he just remembered I'm married to his boss. "Uh ... no. But technically, I haven't clocked in yet, so."

I turn down the steps.

"You're not going to tell him, are you?" he calls after me with alarm.

I choose not to answer him. A little paranoia might do him some good.

Down at the admin building, the front door is unlocked, but the only people inside are the twins whispering at the front desk as Creighton yells in his office, and Billford, who is dawdling at the coffee machine, clearly eavesdropping.

I sidle up to Billford. "Why are the cops here?"

"Creighton called the chief here to tear him a new one." His breath smells like old cigars. "He's fixin' to sue the city."

"Why?"

"You haven't heard the news yet?"

"What news?" I ask, taking out a coffee cup and unfolding its tiny paper wings.

"'Bout the forensics report. Came back yesterday."

I shake my head. He takes the coffee pot and begins pouring my cup for me, a bit carelessly, the scalding water spattering my fingers. I open my mouth to tell him, but he keeps talking.

"That catastrophe in your hubby's office, remember?" he says.

"That's enough," I tell him, nodding to the coffee pot.

He puts it away with a clatter.

"The 'crime' scene." He bends his oil-stained fingers into air quotes. "Just like Creighton said—someone set him up."

My pulse picks up speed. "What do you mean?"

"Animal blood," Billford whispers. "Raccoon."

I blink. That can't be right. I stare at him. He sips his coffee like he just told me the weather forecast.

"And the teeth?" he goes on. "Porcelain. Prosthetics."

If Billford started speaking Turkish to me right now, I think I would understand him just as well.

"Why would someone do that?" I ask, sipping coffee and wincing at the burn.

"Beats the hell outta me."

His walkie-talkie beeps.

"Billford, maintenance can't get this gum out of the hoses these fuckers clogged up at Thunder Cave. You got a drain snake? Over."

"Incontinent pieces of shit," he mutters, but beeps the walkie-talkie and says, "Can't remember where I left it off the top of my noggin. Check the maintenance log." Billford clips the walkie-talkie back to his belt and adds, "If I didn't write every damn thing down, I'd be useless. Gettin' old's a swindle."

He leaves me here, my head swimming. I glance over at Mitch's closed office door, which has a new lock on it and a sign that says AUTHORIZED PERSONNEL ONLY.

Raccoon blood.

Prosthetic teeth.

What the hell?

16

Outside, it's approaching scorching already. I glance at my watch: not even nine a.m. A neon-shirted employee blows bubble gum while listening to her Walkman and sweeping the path. In two hours, this place will be open. The vibes will transform. Crumpled cups will litter the lawns, crows will be scavenging hot dog remnants, and a stampede of half-wet, half-naked tourists and teens will overwhelm every line, path, and ride.

At the top of the steps, I catch my breath and start pulling out my keys to unlock the Ouch Shack when a sound pierces the air.

"Pssst."

I look up. Freddie's there, lurking in the shadows behind the Ouch Shack. He's hunched, pale, and wearing the same Iron Maiden shirt he was wearing when I dropped him off downtown nearly a week ago. There are leaves in his hair, like he slept in the woods.

"What the fuck are you doing here?" I ask in disbelief, my keys still in the air.

"I didn't want to bug you and Mitchy-boy at home."

"Aren't you 86'ed from the park?" I ask, utterly baffled by his presence. "And it's not even open yet. How did you get in?"

"There are places to sneak in. Anyone who worked here the summer of '79 would know that."

"Great," I say sarcastically.

As if Breakneck Bay didn't feel dangerous enough already, now I find out people can sneak in whenever they want. I make a note to tell Billford about this later. The maintenance crew might want to dig into it.

"Look, I'm sorry to bother you," Freddie says, stepping closer, almost wincing at the sunshine. He reminds me of a vampire. "I just need some more cash to tide me over."

"Where have you been staying? I assumed you'd left town."

"I've been around."

"And you spent all the money I gave you already?"

He gives me a sheepish look. I'd like to scream. I can tell from his red eyes that he smoked dope, though the brightness in them makes me wonder if he snorted something, too.

"Freddie, what are you on?"

"I'm hungover, man. Had a little hair of the dog. I'm not on anything." He pauses and corrects himself. "Well, some weed, a few pills—that's it. Nothing hard."

The truth is always a stumble with Freddie.

"What is going on?" I demand. "What did you do? Someone's been calling my house, leaving vaguely threatening messages asking you—I assume it's you—to turn yourself in."

"Wait." His gaze sharpens. "What?"

"Yeah. Mitch was right. Every time you come around, chaos follows. Do me a favor and don't bring it to my job."

"*Mitch was right*," Freddie mocks, then his expression slackens. "Saint Mitch. C'mon, give me a break. Mitch is just as much a loser as I am."

"No, he's not. Mitch had the sense to grow the hell up."

Freddie's dark eyes flash with mischief. "I've got a secret. Wanna hear it?"

"I need to get to work."

"The other night, when Mitch pulled the old vanishing act like the petulant little man-baby he is, I secretly hoped he'd never come home again."

His words land like a slap.

"That is a terrible fucking thing to say," I tell him.

"I hate the games he plays with you and the wedge he drives between us. What I wouldn't give for him to disappear. He's ruining your life."

"*You* are ruining my life. You are."

Freddie's face crumples for one split second before hardening again. "Someday you're going to thank me for being the only person in this world who truly loves you."

"Is that supposed to make me feel good?" I ask in something approaching a shriek. "Thanks a lot. And what do you mean you truly love me? You sponge off me. You borrow money you never repay. You call me when you're in county jail. You show up on my doorstep looking for a place to crash. How is that love?"

Freddie shoots me a look like I'm such a damn shame.

"I don't have any money," I say hoarsely. "You took all my money. I need to work now, so please leave me alone already."

"Someday," he repeats. "You'll look back and see."

"Thanks, Freddie. Thanks a lot."

"Thank me later."

Freddie disappears behind the Ouch Shack, and I hear him scaling down the hill. I close my eyes for one burning second. I consider chasing him to see what hole he crawled through to find me here. Instead, I turn to the Ouch Shack.

"Focus," I tell myself, hand turning the knob.

Wait. The door is unlocked. I didn't unlock it yet, did I?

I push it open. *Lovely. Someone had a party here last night that I'm going to have to clean up.*

But I'm shocked to discover I'm not the first one here: Rhonda's back is to me and she facing the lockers.

"Good morning," I say, her presence in the room cranking my blood pressure. "You surprised me."

She turns. Her eyes are wide behind her glasses. "Likewise."

The moment stretches, and I can't help but notice she's breathing heavily, as if I've caught her in the act of something. I glance behind her. Gloria's old locker is open. A flashlight is on inside, as if Rhonda just dropped it.

I raise my eyebrows. "Is there something I can help you with?"

"I didn't mean to eavesdrop," she blurts.

"It's okay. That was just my brother."

"Yes, he popped in here looking for you a few minutes ago. I assumed he was allowed here at the time, but I heard him tell you he ... snuck into the park?"

"Apparently. We might want to look into that."

"He doesn't sound like he's a big fan of Mitch."

"Rhonda." I'm trying to be patient, but the last thing I feel like doing is explaining my dysfunctional family to her right now. "Why are you here? What can I help you with?"

"Well, I asked if I could look around this morning, and Mr. Marrs said, 'Sure, I don't give a fudge,' although of course, Mr. Marrs didn't say 'fudge.' He—"

"Rhonda," I say, putting a hand on her shoulder. "It's okay."

"Since the police chief is here," she says, dropping her tone, as if we're now having a confidential conversation. "I wanted to see if there was anything new I could give them." She whispers loudly, "About Gloria."

I let this information circle in my brain and sink in. It's far too much for a woman who has only had one cup of coffee. Rhonda's face is flushing, and she's got a barely perceptible quiver in her hands. Is she scared of me? I'm so confused.

"Rhonda, no offense, but I think you're chasing a dead end here. The police told me Gloria isn't actually missing. She just didn't show up to work one day." I put my purse in my locker and shut it.

"It's been bothering me, though," she says. "Since the—the —*box* you disposed of that we won't talk about, which I absolutely, positively did not see. Don't worry." She gives me such an exaggerated a wink it looks more like a tic. "But I wanted to check if there was anything up here related to Gloria. As I told you before, being a student reporter comes with a natural curiosity." She backs away from the open locker, regarding me like I'm a bomb that may or may not explode at any moment. "But I need to curtail it. I've overstepped. My profuse apologies."

I continue watching her scoot toward the doorway. This must be some elaborate performance, because it's utterly bizarre. She had that same expression when she looked at the files I disposed of and saw Gloria's name.

"It's definitely confusing. I get it." I cross to a cabinet to restock the Band-Aids. We'll go through at least a hundred by day's end. "You are more than welcome to look around."

The tight expression on her face melts a little.

"I have no idea what was in the files," I go on. "I'm sure it was nothing."

"Absolutely, I'm sure it was nothing, as well." She folds her hands in front of her fanny pack, and I can practically see the wheels turning in her head. "Shame, though, because seems to be the only paperwork that had her contact info."

Fast-forward twenty years and Rhonda is going to be the nosiest neighbor on the block. Just wait.

She's not wrong, though. *Shit, did I get rid of the only paper-work that had Gloria's contact info on it? How could that be?*

I stuff cotton balls in a jar. "You know that forensics came back, right? Mitch's office? It wasn't human blood. And the teeth weren't real, either."

"I heard that, yes."

"And considering that Dwayne saw Gloria later that night at the pay phone down by the highway ... I think it's safe to assume wherever Gloria is, she's doing just fine."

"Yes, well, it's questionable whether Dwayne is a reliable source."

I don't disagree with her there. Her walkie-talkie blares with Creighton's booming, overblown voice. "Rhonda, where the fuck are my multivitamins?"

"I'd best get back to my station," Rhonda says.

"Wait," I tell her.

I grab the flashlight from the locker and hand it to her.

"Focus on the positive," I tell her with a smile. "My aunt had a saying: 'Keep your face toward the sunshine, and shadows will fall behind you.'"

"That's not your aunt's saying. That's a line from Walt Whitman. But thank you, it's a very nice quote." She opens the door and smiles quickly. "Have a nice day."

The door slams on her way out. I listen to her sneakers thumping down the steps. I chew my cheek, first thinking about the fact that my aunt acted like she made up that line, next ruminating that a seventeen-year-old girl is smarter than I am, and then, finally, replaying that whole strange interaction. To be fair, every interaction with Rhonda is strange, but that was something special.

All day long, as I spray people with iodine, bandage up scrapes, and mop up vomited Mai Tais, I'm distracted. Thinking about Rhonda's fixation with the files and wondering if I'm an idiot for throwing them all away. The sun is shining. I'm surrounded by laughter, adventure, ice cream, and everything smells like tanning lotion. But as I walk through the park when my shift is done, I'm noticing things I usually don't. The older men leering at bikinied girls who still have braces on. The boys chanting *Pussy! Pussy!* at each other on the Jungle Swing. The clearly drunk girls, who can't be over fifteen, stumbling past the tiki torches at the Wet and Wild Bar.

My voice echoes in my mind: *I'm sure wherever Gloria is, she's doing just fine.*

Right? There's no reason to assume she's not. I don't know why that conversation with Rhonda earlier is making the question itch again. Clearly, the office scene was a hoax. Gloria was never actually missing. Plough told me himself.

The timing of it all is just so odd.

Up in the parking lot, under the tall pines and away from the crowds, it's at least ten degrees cooler. I get an unpleasant taste in my mouth. Something is off. Something isn't right. I can feel it in the air, the same way you might sense a coming storm before the clouds blacken.

I dismiss my paranoia and drive home. Sitting at a stoplight where the road meets the highway, I turn on the radio. It's that corny "867-5309/Jenny" song. I'm about to turn it back off again when I'm zinged with a memory. Gloria's application—her phone number. It was a local number that ended with 5309. How could I have forgotten? There's only one prefix in this area —which means I can figure out her phone number.

I spot The NED'S DINER sign flashing red against the setting sun and my eyes land on the phone booth ahead—the one I pass to and from work every day and hardly blink at. The one where Dwayne claims he saw Gloria.

The light turns green and I make a sudden turn ahead into the parking lot, fish a dime from the center console, and jump out of the car. Inside the phone booth, my chlorine-tinged sweat stink hits me. Sheesh, I need a shower. The dial tone ringing in my ear, I plunk a dime into the slot and wait until it clicks. Then I punch in 555-5309.

For a flash, I imagine that this is all it will take. Gloria will answer the phone, and the story will be over. We can all move on with our lives and stop wasting precious time on a teenager who left work one day and never returned.

It rings twice, and a woman's voice picks up. She sounds cranky and tired, like I woke her up from a nap. "Hello?"

"Hi," I say, fluffing my bangs in the distorted silver reflection of the phone. "May I speak with Gloria, please?"

"Ain't no Gloria here."

"Oh ..." I exchange a wide-eyed look with my reflection. "Are you sure?"

"You think I don't know who lives in my own damn house?"

Confused, I squint at the paper again. "Is your number 555-5309?"

"You're talkin' to me, ain'tcha? Lived in this house and had this number for damn near forty years. Ain't no Gloria here."

"Any ... teenage girls? With short, spiky hair?"

"What is this, some kind of prank call?"

The woman yells a string of profanities, and I flinch.

"Sorry," I murmur, hanging up the phone.

Slowly, I walk out to the car. Gloria's number is fake. It has to be. What are the chances someone writes their phone number down wrong?

That creeping feeling that overcame me at the park earlier only gets worse as I drive home. Twilight purples the sky. A cloud of bats wheels overhead.

I'm nauseous. Confused. I couldn't articulate this feeling if I tried.

I had this feeling once before. The summer I went to sleepaway camp, I woke up in the middle of the night in my cabin, slicked with sweat. I complained to my counselor that I was ill. She took my temperature, gave me a cup of water, and made me go back to bed. I lay awake the entire night, teeth chattering from something bigger than sickness. It was a hunch that the entire world was about to come crashing down on me. And it did. The next afternoon, Freddie and I were called into the office. Our aunt was waiting there for us, sobbing.

"Your mother," she started to say, and then shook her head. "Your father..."

No, no, no. I'm not going back there.

I pull onto our dark road, slowing down to mind the bumps and gritting my teeth. After parking behind Mitch's truck, I jump out of the car. I hurry toward the house and am just beginning to relish the relief when I notice the front door is wide open.

"Mitch?" I say, stepping onto the porch.

The second my foot hits the floor, it squeaks. I slip. Something's wet. I look down.

First, I see his feet. Bare, splayed out.

Then his jeans, spattered.

His Eagles T-shirt, stained.

And then—the blood.

So much blood.

"No," I whisper, my stomach plummeting.

And then there's his face. A wound gapes on one side of his face—and where his eye should be, it looks like ground meat.

My hands fly to my mouth, and I look away, but it's too late.

I puke everywhere.

"Mitch," I say, crouching, shaking his leg, scared to touch him and scared to leave him. "Mitch, baby. Mitch. No. Don't do this, Mitch, don't. Don't. This can't be real."

I hear a faint gurgle and turn my head. I gasp when I swear I see him just barely move his neck from side to side—and I spot an ear, a perfectly intact ear, next to the wretched, bloody mess that was his right eye. His left eye is still there, clear and staring at nothing.

One side of his face is unrecognizable. The other is still Mitch.

"You're alive! Baby, can you hear me?" I crawl toward him through a puddle, blood soaking the knees of my jeans. I don't concentrate on his face. I concentrate on his ear. I concentrate on the eye that still looks normal. My gaze drifts to his left hand. His wedding ring is still there. His hands are mostly clean. How?

"Baby?" I try.

He gurgles again, and it's truly a sound from hell—a bloody, babbling brook that shouldn't exist in his throat.

"Stay here. Stay with me. Stay with me, baby," I say, slowly getting up.

I back away from him, from the horrid horror scene in my home, and pick up the phone. There's blood all over my hands. Crimson handprints on my jeans. The powerful, iron stink in the air makes me dizzy.

I dial 9-1-1 and when someone picks up, all I can do is scream, "Help him! He's dying! My husband is dying. Somebody help him!"

HAWK

1970

Rage rockets inside Hawk as he speeds up the freeway.

The road stretches ahead of him, a tarry black river. He's not going back there. Screw that town. His jaw clenches, his muscles tighten. The throb of the blood in his veins *tick, tick, tick*s. He drives exactly the speed limit, bandaged hand strangling the steering wheel, and blows past the sign welcoming him to Washington state. The view could be a painting: rain clouds hovering, delicate as jellyfish, above rolling green hills dotted with cottonwoods. He would set it all on fire if he could.

"Little bitch," he spits, glancing at his hand, which still stings.

Back in Medford, his first hunt got away.

But it isn't the girl's fault for biting him and running; Hawk knows this. The fault is his. A hunter can't blame the doe for fleeing, and the eagle can't begrudge a wriggling mouse.

The problem is that the urge has intensified. It's a pressure that almost feels external, pressing in on him from all sides. He needs to relieve himself. He can't fail this time.

When he sees the pigtailed teen with her thumb out at a

rest stop near Olympia, he notices how frail she is, how alone, how she slouches and holds her arms like she isn't sure of herself. And he knows, he just knows. He can almost smell the weak ones. Time to strike and not miss. This time, Hawk will not fail.

He turns off the radio as the girl opens his passenger door. She's pale and petite and can't be over seventeen. Ripening, but still naïve. Runaway, maybe. He observes how slender her neck is, and his hands pulse with need.

Hawk offers her his best smile.

"Going to Seattle?" she asks.

"Sure am. Hop on in."

The girl's blue eyes sparkle. She cranes her neck to eye the highway as if she's reconsidering, but then she jumps in. She wears a knapsack, sandals, a broomstick skirt, and a peasant blouse. A scent of lemon and patchouli wafts in with her. She carries what appears to be an amethyst crystal in her hand.

"I'm Jenny," she says. "Bitchin' ride."

He holds out his hand and introduces himself as Hawk.

"Hawk," she says in awe. "Wow. That your given name?"

Hawk pulls onto the highway and lets a beat pass. "Yep."

"Far out."

Hawk can sense that the girl is ever so slightly wary of him. He's bad at reading faces, but an expert in body language. The way her knees lean toward the window and away from him. How tightly she clutches her crystal.

"Okay if I turn on the radio?" he asks.

"I don't mind."

He flicks on the radio dial. It's the rattlesnake drum and the slithering bass line of the Beatles' "Come Together."

"I love this song," he says. "It's my son's favorite."

"Aww, you have a son?" She turns to look at him as if he just stepped into a new light.

On the horizon, the jellyfish clouds blacken over unpeopled farmland.

"Sure do. Otis. Six years old." He points to the school picture that hangs from his rearview—a little blond boy with hair that sticks out on end and a missing front tooth. "Just about the cutest kid you've ever seen in your life. My objective opinion, of course."

She laughs. Her grip on the crystal loosens as she leans in and studies the photo. "He *is* cute." The girl turns to Hawk and studies him now, as if that whiff of skepticism has returned. "Aren't you a little ... young to have a kid his age?"

"Aren't you a little young to be hitchhiking?" he shoots back, jokingly.

She lets out a nervous *heh*.

"No, his mom and I were high-school sweethearts," he says. "She had him right after we graduated."

"That's sweet. Got any other kids?"

"I wish." He lets his face slacken and his voice soften. "My wife ... passed away a few years ago. Cancer. It's just me and little Otie now."

Out of the corner of his eye, he sees the shadow of pity pass over her face. "I'm so sorry to hear that."

"Yeah, not gonna lie, it's been hard. But got to look on the bright side, you know? I have this guy to think about." He taps the picture with his pointer finger and sighs. "Anyway, let's talk about something else. Tell me about yourself."

The girl spills mundane details about her life. Something about Utah and visiting her cousin in Seattle and an anti-war protest, but Hawk's thoughts are much louder than the nasal drone of her voice. He's thinking about all the things he's going to do to her. About where to pull off and the pros and cons of strangling her versus knocking her out. The anticipation is like a starving man finding a gourmet meal. He isn't sure where to start, but he knows he's going to tear into this lovely thing seated next to him.

His blood pressure rises. An electric current of desire pulses, and he grits his teeth, scanning the upcoming road for an off-ramp. It would be smarter to destroy her quickly. The longer she stays in his car, the longer he has to hear her yammer on and smell her perfume, the more human she becomes. And someone passing by might witness her in his van. Last time, he was too calculating. He watched the girl for days, and then, when he saw how young she was up close and realized she wasn't how he imagined, he hesitated just a split second. That was where it all fell apart.

"Um ... Hawk?" the girl is saying. "Can you hear me?"

Hawk switches to the right lane. He forces a chuckle and a sheepish grin. "I'm sorry. What were you saying?"

"I was asking what happened to your hand," she says with wide-eyed concern.

Hawk notices how she still clutches the crystal. He needs to get it away from her somehow before he makes his move. It's big enough that she could use it as a weapon. He wiggles his bandage.

"Tried to help a dog out of a trap," he says. "Got bitten."

"How awful."

"Yeah, poor thing didn't know any better."

She nods.

Hawk flicks on his signal, *tick-tick-tick*.

"Wait, what's happening?" the girl asks.

Hawk turns down the music. "My apologies, nature's calling."

"Oh."

There's a single ice cube in her tone, just a slight coldness that makes him wonder if she senses danger.

"Too much coffee this morning, I guess."

She says nothing as he turns to drive up a tree-lined road, but her grasp tightens on the crystal.

"You want me to put some of your things in the back while we're stopped?" he asks. "Give you a little more legroom?"

"No, that's okay."

Dang. He was hoping to get the crystal out of her hand. That thing has violet, jagged teeth. He turns the music to a whisper now. The rain has just started, less a downpour and more a twinkle in the air. They drive up the country road between farmland to the right and a black oak forest to the left. The trees are twisted, dark, and menacing. They're beautiful.

Her suspicion is mounting. He feels it like you feel a storm brewing in the air. The girl is on alert. She isn't as weak and inexperienced as he first thought. The only way he got her to soften up was when he talked about his nonexistent son, pointing to that silly little photo he swiped from someone's wallet.

Hawk suddenly knows just how he can trap her. He checks his rearview to make sure no one is following and turns left, off the road and into the trees.

"Sorry to go so off the beaten path," he says as he yanks the emergency brake. "I'm modest. Don't want anyone to see."

"Okay." She glances longingly out the window as if she's thinking of bolting.

"I'm leaving my keys in here." He opens his door and then hesitates. "Hope you're not some juvenile delinquent about to take my van for a joyride."

She smiles, seemingly warmed for a moment. "'Course not. I'll be right here."

He shuts his door and pretends to scope out a spot to relieve himself. He heads behind an oak, peers over his shoulder to make sure he's still in her line of vision, and pretends to trip over a branch. He falls face-first to the ground, palms stinging from the oak leaves.

"Ouch!" he shouts. He stays there and closes his eyes, pretending to roll around, clutching his ankle in imagined pain. "Oh, Lord!"

Soon, just as he hoped, he hears the van's door open, then footsteps.

"Hawk?" she says, her voice getting closer.

He wrenches his face and rolls to his back, squeezing his ankle. He moans and waits for her.

She squats next to him. "Geez, are you okay?"

He opens his eyes and immediately sees she's still clutching the crystal. Shoot. He continues contorting his face and holding his left ankle.

"It's my—my—ankle. I might've broken it." He squeezes some tears out, delighted that they come so easily. "It's so painful. C-c-can you look? I might need to go to a hospital."

"Oh gosh. I don't know if I can help, but I'll try. I was a Girl Scout and learned some first aid ..."

Blah, blah, blah. Hawk ignores this. He doesn't want to know about her life. As he props himself up on his hands, she gently sets the crystal down next to her. That's all he cares about. Her hands are free. She's unarmed.

Victory!

The spiky, twinkling amethyst fills him with a monstrous lust.

Grimacing, she rolls up his pant leg to inspect his ankle. "Looks okay to me—"

It takes less than a second for him to grab the crystal from the ground and smash her skull with it. She falls forward on her knees and makes a sound between a grunt and a scream, blocking her head like a schoolgirl in a duck-and-cover drill. As he circles his hands around her throat from behind and squeezes as hard as he can, something in Hawk releases. It's the most intense pleasure he's ever felt in his life. Better than drugs. Better than sex. Better than the majesty of Mother Nature. She isn't trying to scream anymore, just clawing at his arms with sharp nails, frantic as a mouse trapped in a cage.

"Be still, or I'll hurt you," he whispers in her ear.

And she does. She squirms and thrashes at first, but then her body goes rigid and silent.

"Good," he says.

He allows her a few breaths of air, gasping and coughing, but keeps his hands around her neck and applies pressure to keep her obedient. The more she fights, the harder he squeezes. Then, Hawk does what he's dreamt of doing for a long time. He makes her do what he wants. He takes what is his. This isn't a girl anymore; this is a prize, belonging to him. Power, rage, possession, all rolled in one. The more she hurts, the better he feels.

When he's done, he smashes her head again with the crystal, and this time she goes still. His heartbeat continues racing in his chest as he watches her body pitch forward in the dirt. He stands up and buckles his belt. He kicks the body, and it doesn't move. In the silence, the freeway noise rises and falls. It's raining now, misty and smothering from all sides.

He strips the body of clothing with the emotionlessness of someone taking out the garbage. Balling up her skirt and blouse, he jogs to his van and tosses them on the floor. He takes a lighter out of the glove compartment and returns to the body. He sits with it, carefully burning each fingertip to make her harder to identify. Hawk has read stories in the paper. He knows how murderers get caught. The longer it takes to identify the body, the more time he has to get away. After a few seconds of hesitation, he turns the body over, face up. He tries not to look at its pale skin and unblinking eyes as he smashes the crystal into the middle of the head to make it harder to identify. He wants to rid it of all the marks that make it special. He thinks of butchers skinning animals, turning an individual creature into nothing but meat.

He sits with the body for just a few minutes, touching its skin with curiosity as it chills. He wishes he could stay longer. Seems wrong to just leave it here out in the open. Before he leaves, he picks up a bloody canine tooth scattered with flesh and bone in the oak leaves. He puts it in his pocket and fondles it like a sharp pebble as he whistles "Take Me Away" and heads back to his van.

The release, the relief, the sweet letdown, makes him feel the urge disappearing. Hawk is fed. He lets out the longest sigh as he slides back into the driver's seat. In the mirror, he isn't sure who he's staring at. He did it. He finally did the thing he always dreamt of doing. The hunger is satiated. Now he can dispose of the evidence—the bag, the clothing, the crystal— and shapeshift back into a normal man again and live a normal life. He just needed to get this out of his system, release the pressure.

As he drives, humming along with Creedence Clearwater Revival's "Green River," he keeps his bandaged hand on the wheel and his other hand in his pocket, where the tooth is. He rubs it between his fingertips.

Maybe he can let himself keep it. A memento of his first kill.

Because who's he kidding? Hibernation is a temporary state.

Hawk has only just begun.

HILL VALLEY GENERAL HOSPITAL PATIENT INTAKE FORM

Date: July 5, 1982

Time of Arrival: 6:47 PM

Patient Name: MITCHELL "MITCH" BLUE

Age: 33

Sex: Male

Chief Complaint: Gunshot wound to the head, extensive facial trauma, severe hemorrhaging.

Triage Level: Critical

Presenting Symptoms: Unconscious upon arrival, severe facial and cranial trauma, massive blood loss, exposed bone and tissue, fluctuating vitals.

Treatment Initiated: Emergency transfusion, intubation, stabilization of cranial injuries, preparation for surgical intervention.

Next of Kin: KATHERINE "KIT" BLUE (spouse)

Notes: Police on-site. Pending investigation.

17

I've been here before. Not this hospital, not this intensive care unit, but to this lost place. It's an empty field that stretches forever, and I'm in the middle of it, alone. It doesn't matter who is here with me in this gleaming linoleum hallway. My body is in Hill Valley General Hospital, but my mind is not. And my heart is shattered beyond repair.

Machines beep from open doorways, along with the indistinct murmurs of nurses and the occasional bumps and squeaks of gurney wheels. The eye-watering scent of lemon antiseptic burns the air. I fight another wave of nausea. I'm seated on the floor, hugging my knees, wishing I could disappear. Of all the people in the world, it's Detective Plough here with me.

"Mrs. Blue," he says again. "I know you're going through a lot right now. I know you're worried about your husband. But doctors are doing everything they can for him, and you sitting out here in the hallway blocking traffic won't bring him back any sooner."

He's crouched next to me. I smell coffee breath and musky cologne.

"You want to help your husband?" he asks gently.

I nod and choke back a sob.

"Then come with me and answer some questions," he says. "We'll let the nurse know where we are, and she'll come the second there are any updates. We're just going right down the hall."

I'm in such a state, so dizzy with emotion, so sick with worry, that I don't even have the energy to dislike Plough. In fact, he's almost a comfort—a familiar and surprisingly sympathetic face. He's holding his hat in his hands, revealing a balding head of graying hair, and for just a flash, I imagine he's someone's father. Maybe if Mitch were awake, he'd tell me not to talk to detectives. Fourth Amendment. But Mitch is fighting for his life behind closed doors. I don't know what else to do.

"Okay," I whisper finally.

Plough escorts me to a meeting room at the end of the hallway with a long table and plastic chairs. It's blindingly white. We sit down. He takes out his notepad and a pen, dropping them on the table with a *clack*.

"Look, I know you spoke with Detective Gomez at the scene when we arrived, but I want to go over a few things again. The more you can tell me, the more honest you are, the faster we can figure out what happened today."

I don't breathe, afraid if I do, the sobs will start and never stop. I nod.

"Tell me again how you found him."

"I came home from work," I say. "Front door was open. He was there, on the floor. I called 9-1-1 right away."

"Does Mitch own a gun?"

I hesitate, protective of Mitch. "A hunting rifle."

"Any handguns?"

"No."

I say it so certainly, but the thought crosses my mind. He

could have bought one and not told me. Maybe he bought one when he disappeared that one night recently. I have no idea what he was doing. It stings, imagining all I don't know about him and everything I can't ask him. That maybe he did this to himself, and I missed all the signs.

Plough waits for me to elaborate. When I don't, he leans in. "What was his state of mind these past few days?"

"He was ..." I swallow. "He's been having a rough time."

Plough jots this down. "Can you be more specific?"

Mitch is a private person. He barely even tells *me* anything, and he doesn't trust authority figures. He would absolutely hate this, but I reluctantly fill Plough in with the details of the past few weeks. How exhausted and stressed Mitch has been, and that I've been worried about his mental state. As I blurt this aloud, more details float to mind and add up—his temptation to drink again, his relapse, the stress of the investigation—and a story comes together in my mind.

Holy hell.

My heart nearly stops as I press my fingers to my lips. "Did Mitch shoot himself?"

Plough lights a cigarette. "Well. Kinda unusual to have a gun missing from a suicide scene, don't you think?"

He says it gently, but there's a barb to it. My mouth twitches in confusion.

"I don't understand," I say finally.

Exhaling smoke through his nostrils like a dragon, Plough taps his pen on his paper and studies me. His eyes might be kind, but his mouth is a permanent hard line.

"Know anyone who might have had a reason to do this to him?" he asks.

An invisible hand slaps me from nowhere—my last conversation with Freddie. But I clamp my mouth shut and shake my head vehemently.

"No," I say. No, no, absolutely not. He would not.

"Not anyone?"

"No."

Plough remains frozen, watching, cigarette smoke clouding the surrounding air. "Walk me through this one more time. You come up to the house, door's open. You see anything suspicious? A car parked nearby, voices, a shadowy figure in the bushes?"

"I already told you everything," I say, my voice tight.

"Tell it to me again."

My heart is beating so fast. The way he's watching me, like he's trying to bore a hole in my head so he can see inside, is making me writhe, even though I did nothing wrong.

"Can we do this later?" I ask, wiping my eyes. "I can't think right now. I just want to see my husband."

"Of course." His expression relaxes into something resembling sympathy. "Let's take a break. You want a soda or something? Water?"

I shake my head.

"Just one quick, last question." He drops his cigarette butt in a paper cup next to him, and it sizzles out with a little *sss*. "Can you tell me where you were when all this happened?"

My belly pitches as if I'm falling, even though I'm sitting down. "I was working. I got off at five, and I drove home."

"Straight home?"

I nod automatically but realize, after I've started, that it wasn't *straight home*—I stopped to call Gloria's number. Do I need to tell him that? What would it matter? A mental hurricane spirals. A knock rescues me from Plough's laser-eyed focus, and when the door opens, it's like someone letting oxygen into the room again.

"Mrs. Blue?" a nurse says. "The doctor has an update on your husband."

"Oh, thank God," I say, getting up and following her out the door.

I meet a man in a white uniform out in the hallway. I brace myself when I see his tired smile and the pitying stare behind his horn-rimmed glasses.

Please be good news. Please, please, please.

"Your husband is in the OR," he explains. "We're moving ahead with a craniotomy right now to remove debris. It appears we're dealing with a perforating wound, which means the projectile entered and exited the cranium."

I don't know what a single word he said means. It sounds promising, but the look on his face says otherwise.

"That's good, right?" I stand up straighter, trying to read his expression.

"Well, he's in a comatose state and his condition is critical. We can't know the extent of the damage yet."

"Is he ... going to survive?"

He squeezes my arm. "I promise, we'll update you as soon as we have more information. It's going to be a couple of hours, at least, before we know more. Get some rest in the meantime."

"I can't rest," I whisper.

His words ring in my ears, along with the taps of his shiny black shoes clicking down the hallway—quiet, quieter, and then gone altogether.

I've never been much good at praying. I put my hands together and arch my neck back. My blurry eyes fixate on the lights flickering in the ceiling.

Please, I silently beg.

But only the Big Empty replies.

18

In the ICU, there are no windows, just a fluorescent glow as if we're locked in endless artificial sunshine. I pace the halls, too upset to stew in the waiting room, instead circling the nurse's station like a shark, hoping I'll get an update soon. I can't eat, drink, or sleep. I feel guilty even going to the bathroom, afraid I'll miss an update. As if to complete the timeless nature of this hellish night, my watch battery stops working at one a.m. Suddenly, with a mental strike of lightning, I remember Bowie. How could I have forgotten? What kind of pet owner am I? Bowie wasn't there when I came home today. Where the hell is my dog? I sit on the floor of the hall and bawl.

I've never felt so alone, yet I'm far from it. Strangers keep coming by and checking up on me, worried about my state of mind. Nurses kneel to encourage me to move to the waiting room. A woman in white pumps asks me to sign some paperwork. Just when my eyes can't stay open any longer, Plough returns with my purse and keys, which I left at the scene.

"Cleared these for you. We bagged your jacket as evidence, though."

I examine my purse. There's a smear of brown-red blood dried at the bottom. I turn the purse around to hide it, nauseated. For the hundredth time, I ask myself if this is a bad dream.

"What time is it?" I ask.

"Five-thirty. Any updates?"

"No. Not yet."

"Is there someone I can call for you?"

I shake my head, biting the side of my tongue as hard as I can.

"He's my someone," I whisper, nodding toward the direction where hospital staff wheeled his body away so long ago now.

"A family member, maybe?" Plough tries.

For a split second, Freddie comes to mind, but there's no way I'm sending a detective his way. Freddie would run as soon as he saw the badge. "No."

"A girlfriend?"

I shake my head again.

"This could take some time, you know," Plough says. "Some sleep might do you good. Your house is still a mess, even though we cleared it this morning. If you want to—"

"My dog," I say suddenly, looking up. "Did you see my dog? He wasn't there when I came home. I'm afraid he's lost in the woods since the door was left open. There are coyotes."

"Listen. How 'bout this. You and I go to the station. You give me an official statement, and we check to see if anyone spotted your dog. Sound good?"

"No." I wipe my eyes. "I'm staying here until Mitch is out."

The muscles tense in his jaw. "Suit yourself. I'll check back in soon."

Watching his alligator-skin boots click away down the hall, I blow out a long sigh.

My head is heavy with exhaustion. I close my eyes, and

there's Mitch on the floor of the entryway again. There he is, smiling on our wedding day in his linen shirt and pants, barefoot in the sand. His beautiful face, perpetually tanned from being out in the sunshine. The way he seems to know a little of everything and can do anything artfully, from fixing a broken toaster to patching up holes in the roof. The chair he refinished and painted in my favorite shade of red. The maraca he made and gave to me on our wedding day. Our one-month anniversary, when he shocked me by writing me a poem. Mitch is mysterious, full of surprises, and he keeps me on my toes. He's held me close in a way no one else has in my life.

I can't lose him.

I put my hands together and beam every positive vibe I have in my soul his way. While I've never been much of a prayer, I've always been an optimist. I believe people are good and strong and can survive unthinkable tragedies—and I think love can be a savior. Mitch and I will get through this. I know it.

As if on cue, the doctor comes out of the swinging doors at the end of the hall—the same doctor in the horn-rimmed glasses.

"There she is," he says with a smile.

A smile—that's a good sign. I scramble to my feet.

"How is he?" I ask.

"Your husband's craniotomy went well."

"Can I see him?"

"He's being moved to a room, and then, yes, you can go sit with him."

I put a hand to my chest. The sheer relief is almost dizzying. "So, he's okay?"

"He's stabilized," the doctor says again. "But ... from here, we have to wait and see."

"Wait and see about what?"

"He's comatose," the doctor reminds me, smile weakening. "He still has brain activity, and he's not on a ventilator—the bullet didn't hit the brainstem, which is good news. But we'll not know the extent of the damage for some time."

My shoulders slump. "Comatose."

Somehow, I hoped he would make it through surgery and then wake up again soon after. But the look on this doctor's face tells me this is only the beginning of a long recovery.

"He could come out of it at any moment," the doctor says softly. "Or he could remain this way for some time. There could be permanent brain damage, resulting in disability or requiring physical therapy—or none."

I try to squeeze some hope out of my dry, little heart. "What would you guess will happen? Based on what you've seen?"

He sighs. "You know, I wish I were a fortune teller and not a doctor sometimes." He pats my arm. "Look at the bright side: He's extremely lucky to be alive. He's already beaten the odds."

I wipe my eyes, take a deep breath. "True. Thank you."

The doctor disappears down the hall. My ears are ringing, my face is numb. And it hits me. No—it doesn't just hit me; it buries me. An avalanche to the soul.

Even if Mitch survives, nothing will ever be the same again.

19

I'm not looking at my husband.

Nope. Absolutely not. The man in front of me—head bandaged, tiny sliver of his purple, swollen face visible—is not the man I married. There are tubes in his nose, tubes snaking out of his arms, tubes poking from under his blankets. Not only does he not look like Mitch, but he barely looks human. He's some alien creature in a sci-fi movie, and I'm on a spaceship, surrounded by beeping machines I don't understand.

"Hi, babe," I whisper, cautiously taking a seat next to him.

I scoot closer, afraid to examine his face too closely. It's painful to look at and terrifying to imagine what's under the gauze. Instead, I focus on placing my hand on his, comforted by his familiar warmth. That part of him is the same. If I don't move my gaze, it's like nothing has changed. Except for his ring finger, which has a band of white where his ring used to be. The doctors must have removed it.

The stillness of the room gives me goosebumps. My posture melts. I squeeze his hand, tracing over his bare ring finger again.

I hang my head and take a second to gather myself before speaking. I don't want to weep, not when he can hear me. That won't help him. I need to channel the hope that keeps slipping away from me.

"Everything's going to be fine, Mitch," I say, squeezing his hand.

The only response is the sound of his heart-rate monitor. *Beep-beep-beep.* I flick my gaze to it and observe the miniature roller coaster of his heartbeat. Then I dare myself to focus on his face, horrific as it is. Something in me softens at the sight of his delicate eyelashes, the shape of his eyebrow. He might be puffy and bruised, but it's still him.

"You're going to get through this. Okay? You're one of the strongest people I know. And I'm here with you, every step of the way."

Beep-beep-beep.

"I just don't understand what happened," I say, reaching up to pat his arm. His muscular arm just lies there, limp. "What *happened?*"

Beep-beep-beep.

"You need to wake up and tell me, so we can figure it out."

Beep-beep-beep.

"Did you do this to yourself, or did someone else shoot you? Who would have shot you?"

Once again, Freddie is still the only name that comes to mind. I hate the thought so much I hold my breath until it passes. The machine keeps beeping. Same, steady electronic drumbeat. I could make a terrible song out of it.

"I'm going to get some coffee," I say. "Be right back."

I wander out to the hall to a silver dispenser next to the elevators. My hands are shaking as I fill the Styrofoam cup. There's too much going on. I can't do this. I don't know what to do. Nothing feels real; nothing makes sense. Mitch always told me I was unbreakable. But I think he's finally broken me.

"Mrs. Blue?" a voice says.

I turn the other way, where a woman stands in front of the elevators. Not a woman—a girl, one whom I take a couple of blinks to recognize. The round glasses. The pantyhosed legs and clean, white sneakers.

It's Rhonda, wearing a pleated, red-and-white striped dress.

"Rhonda?" I ask, confused.

I'm in some strange fever dream. Why am I standing in a hospital hallway? Why is Rhonda here, and why is she dressed that way?

She adjusts her glasses. "Why are you here?"

"Why are *you* here?"

"I volunteer two days a week as a candy striper." She points proudly to her lanyard that says VOLUNTEER.

I should have put two and two together, but I'm in shambles. She studies my face.

"Mrs. Blue, are you okay?"

I shake my head.

"Did something happen?" she asks.

"Mitch," I say thickly. "He—"

I can't even get the words out. They're stuck. I don't know how to say what Mitch is. He's not dead, but he's not alive either. He did this to himself, or someone else did it to him. For a moment, the sight of his maimed face flashes through me like an electric shock, and I can't speak.

"What happened?" she asks. "Take your time."

"Mitch was shot," I finally whisper, the words sounding so weird it's like I made them up. They're not actual words. They're gibberish.

"My goodness. Is he—"

"He's alive. He's in a coma." I look behind her, toward his doorway down the hall. "I need to get back to him."

For once, I seem to have rendered Rhonda speechless. "My condolences. Sincerely. What can I do to help you?"

I shake my head. C-3PO has more warmth than Rhonda, but she's trying.

"Can I get you some food?"

I shake my head again.

"Does Mr. Marrs know? Should I call him?"

I'm shaking my head so much I'm dizzy. He's the last person I want to talk to right now. There's only one other person in my life I want here, and he doesn't have a phone.

"Is there anyone else I can contact for you? Your brother? I saw him just a little while ago when I was parking my car. In the park?"

"What park?"

"Here. Downtown."

"Just a few blocks away?"

She nods.

"Actually, yes," I say, stunned.

She pats my back awkwardly. "I'll find him, and we'll be back in a jiffy."

"Thanks."

I watch her sneakers squeak down the hall before she's swallowed by the elevator.

I need Freddie right now. I need someone to tell me it's going to be okay.

But there's another reason I need him here. Freddie's voice comes into my head, clear as a bell. *What I wouldn't give for him to disappear one day and never come home again.*

I need to find out if he has anything to do with this.

HAWK

1971

Six months pass.

Six months of tumbleweed towns in the Southwest, odd jobs picking apples or washing cars, a carpentry apprenticeship outside Dallas, a camping trip in the Ozarks. He cracks jokes and makes people smile. Fixes broken machines. Sits in church pews and studies the stained glass as the sounds of a pipe organ tickle his eardrums. Scatters away when he hears sirens. Kisses drunk girls in alleys behind honky-tonk bars. Grows his hair longer, a beard, wears a pouch around his neck, where, every so often, he pulls the tooth out and savors the sharpness between his fingertips.

But Hawk stays quiet, still, and the girl he once hunted becomes nothing but a black-and-white dream. A movie he saw, maybe. A spot on a map of the Pacific Northwest. A news article about a body. Sometimes the memory flickers back with intensity and vivid sound and color, making his heart beat wildly and his mouth water. Sometimes he sees a lonely girl at a bus stop and fights the urge to pull over and choke her and leave her naked body in a field.

The urge starts as a whisper, and its volume cranks up day by day. It burns deep under his skin somewhere—a carnal distraction that mounts in intensity. A hot pride, the sly knowledge that he got away with something so deeply, deliciously wicked, that he's smarter and better than the rest of them. He returns to Olympia twice to scour the local papers and check if they still talked about what he had done. He returns to the spot and sits on the log, gets on his hands and knees in the dirt to sniff it for memories. But it's as if it never happened.

He wonders what the body looked like when they found it, and a rage stirs, because that body belongs to him. And the first girl who got away—sometimes he experiences a wistful twinge that he never felt the crack of her skull. It burrows underneath his skin that she escaped him, outsmarted him, and outran him.

That will never happen again.

It's spring when the snow disappears off the mountain-tops. The rain paints the meadows in wildflowers, screaming yellow and blood-red and bruised blue. He's been staying with a friend at his ranch in southern Idaho, helping renovate some rooms, and living in a trailer off the property for a month. It's a mile away from the only school in town— kindergarten through senior year—and he finds reasons to drive by it often, the wolf in him awakening as he spots the high school girls lounging out by the bus loop with their long legs and big eyes. He circles the block again, again, and drives home frustrated.

But on his last day in town, his bags packed, the jagged wheel in him turns. He knows how easy it would be. He's leaving for another project in Texas tomorrow morning.

When Hawk gets hungry, he just can't help himself.

It's late afternoon when he sees her: a teenage girl with the hair parted in the middle, plaid skirt, bookbag slung over her shoulder. A straggler, the school nearly empty. She's crying and walking home. Her tears are blood in the water to a hungry shark.

"Hey there, are you okay?" He slows down and leans out his window. "Can I give you a ride somewhere?"

She sniffs and shakes her head, stiffening up and walking faster.

"Hey," he says, louder, offended she doesn't answer him. He pulls over, and the girl stops to fully look at him. "I was actually looking for help. I'm lost. I'm hoping you can help me get to a gas station because I'm about to run out."

"Up the road." She wipes her eyes. "Turn right on Connor Avenue until you hit the highway."

"I just came from Connor and ..." He shakes his head, bites his lip. He fakes a wince. "Man, it's so frustrating." He doesn't blink his eyes, hoping they might get dry enough that he can eke out a tear or two. "This injury of mine ... went to 'Nam and now I get spun around everywhere I go. At this point, I'm going to be late to go see my little boy."

The girl adjusts the strap of her backpack, her daisy earrings dangling. He notices her freckles and her tiny wrists. How easily they could snap with a quick twist of his fingers.

"Timmy," he says, pulling the picture of the boy out from his rearview.

"It's just right up the road," the girl says, but her voice softens as her eyes fall on the picture.

"I don't suppose you'd show me where? I'd gladly take you home for your trouble."

She shakes her head. "That's all right."

He pretends to sniff his armpit. "What, do I smell or something?"

The girl breaks into a giggle, revealing her crooked teeth. She looks younger now—thirteen or fourteen, maybe. "'Course not."

"Then get in and help me get some gas so I can see my kid," he says. "Pretty please?"

The girl glances down the road. "I live pretty close to the gas station."

"Well, perfect. Come on in. I won't bite."

With a dramatic sigh, the girl climbs into the passenger seat. His pulse races as he tucks the picture of "Timmy" back in his rearview mirror. Too easy. If God doesn't want him to do this, then why does He make it so easy? If God doesn't want the bunnies to die, why'd he invent the hawk? His stomach rumbles, but it isn't food he wants.

He spins small talk, asking about school. About two minutes into the drive, the girl's gaze flicks to his gas gauge, and a thick silence fills the air. She must notice it isn't anywhere near empty.

And then, when he doesn't turn on Connor, she hovers her hand over the door handle.

"Could you please pull over?" she asks in a shaky voice.

"I'm sorry, I'm all turned around," he says amiably. "Missed the turnoff."

But she isn't smiling. She's rigid, sensing danger. He feels the energy shift. And then she cries again, softly, hand trembling on the door handle. He almost hears the *tick-tick* of her frantic thoughts, wondering if it'd hurt more to stay here in the car or jump and go hurtling down the highway.

"I wouldn't do that if I were you, precious," he says to her sadly, putting a hand on her bony knee with an anticipatory shiver. "What's your name?"

She doesn't answer, sniffling into her hair.

"Mine's Hawk," he says with a wide grin, and presses his foot harder on the gas.

20

Hours later, I'm still in the hospital, parked next to Mitch. No movement, no updates. Thanks to countless Styrofoam cups filled with burnt coffee, I've been awake so long now I might be having an out-of-body experience. Staring out the window at the back parking lot for just a minute, I think I'm in my old apartment back in Los Angeles. Then fantasy disintegrates, and reality hits me with its sledgehammer.

At least the *beep-beep-beep*ing has stopped. After I complained about it a while ago, a nurse came and pressed a mute button on the machine. The silence is golden.

"Mrs. Blue?" a voice says.

I spin around, spooked. It's Rhonda poking her head in the doorway.

"Freddie is here," she says. "I need to go attend to my duties, but I'll check in again soon."

She hurries off, and Freddie steps inside, looking both very stoned and very concerned.

"Kit," he says. "Holy shit. Can I come in?"

I nod, unable to even utter a single word. Relief is a flood.

He steps inside and hugs me tightly. I bury my face in the shoulder of his jacket, which smells like cigarette smoke and beer, but I don't care right now. I'm just so glad to have someone holding me for a minute.

"What in the fucking fuck happened, man?" he asks.

I pull back and wipe my eyes. It takes less than one second for me to know in my heart Freddie has nothing to do with this. His expression—ghost-white, shocked, almost sick-looking—says it all. And I'm so relieved that I cry. What was wrong with me, to even suspect Freddie for a second? I must be losing my mind. The exhaustion is making me paranoid.

"Mitch shot himself, or someone shot him." I wipe my eyes. "I don't know."

"I just—can't wrap my head around this. This is crazy."

"I know."

After a long pause, we sit down in plastic chairs facing the bed, the saddest little audience. Mitch lies in front of us, lifeless except for his chest moving up and down.

Now that Freddie's here, the silence that has been crushing me since I entered this hospital room vanishes. A gush pours out of me. I tell Freddie how I found Mitch in the entryway. How the police and paramedics arrived, and then the ambulance ride. The emergency surgery, the mystery of when he'll wake up, and what he'll be like when he does. I unload nearly every worry I have, right down to where my dog might have run off to and whether he's okay. Freddie responds monosyllabically: *shit, fuck, damn,* and, when I tell him about Plough questioning me with something approaching suspicion, he utters a single *motherfucker.* Freddie's never been one for advice. He's a listener. A validator.

Sometimes, that's all I need. Finally, I've run out of things to say. I catch my breath as if I've just run a marathon.

"What have you been up to?" I ask.

It sounds ridiculous, considering everything, me trying to make cheerful small talk here when my husband's in a coma after a bullet went through his brain. Freddie must agree, because he scoffs.

"Do you really want to know, Kit?" he asks. "I don't think you do."

My brow wrinkles. I turn to him, to those brown eyes that match mine. And in a jarring lightning of emotion, he reminds me of our father. I bury the thought.

"You need to get some sleep," he says.

I shake my head.

"What good are you to him if you lose your mind, Kit? Everybody needs sleep."

I shake my head.

"Let me take you home, feed you a meal, and help you find your dog. Take a nap and recharge so you can come back here tonight."

I lean my head back and eyeball the ceiling, as if there might be an answer dangling somewhere up there. Freddie's right. I'm going to lose it soon if I don't attend to my basic bodily functions. If I don't take care of myself, I can't take care of anyone else.

"He's in safe hands here. Shit, the safest hands, you know? They'll call you if—when—he wakes up."

"I want to be here, though." I blow out a long sigh. "But yeah, you're right. I just—I don't even have my car. I have to think this through."

"I can give you a ride, Mrs. Blue," Rhonda says from the doorway, raising her hand as if she's in school.

I didn't even realize she was still there. Jesus. How long has she been standing there?

"Oh," I say.

"Sorry to startle you—just swinging by again to check in. I couldn't help but overhear what you said about needing a ride."

Under different circumstances, Rhonda's tendency to eavesdrop might annoy me. But I don't have it in me right now.

"Really, it's no trouble at all," Rhonda insists. "I like to be of service."

Freddie squeezes my shoulder. "You should say yes. Yes," he says louder, this time to Rhonda. "Yes, thank you."

I speak with the nurse, triple-checking that they have my correct telephone number. I kiss Mitch on the cheek and whisper in his good ear that I'll be back soon. Then I join Rhonda and Freddie in the elevator, where they're waiting. As we start our descent, my exhaustion hits me with a gravity so strong I lean against the silver wall for support.

"AC/DC," Rhonda says, eyeing Freddie's T-shirt. "Are you an electrician?"

"No, I just like to rock," he says.

An awkward silence ensues. It continues throughout the walk to the car and the drive home. Rhonda drives her Pinto like an old lady, five miles below the speed limit, and news sputters from the AM radio channel. The words might as well be a foreign language to me right now: Pan Am Flight 759. Ronald Reagan. World Cup. A baby born from a test tube.

"Here," I tell her, pointing out my house when the excruciatingly long ride is over.

Rhonda pulls into my driveway, using her signal even though there's no one else around. Yellow crime scene tape blows in the wind around my front porch. The sight of it sours my stomach. It's real. This happened. The last time I was here, Mitch was nearly dead on the other side of our front door.

"Wow," Rhonda says, craning her neck. "The scene of the crime."

She unbuckles her seatbelt, as if she thinks she's coming inside, but I put a stop to that line of thinking quickly.

"Thanks so much." I pop open my car door. "Really appreciate the ride. I'll see you at work ..." I stop, one foot on the ground, squinting at her. "What day is it again?"

"Tuesday."

I note the time on her dash clock: three in the afternoon.

"Oh shit, I need to call in to work," I say.

"Don't worry," she replies. "I already spoke with Mr. Marrs and explained the situation."

I'm one part annoyed, one part grateful. "Thank you," I say. "See you ... soon."

I emerge from the car, but Freddie has passed out in the backseat. I knock on the window, startling him, and he has the same look on his face that he did when he was a kid with a bowl cut—like he has absolutely no idea where or who he is for a split second before the world comes into focus.

Freddie comes out and joins me, saying a few *fuck*s as we step through the crunchy leaves and branches and get to the front porch. He says a few more when he sees the bloody mess that awaits us as soon as I open the front door. The smell hits— a gut-churning rot.

"I can't deal with this right now," I whisper.

"Don't worry. I'll deal with it." Freddie puts his hand on my back and helps me step past the carnage, into the house. "Go lie down. I'll make you a sandwich or something."

"Bowie ..."

"I'll find the dog, too. Don't worry, Kit, I've got you."

I can't tell you what a load those words take off of me. I'm so grateful I could cry. Freddie disappears into the kitchen and opens the fridge, muttering, "Where's the fuckin' peanut butter?" I pan around, taking everything in, so surreal, it's like I walked into someone else's house. The furniture has been moved, the rug peeled back, and there are dusty footprints on the hardwood. Drawers left open, a potted plant broken on the living room floor. I imagine Mitch's voice in my head. *You let cops in here? Without a warrant?*

Yes, I imagine saying back. *Because you shot yourself in the entrance to our fucking house.*

I'm having imaginary conversations now. I do a death march down the hallway and into our bedroom and face-plant on the quilt.

One would think that, after being awake for nearly forty hours, or however long it's been, I would fall right asleep. But I don't. As Freddie clatters around my kitchen, all I can think of is Mitch. My heartbeat reminds me of him. I can almost still hear the beeping. When Freddie slips in and puts a sandwich on my bedside table, I don't move. I stay tucked safely in this dark place.

For a long time, my thoughts loop. I find Mitch on the ground again and again. I remember bits and pieces from the hospital in random order—snippets of my conversation with Plough, the doctor's grave expression, a nurse with lipstick on her teeth. And one line keeps repeating in my head, over and over, like a digital delay effect: *Kinda unusual to have a gun missing from a suicide scene, don't you think?* The truth of it hits me with full force. Mitch didn't do this. Mitch *wouldn't* do this. I know Mitch, and he wouldn't shoot himself in the head. Someone did this to him.

Freddie's listening to records in my living room now.

He is singing along to the Wipers. His footsteps rise and fall, up and down the hall. Murmuring to himself. The flush of a toilet.

Why does he sound so normal?

I must have drifted off, because I awaken with a startle and a face covered in drool. My room is dim. I take a moment to orient myself, hearing birds singing and the shy light of morning. How did so much time pass? My heart pounds, and I sit up. I'm in bed, alone.

"Mitch?"

The Big Empty punches me straightaway. Then the memories kick in.

I get up. The house is quiet, lights off. Panic prickles like a hot rash. I hurry out to the living room. My brother's asleep on the couch with Bowie on his lap, records splayed on the floor.

"Bowie!" I say, shocked.

My dog comes running, happy to see me, so innocent, with no idea of the harsh, real world. It undoes something in me as I bend down, and he licks my face. A teary laugh escapes my lips.

Freddie stirs on the couch. I dare to steal a peek at the entryway—he cleaned it up. I step closer, examining the floorboards, the entrance. You'd never know there was so much blood there hours ago. The entire room smells like Pine Sol.

"Hey," Freddie says with a groggy smile, sitting up on the couch. "Passed out there."

"Where'd you find Bowie?" I ask him, scratching my dog's head. "I'm so happy to see you, buddy."

"He was there in the studio."

I stop petting Bowie's head, taken aback. "In the studio?"

"Yep. Sorry to say he left you a few stinky candy bars while he was out there."

I wrinkle my nose both at the news and that description.

"I can't believe ... why was he in the studio?" I ask.

"The fuck do I know?" Freddie says, pulling a sad, half-smoked joint from the pocket of his black jeans.

My head swims. Who put Bowie in the studio? It sounds like something Mitch would do if Mitch were going to kill himself. But Mitch didn't kill himself. It would make zero sense to kill yourself in the entrance to your house with your door wide open, and I agree with Plough that a gun missing from a suicide scene is baffling.

Who else would take the time to put Bowie in the studio? I get a shiver. Freddie. The confidence I felt earlier melts a little. My gut says he didn't do this, but the facts are staring me in the face. What if my gut is wrong?

"Freddie ..." I say.

How on earth do I finish that sentence? How do I ask my brother, the closest person to me in the entire world, if he shot my husband? It's as if I've forgotten English. I can't say what I mean.

Doesn't matter anyway, because a sharp knock on the door interrupts the conversation. I flinch at the sound of it.

"Who is it?" Freddie asks, eyes widening.

I cross to the window and peek out the curtain. There's an unmarked vehicle parked in our driveway.

"Detective," I say.

It's Plough, I know it. He's come to find me twice yesterday at the hospital, and both times I narrowly missed him.

"Shit," Freddie says, raking his hands through his frizzy hair. "Wait a second."

I go to the entryway. "I need to talk to him, Freddie."

"Well, I'm getting the fuck out of here, then," he says, rushing to the couch and grabbing his backpack. "I have a warrant out for me, remember? I was never here."

My mouth hangs open as my brother runs out of the living room, through the hallway, into my bedroom, and slams the door. Rage throbs behind my eyes, threatening tears. I should have known reaching out to Freddie would only make every-thing more chaotic.

If Mitch were here, he'd say, *I told you so.*

I open the door for Plough.

"Howdy, Kit," Plough says. "How you holdin' up?"

"I've been better," I say.

"I can imagine." When he takes his hat off, he resembles a kind, older man more than a drugstore cowboy. "Mind if I come in and ask a few questions?"

I open the door wider for him. "Sure."

He steps inside, studying the floor. "You got the place nice and cleaned up, I see. How's Mitch?"

"Same." I lead him to the kitchen table. "You want some tea or something?"

"Sure." Plough takes a seat and slaps his notebook in front of him on the table as I put the teapot on. He sniffs the air. "Smells ... funky."

At first, I think he means the lingering scent of bleach, but then I realize Freddie was just in here. And wherever Freddie goes, the scent of marijuana follows. *Damn it, Freddie.* My cheeks blaze, and my heart races—the last thing I want is for Plough to think I'm a druggie.

"My brother was here," is all I say, hoping that will suffice.

"You got a brother?" Plough asks with surprise, opening his notebook to a fresh page. "I didn't know that. He live with you?"

"Not officially. He stays here sometimes."

His bushy eyebrows go up. "Was he staying here when someone shot Mitch?"

I shake my head.

"How do he and Mitch get along?" Plough asks.

My mouth goes dry. All I can do is shrug.

"You have his contact info?" Plough leans in on his elbows. "I'd really like to meet him and ask a few questions."

"He's ... in between places right now. Couch surfing."

My throat constricts. I glance at the hallway where my brother disappeared only minutes ago. I'm paralyzed, not sure what to do—should I tell Plough he's here?

Plough seems to read my mind. "He here right now?"

A long pause stretches. I scramble for the right answer. But sometimes, the only thing left to do is tell the truth.

I nod.

"Can I talk to him?"

"I don't think he's going to want to talk to you."

"You mind askin' him for me?"

In the pause, my stomach sinks. I can't tell you why exactly, but I have a feeling I just opened Pandora's box.

"I can try," I say, getting up.

Slowly, I make my way through the living room and hallway. I go to my bedroom and push open the door.

"Freddie?" I say.

The room is still; no sign of him, but the bathroom door is closed. I knock.

"Freddie?"

Nothing.

"Freddie, answer me."

In the silence, my dread expands.

"If you don't, I'm going to open the door on you." I swallow, waiting. "You'd better not have your pants down." I give him one last chance to speak up before saying, "One, two, three."

I push the door open.

The bathroom is empty: window wide open, breeze tossing the curtains. Dirty footprints smear the toilet seat cover.

He ran.

I breathe in deeply and blow the sigh out. I can't say I'm surprised—just disappointed.

And as I stare at that open window, a worse thought creeps in.

Freddie might be much more dangerous than I ever imagined.

21

I return to the kitchen and tell Plough the bad news. "It appears my brother took off through my bathroom window."

Plough stares at me so long I'm not sure if he heard me. "He …"

I swallow hard. Time for the full story. "He has a warrant out for him. He doesn't want to get picked up."

"He has a *warrant* out for him?" Plough gets up from his seat, the chair scraping the floor with a scream. "And you didn't think to tell me this?"

"I …"

But Plough's already out the door and heading to his car for his radio. Ten minutes later, he's had a conversation with the dispatcher, and backup is on its way. Plough comes back into my house, sweaty-shiny and pink as an Easter ham. He grabs his notebook and hat.

"You're telling me you've got a brother who was staying with you who had two warrants out for his arrest for felony aggravated assault and failure to appear and you didn't think, *gee, maybe I should tell that nice detective who keeps asking me questions?*"

His words steal the wind from me. "Aggravated assault?"

"He beat a woman in Burbank and then jumped bail. You didn't know this?"

My jaw drops. "No. I didn't."

Plough doesn't blink, his flame-blue gaze searing into me.

My cheeks flush. "That doesn't sound like him," I try to explain. "He's—he gets in trouble, but he's not usually violent."

"Not usually violent?" Plough wipes his brow. "The rap sheet on this guy's a mile long."

"I didn't know about the assault," I repeat, my voice shrinking.

My heart just found a brand-new way to break.

The morning unravels into dizzying confusion. Backup arrives soon after: two more squad cars in my driveway, police combing the woods for Freddie. No one finds him—not a footprint, nothing. I tell them everything I know about Freddie since he came to town. I tell them about Mitch's truck being vandalized, about Freddie showing up to Breakneck Bay and confronting me, and his vague threat. I hold nothing back. I'm shattered, exhausted, and done protecting him.

"This guy's already seriously hurt someone," Plough tells me. "He's capable of violence. He had a motive to shoot Mitch. It all adds up."

I nod, wiping my eyes.

"No more protecting your big brother, Kit," Plough says as he heads back to his car. "See what happens when you do? People get hurt. You don't want more people hurt, do you?"

I shake my head.

"Then promise me I am the *first* person you call when anything happens. You hear a whisper from Freddie, and you'd better be running to call me."

I promise.

In a daze, as twilight settles in, I drive to visit Mitch and sit beside him. His state is the same—stable, but comatose. I watch him, feeling sorrier than I ever have before—what if I'm the reason he got hurt? What if me letting Freddie back into our life meant I was inviting violence into our home? I wipe my eyes, my chest throbbing. I want to implode.

When I return home, night has drowned the world. I'm not Kit anymore. I'm a husk. I'm as empty and quiet and dim and messy as this house. I kick my shoes off and sit on the couch, stunned, petting Bowie's head. I don't know what to think anymore. But there's also this overwhelming relief beneath it all, as if the floor is steadying beneath my feet. It's so weird and backward to sit here alone in the lamplight, succumbed to the Big Empty, and yet ... I feel *safer*.

Because Freddie's gone now.

I know Freddie. He got a whiff of police and bolted the second he smelled trouble. He probably scaled the hill to the interstate, hitchhiked, and crossed state lines at this point.

It's as if a violent storm has passed. The peace in the air, in my bloodstream, is palpable. Freddie shot Mitch. There it is: the ugly answer. The horrid truth. It just adds up. Freddie's unstable, a criminal, and jealous. He hates Mitch. The police will catch up with him, eventually. He'll die in prison or in the gutter in the not-too-distant future. It kills me to think that, but it's true. Freddie's fate was written years ago.

And I can't save him anymore.

Now, I need to focus on what's important: helping Mitch heal. Getting our life back together. Being a normal person again, one who eats meals and showers and goes to work and remembers to feed her dog. That kind of thing.

"You hungry, Bow?" I ask, getting up from the couch.

I cross to the kitchen, where his silver bowl is empty. Bad dog mom. Very bad dog mom. I fill his bowl with kibble. He trembles with excitement as I put it on the floor, then wolfs it down.

That's when I notice the little red light blinking on the answering machine.

Thinking it might be the hospital telling me Mitch suddenly woke up—*please, please, please*—or some update about Freddie's whereabouts, I trip over my own two feet to listen to it.

I press play. Static crackles, then heavy breathing.

The back of my neck tingles.

"Mrs. Blue," a voice starts.

It's a female voice, one I don't recognize—fragile, weepy, and slurred. There's a silence so long I think that's all there is. But then ...

"... sorry I shot your husband," it sounds like she says.

Click.

In a single second, my blood turns to ice.

I must have misheard her. That can't be what she said. It was distorted. My exhausted mind's playing tricks on me. Her voice was hard to understand.

I replay it.

"Mrs. Blue ... sorry I shot your husband."

Though the tape makes it sound garbled and distant, this time I'm sure of it. Horror squeezes my heart.

"What?" I whisper, staring at the machine, as if it can answer.

I listen to it one more time, holding my breath. Do I know that voice? It seems familiar, but I truly don't know. She sounds young. And drunk, maybe. The weepiness I heard the first time sounds like it's maybe even laughing—I can't tell.

I stand still for a long time. It's like the earth pumps the brakes and comes to a complete, full stop. My mind goes blank, until a memory blows through. A month ago, Mitch got a couple of prank calls. Stupid crap: a giggling guy asking for Mike Hunt. A heavy breather who said, "I'm watching you" and then burst into laughter and hung up.

That must be what this is. Some asshole who thinks it's funny to prank call me right now.

"Not cool," I say. "Not the time."

I take out the tape from the answering machine, replace it with a new one, and stash the tape to give to Plough later—just in case.

But for now, I let it go. I have enough to worry about. For one, I need to get a good night's sleep. Tomorrow I'm heading in to work. It's not because the Ouch Shack matters to me—they can cover my shifts just fine. But now that Freddie's become the number one suspect in my mind for who shot Mitch, I'm assuming that he's behind everything: the truck being vandalized. The "crime scene" in Mitch's office. God knows what else.

The rap sheet on this guy's a mile long.

I love him, no matter what. He's my brother. But everything I don't know about him terrifies me.

I need to find out more about his connection to Breakneck Bay that might link him to Mitch's vandalized office. And talk to Creighton.

After getting ready for bed, I dig into our bedroom closet, popping the light bulb on overhead. There are a few dusty footprints, like the police were here at some point. Mitch's hunting rifle is still in the corner next to his fishing pole. I shudder at the sight of his belongings—he has so few of them. On my side, there are bright dresses and tall boots and purses, and scarves. But he just has this one corner. I can't stare at it, or I'll cry. Instead, I grab the hunting rifle.

"You'll be back soon, baby," I say, closing the closet door.

I have to keep myself together. Tomorrow is another day.

I slide the rifle to Mitch's side of the bed, take two sleeping pills, and try to forget for a little while.

22

I'm pulled together this morning by under-eye concealer, a cemented fake smile, and a lot of talking to myself aloud as I drive to work. I fight carsickness, but it's not the hairpin curves in the road. I have a feeling this malaise is permanent.

I can't believe it's been less than three days since Mitch was shot. It feels like a tiny eternity.

"Everything's going to be fine," I tell myself in the rearview. "We made it through the night. The hospital said Mitch is doing just fine, and they'll call us as soon as there's any update." I blink back tears and force myself to smile wider. Sometimes the action comes first, and the emotion follows. "Think positively."

I should be driving to the hospital. But this morning, I woke up in a new, fresh panic as the reality of our situation hit me like a firehose. I've been in such a daze the logistics hadn't even hit me yet—like, how will I survive and pay rent and hospital bills with one income? How will I afford expensive physical therapy for Mitch once he wakes up? The thought of having to deal with everything all on my own is so overwhelming that all I could think to do is go to work. I need the money, but even more than that, I need to talk to Creighton about the bills we're facing. If there's anyone who can help, it's him. And who knows, maybe he'll have some thoughts on the Freddie situation, too.

I've never been so relieved to spot the Breakneck Bay sign ahead of me, the bright, cartoonish entrance, the artificial pools and rivers sparkling in the morning sunshine. It's normalcy. It's summertime. It's everything I forgot about since Mitch got shot, and my world stopped spinning on its axis days ago. And even though a part of me doubted coming here today, thinking I couldn't face everyone—now that I'm pulling up into my familiar space in the employee parking lot, I'm calmed.

"Good morning," I chirp, waving at a girl in a neon shirt who is sweeping the stairs.

She does a double-take when she sees me. I choose to ignore it.

Down the stairs, I hurry toward the admin building. Ah, the electric hum of wave machines and the smell of chlorine. The stand with the painted hot dog in sunglasses giving a thumbs-up. The vague smell of deep-fried everything. I pass a couple of neon-shirted employees who are hosing down the sidewalks and encouraging yesterday's puddles down the drain. They stop talking when they see me, jaws unhinged.

"Morning!" I sing.

Billford almost trips off a ladder near the Rapid Danger ride when I wave at him. Everyone is staring at me. I'm trying to ignore it. I march into the admin building, and a conversation happening between Dwayne, Creighton, Rhonda, the twins, and a few other ride operators ceases.

"Good morning," I say, heading over to the coffee machine.

As I pour myself a cup, Creighton ambles over. He's in Bermuda shorts, flip-flops, and a shirt that says *Coke Is It!*

"What the fuck are you doing here?" Creighton asks me quietly. "How's Mitch?"

"Same. Stable, but still hasn't woken up."

"You don't need to work. Go to the hospital and be with your husband. Jesus."

"I can't right now. Can we talk?"

I meet his beady stare, and without warning, my eyes fill. I can't help it. Please, not this. Of all people to spill myself to—of all the places to spill—not here, not now. Creighton seems to sense that I'm about to break down because he pushes me toward his office, past the gawking teenagers who are whispering and watching us.

"Of course. Let's sit down for a minute," he says, ushering me in and shutting the door.

He steers me to a red leather chair and gently pushes me down onto it. He circles his giant oak desk and plunks into his swivel chair and eyes me with concern. It's an impressive room, one I have spent little time in—plush carpeting, shelves of framed photos, a wall of plaques with his name on them. An enormous full-color painting of a hawk in flight looming over his desk. Oh, and a bust of himself in the corner, of course.

"What the fuck happened?" he asks, genuinely. "What's going on? Is Mitch gonna make it, or what?"

I'm used to Creighton yelling, barking, booming. When he gets this sincere, it's uncanny.

"I honestly don't know," I say. "They say he could wake up at any moment. He could be okay, or he could not be. He could be —disabled—brain damaged—" I flinch as I say the words I've been avoiding even thinking for the past forty-eight hours. "Or he could recover. I just don't know."

"When can I visit him?"

"Not until he's moved to a regular room."

"Is he still in ICU?"

"He's in 'intermediary care' right now. It's like a step between ICU and getting a room, I guess." My pitch rises. "I'm so worried about him, Creighton. I don't know how long he'll be in there. And the bills ... I don't know how I'm going to manage the costs of his stay. I mean, we have insurance, but—"

"Kit, the last thing you need to worry about right now is money."

Easy for a rich guy to say.

"Seriously," Creighton says. "Mitch is my main man. Whatever his stay costs, whatever the bills are, I'll cover it. Hundred percent."

The relief hits me like a stuff drink. I feel myself able to actually exhale fully for the first time in I don't even know how long.

"You're so kind," I tell Creighton.

He waves off this remark as if it's an annoyance. "So, I have to ask. Did he shoot himself?"

I shake my head. "I don't think so."

"Who the fuck shot him, then?"

I know the answer, but I can't speak it. My brother's name is stuck in my throat like a nasty bite of food.

"Kit, it wasn't you, right?" Creighton asks, leaning on his elbows. "Please tell me it wasn't you."

My mouth drops. "Of course, it wasn't me—"

"I know, I know, I had to ask." Creighton blows out a sigh. "I ask because Detective Buckaroo was out here yesterday asking questions about you."

I'm shocked; I don't know what to say. Plough was asking questions about me? I thought he was on my side.

"I know you did nothing, sweetheart," he continues. "But these cops are a bunch of bunglers. He interviewed everyone yesterday and seemed hellbent on knowing all about you and Mitch, how your marriage seems, and if anything was going on."

"What time was this?"

"Late morning, early afternoon."

"Oh. Well, a lot's happened since then. I don't think I'm really under suspicion."

I'd better not be, anyway. I'm dealing with enough right now —having a shadow cast over me as a suspect is a twist I can't handle.

"What the hell happened since then?" Creighton asks, leaning back and folding his hands behind his head.

"That's what I wanted to talk to you about."

"Spill it, sweetheart."

"It's Freddie," I say. "I'm pretty sure he did it."

Creighton's furrowed brow and frozen expression tells me he doesn't know who I'm talking about.

"My brother?" I remind him. "Freddie, who used to work here?"

"Oh, that deadbeat. Freddie the Fuck-Up." Creighton's expression changes, as if he tasted something sour. "Christ, I haven't thought of him in years. Now, why in the hell would he …?"

"They hate each other."

"Well, of course they do. Everyone hates Freddie; he's a cockroach."

My instinct is to defend my brother, but my loyalty to him has dried all the way up in the last twenty-four hours. I let the insults slide. "I'm wondering if not only did he shoot Mitch, but if he's the one who messed up his office, too."

"Wasn't he 86'ed?"

"Yes, but … how hard would it be for him to come into the park? It's not like most people who work here at this point would recognize him."

I don't tell Creighton about Freddie bragging about sneaking in. That would just make Creighton fly off the handle.

"Why would he do that?" Creighton asks, squinting. "Throw a bunch of animal blood and fake teeth everywhere? Makes no sense." He snaps his fingers. A light bulb pops off in his head. "Unless ..."

I wait for him to finish. Creighton's staring into the air.

"What a piece of shit," he mutters.

"What?"

"I always knew he was a ticking time bomb." Creighton's jaw tightens. "From the moment I laid eyes on his greasy little face." He snorts. "You know where Mitch and I met the guy, right? He was sparing change on the fucking side of the road."

"Yes, I've heard this be—"

"Mitch always had a soft spot for lowlifes. Honestly, I thought he'd become a preacher with all the times he dragged me to church. He picked up Freddie on the side of the road and got him a job with us working in construction. He worked a few days and then was a no-show, and we didn't see him again for a couple of years. Then we run into him somewhere else—Texas? Can't remember. At a bar one night. He was a roadie for some heavy metal band where the singer sounded like a sheep being tortured in front of a live audience. Venom Lung, I think they were called. God, they were awful."

"Right. I know the story—"

"Then he shows up here randomly a few years ago, asking about a job. Mitch felt sorry for him—I think at that point you'd stepped into the picture. Mitch wanted to do you a favor —so we hired him. I told Mitch it wasn't a good idea. I never liked the guy, but hey, we gave it a shot." He shakes his head. "Then he stole the entire fucking cash register and took off. Took a shit on my desk before he left, too. Know that? I could never prove he did that—the timing, though. No doubt in my mind."

During this monologue, Creighton's face has gradually deepened from its usual peach-pink color to an angry red.

"I get it now," Creighton says quietly, more to himself than me. "So, *he* was the one who fucked up Mitch's office. Of course he was. Leaving a message like that for me, trying to make me look bad. Trying to expose me. He thought he could take me down."

What? Why is Creighton thinking Freddie is targeting *him*? Bewildered, I look for a response but come up blank.

"Where's Freddie, anyway?" Creighton asks, tightening his fists on the table. He has a look on his face I've never seen before.

Honestly, it's terrifying.

"He's on the run. He's got a warrant out for something else."

Creighton shakes his head. "Hope those clowns at the PD can do their job this time and catch him. I won't hold my breath. You know, he was a real creep when he worked here, too. Leering at teenage girls and shit. There was some problem the first week he was here. I can't even remember what it was— we had to transfer him from working rides to food service. I should have followed my goddamn gut." Finally, Creighton meets my eyes again. The rage drains from his face. His tone softens. "How in the hell did such a nice, pretty girl like you end up with a brother like him?"

Because the unthinkable tragedy of having our parents die in a murder-suicide when we were kids destroyed his faith in the world. But I need to stop thinking that way. Many people have awful childhoods. Most of them don't become monsters.

"Who knows," I say.

"Anyway, Mitch is a tough son of a bitch; he'll make it through anything." Creighton takes a tin of mints out of his pocket and eats what looks like a handful, crunching them between his teeth. "This'll be a story he tells someday over a bonfire. But what we were talking about before, detectives coming around here every other goddamn day, hammering my staff with questions. Looks bad, you know? It's gonna drive customers away if every time they come here, they see a bunch of squad cards and little piggies crawling around."

The blood thumps in my ears. There's a quiet shift in me as I remember something: Creighton Marrs only cares about himself.

"I need this to go away," he tells me. "Understand? I need it to stop. I don't know what the fuck happened with Mitch, but I need it to stay out there, not in here. I'm ready to give you as much time off as you need. When are you scheduled to work again?"

"Tomorrow, I think?"

"Don't worry about it."

I consider this for a split second, but there's so much I want to dig into here. This implication that Freddie was a creep is new to me. I've never seen him behave that way with girls, but now that I know about his arrest for aggravated assault and his fight with a woman? Anything's possible. I remember his file, how it said his original station was Scream River. It's coming together in my mind.

But I need to know the full story. And the full story is somewhere here in Breakneck Bay.

"I actually *want* to work," I tell Creighton.

"Just take a few days."

"I need something to do, or I'll lose my mind."

I say it so desperately that it seems to slice the air.

Creighton watches me like he's internally shaking his head at my naivety. "All right, then. Suit yourself, you crazy woman." He stands up, saunters over to me, and gives me a gruff hug heavy with cologne. He claps my back hard enough to make me wince. "At least let me and Kimber have you over for dinner. Will you at least do that?"

Ordinarily, nothing would sound less fun to me than going over to Creighton's house for dinner. His wife, Kimber, is ... to put it nicely, a few chords short of a pop song. But I'm so desperate right now that I'll gladly take any kindness the world's willing to hand me.

"Sure," I say.

"Saturday? Great."

And that, right there, is how Creighton Marrs negotiates.

POLICE FEAR HIGHWAY BODY FOUND IS ANOTHER VICTIM OF THE 'CANINE KILLER.'

October 1972

By Trudy Vexler, Special Correspondent, Kansas Crime Wire

A gruesome discovery has reignited fears that the infamous "Canine Killer" is still at large. The body of a young woman, believed to be in her late teens or early twenties, was found tangled in brush just off Route 81 Tuesday morning. Local deputies say the condition of the remains mirrors past slayings linked to the elusive predator—including the signature removal of one of the victim's canine teeth.

"We've seen this before," said an officer close to the investigation, who spoke on condition of anonymity. "If this is what it looks like, we've got a serial on our hands—and he's hunting again."

Locals are being urged to stay alert, especially young women traveling alone. "The worst part?" one bystander told *Kansas Crime Wire*. "Nobody ever sees him coming."

HAWK

1972

A girl in a bandanna and hoop earrings gets into Hawk's car one night with a name, a story, and a dream for the future. Not an hour later, she's just another naked Jane Doe in a corn field with a missing canine tooth. Nothing but a few stains on his blue jeans and a *rattle rattle* in his pouch.

By his fourth hunt, he's grown. He traded his camper van for a wood-paneled station wagon—it makes him look like a family man. A knapsack in his trunk holds an assortment of useful items: a bottle of liquid courage, duct tape, pliers, and a paring knife. He washes dishes in a motel kitchen and hangs around town just long enough to rip the article from the local paper that says POLICE FEAR HIGHWAY BODY FOUND IS ANOTHER VICTIM OF THE 'CANINE KILLER.'

"Canine Killer," he says aloud, exchanging a wicked glance with himself in the rearview.

He drives to Tulsa. Trades the station wagon for a Chrysler, sees a cross glowing high on a hill with a hawk circling about, and decides it's a sign. He waves brazenly at cops, sure he's protected by the Holy Spirit.

In the fall, he returns to his hometown to attend his five-year high school reunion. He's going to blow them all away when they see how handsome he is, how many skills he's gained, and how worldly he is now, having traveled through thirteen U.S. states.

"What are you up to these days?" asks a girl he barely remembers, Deb, who looks like a blowsy secretary now because she is one.

"I'm a detective," he says.

That impresses her. She fluffs her hair. He debates taking her outside and strangling her in the alleyway, but she's not his type. Too homely and familiar. And more importantly, she would squeal like a hog.

Julie Preston turns him down for a dance, saying she's engaged to an Air Force pilot now, and that puts him in a terrible mood. If she had any idea what he was capable of, she would wipe that glossy simper off her lips.

He lurks in the corner, sipping punch, flask in his jacket pocket, watching the dancers in the dim light. He considers the possibility that he's not the smartest man in the room, but the dumbest and the loneliest. He hates when bitches make him feel that way. When the Jackie DeShannon song comes on, he shudders with arousal. He's reminded that no matter what he calls himself or where he comes from, Hawk's there, his shadow always lurking a few steps away. He tosses the carnation on his lapel into the garbage and wanders out to the dark street.

When he's not Hawk, there's a sickening stickiness to his memories. He tries to shut the door to them, but when they strike, even a splash of the color red can make him lose his appetite.

After the reunion, a trucking job out of Houston keeps him busy until Christmas. He's eating a hot dog in the Midwest, excited to revisit the spot where he killed the bandanna girl, when he spots the police sketch on the bulletin board. He slows his chewing, the hot dog a lump in his throat. It looks an awful lot like him, and the FBI is offering reward of twenty thousand dollars. WANTED, DEAD OR ALIVE. Someone must have witnessed them together in the car and remembered his face. He stares at it in awe, heart skipping a beat, wiping ketchup from his lip. What a terrified pride it is to be famous and anonymous at the same time.

Still, he knows when to lay low.

That night, he has a dream he's married to Julie Preston. She wears hoop earrings and a peasant blouse. It's all going well until Hawk runs his tongue along his teeth and finds his canines are loose. He pulls one out with a wet *pop*, its forked roots pink and fleshy. He wakes up woozy. His sweat smells like blood.

He runs his tongue along his intact smile. He reaches for the pouch on his bedside table and fondles the teeth in there, sharp little stones. The feel of them is cozy. But there's a danger blowing like a low breeze in his ears.

Maybe he'll give up Hawk for his New Year's resolution.

23

After meeting with Creighton, I head to the hospital to sit with Mitch a little while. I sing to him and hold his hand. There's been no movement. My heart is a hole when I sit here looking at him, wondering if he might be like this forever. What then? What if I end up married to a vegetable? I can't stand the thought, so I don't stay long. I tell myself Mitch needs me out there in the world seeking answers more than he needs me sitting beside him waiting for nothing to change.

I go home and call Plough at his office, asking for updates on whether they found Freddie.

"'Fraid not," he says. "But we have an APB out. You call me if you hear anything, and I'll do the same, all right?"

"Sure."

There's a pause. "You doing okay?"

"I mean, as well as one can do."

"You're a strong girl, Kit. I know you'll get through this."

I narrow my eyes at the Big Empty. It's a nice thing to say, but it's so not Plough.

"I, uh ... I was digging and found some info about your parents," he says.

Instantly, it all makes sense. He knows about The Tragedy. I've become an object of pity. This is why I rarely tell people about my parents' deaths—I'd rather just be plain old me than That Poor Girl Whose Dad Murdered Her Mom and Then Killed Himself.

"Okay," I say. "Thanks."

"You know, some people walk through the fire and get drawn into the darkness. Seems like that might have been what happened to your brother. But others—they walk through fire, and they choose the light. And they're stronger for it."

"Sure." I'm not in the mood to pretend Plough is my shrink. I clear my throat. "Well, just wanted to check and see if there were updates. I'll call you if I hear anything. Bye."

I hang up and hold my hand out in the air. It's shaking. I push my childhood back into the basement of my mind and lock the door. And not three seconds after I do, the phone rings.

I blow out a sigh, thinking it's going to be Plough again.

"Yes?" I ask, bracing myself.

"How are you?" a female voice asks.

My brow wrinkles. "Who is this?"

The silence that extends pops with static, as if I'm listening to a radio station and the girl is calling from far away. "I'm so sorry about what you're going through."

I play with the cord, leaning against the counter. "Um, who are you?"

"I know how hard it is to lose people you care about." Her voice is sweet and velvety. And suddenly I recognize it—the prank caller who left that message on the answering machine. I consider hanging up.

"Oh, really?" I say, my voice tight. "Is that why you're prank-called my house?"

"The more I think about it, the more I really think I understand you."

I'm getting annoyed. "Tell me who you are, or I'm hanging up."

"The thing is, sometimes ..." She heaves a sigh into my ear, a breath of white noise. "Sometimes you lose a person before you even realize it."

I'm turning inside out. *Is* this a prank call?

"I'm going to hang up if you don't tell me who this is," I say.

The silence is so long, it's like I've got my ear in a conch shell. I clutch the cradle harder, about to turn and jam it back into the receiver, but her words stop me. Her words steal the breath from my body.

"I'm the woman who shot Mitch."

24

I lean on the counter, my legs becoming weak. If I don't hold on to something, I might float away.

This is just a sick joke. *Freddie* shot Mitch. This is some looney tunes prank caller.

"Why are you doing this to me?" I ask.

"I shot him," the muffled voice says again.

The phone almost slips from my hand. I grab the nearest chair and collapse into it. My thoughts stutter.

"I called to tell you I'm sorry." She sniffs. "You don't deserve this. You didn't ask for this."

My words have run dry.

"Do you know, though?" she asks softly. "Do you know who Mitch really is?"

"You're messing with me." I squeeze my eyes shut tight, as if I'm a child afraid of a monster in my closet. "You're—who is this?"

"You don't know the real Mitch."

"I'm *married* to him."

Who is this terrible woman? What the hell am I supposed

to do? I open my eyes and behold the entryway in front of me, where, just days ago, Mitch lay in a blood-spattered crime scene within an inch of his life. Because of this woman on the phone. So she says. Am I supposed to believe her? Should I hang up, call the police, and tell them?

"He deserved to die," she says. "He's a killer."

What? She's insane. The awful things coming out of this stranger's mouth—I can't even process them.

"I'm calling the cops," I say, getting up from the chair.

"By the time they find me, I'll be dead."

I freeze, my mind a tornado.

She breaks down, sobbing, her words becoming broken. "I'll kill myself before they find me, Mrs. Blue. I have the gun in my hand right now."

Slowly, I sit back down in the chair. "What kind of sick mind game—"

"I'm so sorry for what I did." She sniffles. Is she crying? "But I need you to know something. I saved lives by killing him. I saved *your* life."

"You need help," I respond through clenched teeth, clutching my stomach because I might lose the day's stale coffee and hospital cafeteria sandwiches right now.

"Yeah, but I wasn't born this way."

I ball up my fists, wishing I could punch a wall. Who does this woman think she is? Does she have any idea what she's put Mitch through? What kind of psychopath would shoot him and then call and tell me about it?

"Who are you?" I demand. "How do you know Mitch?"

"Oh, we go way back. I've known him longer than you."

I swallow and pull my hair, just to feel something. "Have you now."

The picture's coming together in my mind: an ex. A fling Mitch had in his vagabond years before me, or someone he slept with when we were "on a break." My stomach turns, and I hope it's not something worse—an affair I never knew about. I've heard of tragedies like this before, a jealous mistress seeking revenge.

"Tell me how you know him, then," I say as evenly as I can. "Do I know you?"

"Do you recognize my voice?"

I burn, exhausted, beaten down by life. The last thing I want to do is play guessing games.

"What about now?" she asks, in a raspier voice.

And my jaw drops. It clicks.

Is it? It can't be.

But it is.

Yes, I know her voice.

"You're the one who's been calling," I say as I realize it. "Medford. Olympia—"

"Omaha, Colorado Springs, Wichita, Bozeman," she interrupts impatiently.

I'm so thrown off, I don't know how to answer.

"What do all these places have in common?" she asks.

"I don't know; you tell me."

Then she laughs a little, bitter, and I wonder if she's intoxicated.

A sob hitches in my lungs, even though all I feel is anger. "Do you know what I've been through this past week? You're— you're saying you shot my husband? You're calling me when I've been sitting in the hospital wondering if he's going to live or die all day long, and you want to play mind games—"

"He's alive?" she asks, her voice seeming to shrink.

That tone—genuine shock. She thought she killed him.

I bite my tongue. I shouldn't even be talking to this woman. I should have hung up and called the police the moment she started spewing this hateful bullshit. But then I hear her entire demeanor change. She weeps in my ear, and even though I know she's horrible, whoever she is, I can't help but feel for her because she sounds like she's in as much pain as I am right now.

"Why does evil keep winning?" she wails.

I stand up, suddenly sure that I should be listening more closely. If this is really the woman who tried to kill Mitch—if what she's saying is true—I should make sure I remember every word of this conversation so I can tell the police later. I grab a pen and a receipt from the countertop and scribble the words *Omaha, Wichita, Bozeman.*

"Mitch ruined my life," she pleads. "He's a predator—"

"Listen, it's okay," I say, using every ounce of willpower to control my voice. I want to scream, but I channel my most soothing tone instead. I need clues. I need to gather as much as I can so we can find this woman. "We can figure this out. What did he do to you?"

She shudders, and I hear a sharp intake of breath. "You really don't know, do you?"

"Know what?"

All I hear is the wind of her breath.

"Who are you?" I ask, stamping my foot on the ground, wishing I could break something. "What is your name? Tell me."

"Gloria," she says.

Click.

A pause. A dial tone.

The line goes dead.

"Gloria?" I say in disbelief.

I hang up the phone.

"Gloria," I tell Bowie, who is sitting on the kitchen floor looking happy as can be. Oh, to be a dog. "Gloria is alive, and she's calling me."

My life is falling apart.

It's as if I'm at the epicenter of some massive earthquake—my husband in the hospital fighting for his life, my brother on the lam, and now these unfathomable accusations hurled at me over the phone. A killer? A predator? Give me a break. She's just jilted.

Do you know who Mitch really is?

I grit my teeth. The gall of that question. I'm his *wife*. And yet, there's something colossal and nasty and nameless here, something so dark I need to hold on to it before figuring out my next move.

Gloria, Patti Smith sings in my head, as if my psyche's jukebox is torturing me. *G-L-O-R-I-A.*

I remember our last conversation, how I tried to help her. How I shared the intimate details of my tragic childhood with her, hoping it might serve as inspiration. And all the while, she's some crazy woman who has some vendetta against Mitch. She's apparently an attempted murderer. I'll bet she trashed Mitch's office, too. And vandalized his truck. I want to throw up.

All I know is that he hired Gloria, he was her boss, but—then what?

They seemed very ... chummy, Rhonda says in my mind.

Gloria wanted to talk to me after work, an imaginary Mitch says.

About what? I ask him.

Road trips.

I shiver. There has to be something more to this. I see Mitch's mess of a face for a blink, and I hear Gloria's sobbing on the phone, and smell Freddie's oddly comforting scent of beer and stale cigarettes, and it's all too much. I need to make it stop.

Guilt roils at the thought of my brother.

If Gloria is telling the truth, I was wrong about him. Freddie didn't shoot Mitch.

I jump up out of my chair and run to the phone. I leave a message on Plough's answering machine.

"Plough, it's me, Kit Blue," I say breathlessly. "I just got a call from a woman claiming to be Gloria who says she shot Mitch. I don't know what to think. Call me back right away."

I wait an hour, but he doesn't call. It's late anyway. I take three sleeping pills and lock my doors and windows, but on second thought—fingers poised above the switch—I keep the lights on tonight.

25

The next morning, as I'm in the middle of teasing and spraying my hair, the phone rings. I'm shell-shocked from last night's call and almost afraid to pick it up, but thankfully it's just Plough calling me back.

I summarize the story for him. Gloria's calls, the cryptic names and dates, the claim she thought Mitch was a killer she was taking down. I tell him about the tape I saved for him with the message saying *sorry I shot your husband.*

"Well, cripes. This puts a whole new spin on the story, doesn't it? Now we've got the 'other woman' thrown into the mix." He sighs. "Was Mitch having an affair with this girl?"

"I don't think so. I really don't."

In the silence, the desperation in my tone echoes. I wonder if Plough believes me. I wonder if he *should* believe me.

"I remember even in the small interactions I had with her, she seemed ... off," I say. "And she sounded drunk or something on the phone. Not right in the head." I snap a finger. "Oh! And I tried calling her phone number I found for her once ... it was a wrong number."

"Hmm. Any word from your brother?"

"Still nothing."

"All right. Hang in there. Here's what I'm thinking: with your permission, we can rig up a recorder on your phone line. If she calls again, we'll get it on tape. Can't promise we'll trace the number unless she stays on the line long enough, but it's a start. You okay with that?"

"Sure, what the hell."

We agree for him to come over in the evening after my shift and visitation hours at the hospital are over. I hang up and get ready for work. And now with this Gloria business, I can't wait to get there. There has to be something there to help me piece together the actual story.

I've never driven to Breakneck Bay so fast in all my life. I practically teleport.

When I get to the admin building, I clock in, get a cup of coffee, and then Creighton intercepts me with Rhonda at his side.

"Talk about a work ethic," he tells Rhonda, pointing to me. "This broad's got a husband in a coma, and she still shows up to work."

If I weren't so desperate for clues, I might not be here. But I accept the compliment and keep my ulterior motive to myself.

"And I want you to work the Ouch Shack today with our friend here," he says to Rhonda, giving me a side hug. "Keep an eye out and make sure she's okay."

I turn to him, jaw fixed. Humiliating. He needs Rhonda to babysit me? Is that how far I've fallen? Good Lord.

"Roger. You ready to head up the hill, Mrs. Blue?" Rhonda says, with the condescending excitement of a camp counselor.

I nod reluctantly.

Outside, the sun's blazing, the pools twinkle, the air smells like soft serve. But I'm still stuck deep in the forest as I make my way up the stairs to the Ouch Shack.

"I think it's great you're staying busy," Rhonda chirps from behind me.

I say nothing, hurrying up the steps, gripping the rail, grateful for the burn in the backs of my calves so I don't feel the pain in my soul.

"One of my very favorite poems is Rudyard Kipling's 'If,'" she goes on. "You know that one?"

I'm not in the mood. Rhonda's voice is getting under my skin. I bite my tongue and fish my keys from my purse to open the door.

Her voice cuts in, an overdramatic trill, as if she's trying out for a Shakespearean play. "'If you can keep your head when all about you are losing theirs and blaming it on you—'"

"Zip it, Rhonda," I snap, pushing the door open.

At once, I know how mean that sounded. I shut my eyes for a split second to gather myself, then open them again and turn around. Rhonda is so bewildered she almost looks like a lost child.

"I'm sorry," I say. "I'm under a lot of pressure. I shouldn't have spoken to you that way."

"I've had much worse," Rhonda says. "It's okay. I work for Mr. Marrs, remember?"

I don't want to be in the same category as Creighton when it comes to how I treat other human beings. Poor Rhonda. I can't even imagine what she's had to put up with, being his assistant. I soften and offer her a smile.

"Thanks for helping today," I try.

Yes, that's much better. Tiny Kit's gearing up for a tantrum, but I'm not letting her. I should be grateful for everything Rhonda's done to be kind to me.

"How's Freddie?" Rhonda asks.

My smile falters. "He left town."

"Oh, really? Where'd he go?"

I open my locker and shove my purse inside. I flick my gaze to Gloria's old locker, pained at the sight of it. "Who knows?"

I hear the scrape of a stool on the floor. Turning, I see that Rhonda's leaning an elbow on her knee and studying me. "You know, Mrs. Blue, I'm a very good confidant."

"Are you."

"It's part of a reporter's repertoire—establishing trust. I've been told I'm incredibly trustworthy. Sources have dilvulged many, many secrets to me over the years. I am a *vault*."

She is a very strange person is what she is. I eye her with my hands on my hips, unsure of what to make of her. Is she trying to tell me something? Now that I think about it, Rhonda works for Creighton. She's his eyes and ears around this park. She probably knows more about everything going on here than even Mitch does at this point.

The hell with it. I'm going to see if I can crack into her.

"Whatever happened to Gloria?" I ask, searching her face for some hidden clue. "Do you have any ideas?"

"Gloria?" Rhonda repeats, taken aback.

That was clearly not what she was expecting.

"No, I don't know," she says, tone still surprised. "Why? Do you?"

"Why would *I* know?"

"Well ..." Rhonda looks around, as if someone might be listening in this tiny place. "The files?" she stage-whispers.

She's lit up like she thinks she's Nancy Drew.

"The files I chucked in a Dumpster downtown. I know nothing, same as you," I tell her, trying to quell her obvious thirst for details. "But I want to find her. I need to talk to her."

"About Mitch?"

I nod.

"Was something going on between them, after all?" she whispers.

The question hurts like a slap.

"I'm sorry," Rhonda says quickly. "I shouldn't have said that. You're in a vulnerable place right now."

I swallow and turn, busying myself with straightening the bandages, cotton balls, and Q-tips. "I'd like to know the answer to that question, too."

"And that's why you want to find Gloria?" Rhonda asks.

God, she's nosy. I'm not about to tell her the entire story right now, so I just nod.

"The police seem to have given up looking for her," Rhonda says. "And, unfortunately, with her file missing, I'm not sure who to ask. Dwayne, maybe? He kept pestering her to go out with him. He claims he never got her phone number, though."

"I actually peeked at her file before I threw it away, and remembered the phone number. I've called it."

I blurt it out without thinking and flush.

"Oh," Rhonda says, coming to where I'm standing, joining me in mindlessly tidying up the station. "And?"

"It was a wrong number."

"What about her address?"

"That I don't have," I say.

Damn. Why didn't I hold onto those files? I could kick myself. I imagine that gold mine of information rotting under a crumpled Coke cans and Big Mac wrappers.

"Rhonda," I ask, slowly. "It's been a couple weeks, but do you think there's any chance the files are still there?"

"Where? In the 'downtown Dumpster?'"

I nod.

"Maybe," she says, eyes widening. She puts a hand to her chest. "Oh, Mrs. Blue—wouldn't that be something?"

"It was kind of a remote area at the end, you know where

the park is? And the Dumpster was pretty empty ..." I say with a little surge of excitement.

"I would happily help you dig through a Dumpster in pursuit of justice," Rhonda says.

My lips twitch. I crack a tiny smile at Rhonda's eagerness. She wants so badly to be helpful.

"Well, do you want to head there with me after work?" I ask, half-jokingly. "Dumpster hangout?"

"Mrs. Blue," Rhonda says, hand to her heart. "I would love nothing more."

What I said half-jokingly just now settles into my mind as a serious idea. I had planned to visit Mitch after work, but I can just check in quickly. Finding the person who shot him seems much more important.

"Okay, then," I say. "We'll do it."

She lights up like I just told her she won a year's supply of chocolate.

"But let's focus on work now," I say, remembering that I'm in charge of this Ouch Shack. I have a job to do today. I clear my throat, pull out the iodine spray, and check my watch. "Park opens in ten."

Rhonda nods and salutes me. Yes, she *salutes* me.

I don't know why I just agreed to take Rhonda with me on a road trip to Gloria's address. I must be losing my damn mind.

My shift can't pass fast enough. I've never been more excited to rummage through garbage in all my life.

26

Rhonda and I plug our noses as we stare into a Dumpster swarming with flies.

"Well, if the stench is any clue," Rhonda says, her voice pinched as she holds her nostrils closed, "it appears that this Dumpster hasn't been emptied in quite some time."

We put on some Latex gloves I took from Mitch's hospital room a few minutes ago and get to work. Banana peels. Soggy newspapers. Dirty diapers. Fast food bags. Wads of gum. Clumps of hair. We're elbows deep in this disgusting mess by the time I feel the shape of a cardboard box between my fingertips near the bottom. I dig deeper and see a file sticking out. WILSON, GLORIA.

"It's here!" I say excitedly. "Over here."

Rhonda and I are so excited, you'd think we were mining for gold. The file folder is wet with something pink and sticky—strawberry soda, I pray—but the paperwork inside is fresh as the last time I saw it.

"It's a miracle," Rhonda breathes.

"That's the number I called," I say, pointing to the 5309 phone number.

"According to her address, she lives in Riverwood," Rhonda says.

"Where's that?"

"Just over the river. My aunt lives there." Rhonda waves a few flies away from her head. "We could be there in fifteen, twenty minutes."

I hesitate, checking my watch. Do I have time? Plough's coming over after seven to tap my phone. That's a little over an hour from now. It makes me sick thinking about facing Gloria if I managed to track her down. But it makes me even sicker to think I might never get the chance. What if she never calls back again?

I need answers, and I need them now.

"Sure," I say, getting into the car. "But we have to be quick."

Do you know who Mitch really is?

Twilight looms. I drive my car along the highway under a pink-smeared sky. In the passenger seat, Rhonda holds the papers and chatters my ear off about her school newspaper so long she becomes nothing but white noise. My brain is a loop pedal. My brain is one echo full of reverb.

Do you know who Mitch really is?

Every time I remember Gloria's staticky voice, I get chills from head to toe. I grip the wheel harder, foot on the gas. This is silly. Why am I driving to her address? Why have I teamed up with Harriet the Spy here? Am I making a fool of myself?

Do you know who Mitch really is?

I didn't recognize him when we swung by the hospital a while ago. They removed the gauze, and the first instinct I had was to turn away, to focus anywhere but his head. I feel terrible about it. But it was such a shock: half his head shaved, his eye patched up, stitches all over his face. The beeps kept beeping.

He lay there, a breathing corpse. The doctor mentioned blindness in his right eye and the need for plastic surgery, but I just nodded, stared at Mitch's hand, and rushed from the room after the update.

Do you know who Mitch really is?

"Why the sudden interest?" Rhonda asks me, yanking me back to the present moment.

"Huh?" I let out a breath. "I'm sorry, Rhonda, I haven't been listening to a word you're saying."

Rhonda has a notebook with a fresh page open on her lap, as if a news story might break at any moment. "It's okay. I know you have a lot on your mind right now. I was just asking why you seem suddenly so focused on Gloria today."

I open my mouth, but close it again, because I'm not about to tell Rhonda about the phone call I got.

"The other times we've spoken about her, you seemed reluctant. But now you're in a bit of a hurry to find her. I can't help but notice the change in behavior."

One steady breath. In and out. "I'm trying to figure out who did this to Mitch."

"And Gloria is a person of interest?"

I don't answer.

"Such a fascinating twist, since after the alleged 'crime scene' in Mitch's office, I wondered if he did something to Gloria. But now you suspect the opposite?"

"I don't know what I suspect. Mitch needs to wake up and tell me."

"Have the doctors given you any kind of prognosis?"

Rhonda reminds me of a woodpecker sometimes. Just ... a relentless *tap-tap-tap* in human form. Still, she's here for a reason. She claims to know where Gloria's house is. And I appreciate moral support in whatever form I can get.

All at once, I miss Freddie by my side. My brother is a

sketchy mess, but he's a sketchy mess who's always been there for me. And if he had nothing to do with Mitch's shooting, the vandalized truck, the "crime scene," then I feel awful for assuming he did. I push the needling thought of him from my mind—my heart only has enough pain for one man in my life today.

A sign tells us Riverwood is five miles away. I blow a relieved sigh when I see it, but my belly squirms. My pulse kicks up a notch. What on earth am I going to say when I see her?

I sneak a quick glance at Rhonda, who has written *Gloria = suspect?* on her paper.

"What do you know about Gloria?" I ask. "I want to know everything. Open the vault."

"Not much, Mrs. Blue," Rhonda says, studying the papers. "I know she was nineteen years old and worked at the park for less than two months. She talked to the twins sometimes in the break room, and Dwayne was trying to 'get in her pants,' as he so eloquently told me."

"Was he, now."

"I don't believe he succeeded." Rhonda holds the photocopy of Gloria's driver's license in the air and squints at it. "I doubt Dwayne's success rate is very high."

"What about ..." I force myself to continue, my knuckles bone-white from how hard I'm squeezing the steering wheel. "What about Gloria and Mitch? Tell me the truth. What was going on, do you think?"

"I have no evidence." She tucks the paper back on her lap, then smells her hand. "I only have hearsay."

The way it comes out of her mouth, so defensive, sinks my stomach.

"Okay." I brace myself. "What's the hearsay?"

The car gets so quiet that all I hear is the hum of the wheels along the road.

"Do you really want to know?" Rhonda asks in an uncharacteristically tender tone.

"Well, we're on our way to meet this woman." The pressure in my head rises as I try to dam the tears. "I'm preparing myself."

She sighs. "There are rumors about Mitch. I assumed you've heard them?"

This is news to me. I shake my head, cheeks growing hot.

"None of them?" she asks, with a touch of disbelief.

"No."

A fever would be cooler than this humiliation. I turn up the air and point the vent directly at my face.

"What rumors?" I ask, my tone sharper.

"That he's flirty with the female teenage employees who are under his direct supervision. That he's had inappropriate relationships with some of them. I never verified if it was true."

The screw in my belly tightens. And it hits me at once, a mudslide of information so overwhelming that, for a flicker, I consider pulling over: Mitch's reluctance to the idea of me working at Breakneck Bay. How stressed out he seemed when I was there, how he set up our schedules to work different hours in different parts of the park. The odd choice to put me in the isolated medic station when I have zero experience. And, of course, the summers before this one where he worked here while I stayed behind in LA. Is this why a long-distance relationship was enough for him?

Tiny Kit has been waiting for this moment. She knew.

The truth hits hard. I try out the thought: *Mitch cheated on me.* With a deranged teenager half his age. It's disgusting, but worse, I hate how easily I accept it. On the surface, I've trusted him. I've believed him when he's told me the only time he was with other women was when we'd broken it off for a few months. But somewhere dark and deep, another me suspected.

Another me knew there was another him I wasn't seeing. I just hoped it wasn't this ugly.

Do you know who Mitch really is?

"I can assure you, Mrs. Blue, he was never anything but a gentleman with me," Rhonda says defensively.

I let out a snort that relieves a little pressure. "I didn't suspect you, Rhonda. I'm thinking of Gloria."

"Yes, precisely. I told you about the chummy chats. *That* I can verify because I saw it with my own two eyes. Everything else is hearsay. Rumors circulated. Some wild conspiracy theories, because last summer—well, you know about Pamela Bronson? Take this exit."

The WELCOME TO RIVERWOOD! sign comes into view. I turn on my signal and head down the off-ramp. *Mitch cheated,* my brain says again, just trying it out. It stings, but I don't squirm. I don't have the will to fight it.

"Pamela ... the dead girl?" I ask, my throat tight.

"Yes. Well, she apparently had some issue with Mitch. She complained to some other employees that he was following her around, being a little too touchy-feely, you know, creeping her out."

"Mitch is friendly with everyone. I think some people mistake it for flirting," I say, but there's a tremble in my voice.

"That might be so. It's a shame the only witnesses who could clarify this for us are comatose or deceased." Rhonda opens a map where she has already highlighted an area. Rhonda is the girl who does her homework and the extra credit assignment, too. "Maple Street is in the hills. A cul-de-sac. 321 Maple Street, you said? Turn right here on Dickinson."

This town is adorable. A green river runs to the side of Dickinson, the main street, and every window has a sign with a cute, punny name. A butcher shop called Nice to Meat You, a bookstore called Prose and Cons, a bakery called Loaf Is All You Need.

"So adorable here," I say.

"Isn't it?" Rhonda asks.

I spot a few squealing kids riding bikes down a sidewalk. A man and a woman walk behind them, holding hands. I get a stunned pang.

Mitch cheated on me.

"Seems like it would be a great place to raise a family," I say.

"Indeed. Even so, it's important to remain vigilant."

I raise an eyebrow.

"As someone who reads a lot of news, I know killers are everywhere."

I give her a sidelong glance. "Are they, though?"

"Yes. Fun fact: Ted Bundy stayed in this area for a time."

"I don't know how fun that fact is."

"I'm very interested in serial killer cases. Especially cold cases. I write a column about them for the *Hill Valley High Beacon* called 'Killer Chronicles.' The Freezer Man—no pun intended—has been a recent obsession of mine. The Canine Killer is another interesting one. Turn left up here on Walnut."

"Canine Killer—a dog murderer?"

"Oh no. That would be awful. No, this is a man who raped and murdered several women. He's called the Canine Killer because he pulled out his victim's teeth postmortem. Here it is! Maple, on the right."

I pull onto the street, anxiety spiking. It's a cul-de-sac, like she said. A quiet one with pastel Victorians bursting with flower gardens. Gloria lives here? She lives in this wealthy neighborhood in this sweet little town and commutes to the waterpark every day? Something doesn't add up.

I squint out the window, looking for answers.

"Rhonda, I think you need some new hobbies," I say as

gently as I can while I slow the car to a crawl. "It's a little weird to be your age and so enthralled with serial killers."

"Not weird if I'm going to grow up to be a crime reporter. Wait. Stop."

I slam on the brakes. Both Rhonda and I must see it because a silence slices the air between us. The placard on the house reads *89 Maple Street*.

"That address only has two digits," Rhonda says.

I blink at it again, as if the problem is my eyes and not the number.

"Maybe the others are different?" I try.

"Maybe. Keep driving."

I don't like how easily she orders me around, but I push the gas and we look at the next house. 87. The next one is 85. After that, 83, 81, and 79. Then, the street is done.

"This whole street's double-digits," I say. "Why would 321 be in the middle of this?"

We loop around again, and a disappointed pause swells between us. My body hasn't caught on to the breaking news. The adrenaline of possibly confronting Gloria is still there, thundering through my veins. But my mind knows.

There is no 321 Maple in Riverwood. There never was.

HAWK

1973

It's not easy carrying a demon inside you.

In the silvery shine of every mirror, a young man smiles back. He still stops to pet dogs; he carves figurines and collects interesting rocks; he's eager to learn new skills, like how to operate a jigsaw and how to tell a dirty joke in Spanish. He expects the spring smell of the earth after a fresh rain. He relishes unbuckling his belt after a meal and the way his muscles ache after a day of hard labor. But that's only half the story. The other half he keeps hidden. The other is a Hawk who only emerges to terrorize, dismember, and devour. But if he could just keep this going—separate the two, let demon and man coexist—perhaps they could share this house that is his body.

The hope of the sixties crashed and burned years ago. Vietnam vets are yelling at themselves in the streets, and heroin is sweeping the cities. Prices are high, and every town is feeling the same. He doesn't know his place in this weird, new world. He's in his mid-twenties now and no place feels like home. He trades his Ford Country Squire for a Monte Carlo. Throws out his cowboy hat and grows a mustache. He tries out Tucson, rents a trailer, takes some night classes, and attends church on Sundays. He meets girls at the drive-in and laughs at the stuff they say. When he's lucky, he takes them home and does the deed, but it's like eating with no taste buds. It never reaches that deep place. The most excitement he feels is when he parks near the high school at lunchtime and watches the girls in the bleachers eating their lunches, their skirts blowing gently in the wind, their delicate, swan-like necks.

That's all it is. Watching.

He's proud of himself for his restraint. If only they knew what a good person he is, the level of evil he protects them from. He could have killed a dozen girls this year. He could have turned them into soulless meat sacks and left them to rot in the woods, but he didn't. He attends church, volunteers, and no one has any idea what a wonderful man he truly is, how deep his sacrifice, how much smarter and stronger he is than the rest of them. His spiritual awakening keeps him righteous through 1973, which he thinks cancels out anything questionable that might have come before it.

Still.

Hawk lurks somewhere.

The spring of 1974 lands like a ton of bricks. The Lord must be testing him, because he gets laid off from a flower shop and loses his youth group position all in the same week. A little horse-faced bitch at church must have misunderstood his intentions, because she reported him for resting his hand on her leg, which he did, but she blew it out of proportion. She was lucky he didn't cave her skull in. He packs up and drives to Colorado to begin again.

Usually, he enjoys moving—shiny, fresh starts, and towns he can get lost in—but this time feels like a failure. Somewhere deep and wordless, he's afraid that something is so wrong with him he doesn't belong in this world. That he can't even fake it—other people see right through him and spot the demon.

Alarm clocks ring. Get dressed, head to work, drive, smile, and say *how are you.* Try to do right. Push the thoughts of violence out. Read the Bible. Eat food. Sleep. Repeat.

Is that all there is?

A bitter taste hangs on the roof of his mouth, and his smile weakens by the day. An itch builds. Starts in his palms, which he rubs absentmindedly on his steering wheel as he drives a van that says PHIL'S FRESH FISH from restaurant to restaurant. The smell of seafood is pungent, raw and sickening, and stirs something deep in him. He drives with a hard-on, goosebumps flaring, the urge a gentle hum beneath him. Every day, the hum gets a little louder. Hawk's shadow crawls a millimeter closer. He drinks from his flask during his lunch break, studying the high school girls through the fence, touching himself. That's all it is—no harm in touching yourself. They don't even know he's there, so who does it hurt? Like peeking into his neighbor's windows and seeing her get undressed. Nothing wrong with a little appreciation.

But his hunger is rising.

The more he watches, the more he wants to touch himself.

The more he touches himself, the more he wants to hurt them.

And then one night, tired and tipsy from a night out at a bar, he spots her. A waitress, judging by her uniform, long hair parted down the middle. Petite, breakable, barely eighteen. The sight of her makes Hawk wake all the way up. He eyes his rearview, sees blackness, and pulls to the shoulder where she is walking, alone, on the side of the road. He's practically shivering as he waves at her and rolls his window down. The urge tingles from his fingertips to his scalp.

She's got the wide-eyed resemblance to a doe in crosshairs.

"I ran out of gas," she says in a sweet Southern accent. "Like some kind of doofus."

He cringes. He doesn't want her to talk, to have a voice, or to be memorable. "There's a station right up the way. Hop on in."

It's a divine similarity to his last kill. A gas station; a helpless girl on the side of the road. The déjà vu takes his breath away.

When she's in the car, he fills the silence with whistling that old tune he hasn't thought about in a while. Hawk's theme. And as she tries to make small talk, he nods and calculates where to pull off the road and how he will take his girl-shaped prize. He's energized, remembering the knapsack buried somewhere in his trunk with his tools in it. He hasn't hunted in so long, he's truly going to savor every moment of her torment. Then he's going to clean up, go home, and have the best night's sleep of his life.

Because when Hawk gets fed, all is well again.

The very next morning, the sun shines as he drops a bloody waitress uniform in a garbage can outside a fast-food restaurant. He whistles and shakes the pouch hanging around his neck, getting tingles. The blue sky is clear. What a blessed man. As he drives to work, the corners of his mouth turn up, and a lightness makes him feel years younger. Perhaps Hawk is a vampire feeding on the blood of beautiful, young women. That makes him laugh to himself until he sees the red-and-blue light twirling in the rearview.

He pulls to the side of the highway with a frown.

"Mistake," he mutters to himself.

But his hands are shaking on the wheel. He's surrounded by cattle ranches on both sides of the highway, and the smell of death is sharp enough to cut a tear to his eye. He stares in disbelief at the cop strutting toward him. No way this blue idiot has any idea what he's done. The body is probably still warm in the riverbed. No one knows she's missing. There's just no way.

"What can I do for you, Officer?" he asks, grinning and leaning out the window.

"Someone reported seeing this girl in your vehicle last night." The cop, wiry and gaunt, pulls out a black-and-white photo that looks like a high school senior portrait. Hawk nearly winces at the sight of her crooked, familiar smile. "You mind coming to the station and answering a few questions?"

His grin melts. His heart forgets how to beat. Hawk spreads his wings and flies away, leaving him behind, and for a moment he is nothing but a stupid human being.

27

I come home from my pointless Riverwood road trip strung out on heartbreak and secrets.

Before we parted, Rhonda begged me for the Gloria file. I gave it to her because apparently it's all lies anyway. The garbage is where it belongs. But Rhonda acted like I'd just given her the Holy Grail.

"Mrs. Blue," she said, voice shaking. "It's an honor to be your trusted associate."

"Good night, Rhonda," I said flatly, and drove homeward—into the belly of the Big Empty.

Now, my house is dark. My dog is attention-starved. My stomach is screaming for a good meal. All I want is a bubble bath to get the Dumpster stink off me and a solid eight hours of sleep. Instead, I eat a piece of stale bread in an empty kitchen and wait around for Plough to show up. I press rewind on my day and go over it again and circle back to the tenderest bruise of all my questions: Did Mitch cheat on me? What don't I know about him? These questions have shaken my faith.

Finally, I hear the crunch of tires in the driveway. I hurry to the door and wave to Plough as he heads up my driveway, oddly relieved at the sight of his swagger and his Marlboro Man silhouette. He carries a tool bag this time and wipes his boots on the mat.

"Come on in," I say, welcoming him inside.

"Hey there, Kit. Any news?"

"Well, kind of. I went and checked out Gloria's supposed address. It doesn't exist."

He drops his bag on my dining room table and gives me a look. "How'd you find that? I thought the girl was a ghost."

I flush. He doesn't know about the files. I kick myself—I should have just given them to Plough when I first got them. At the very least, I wouldn't smell like trash juice right now.

"Just some paperwork I found. It had her phone number and address. Neither are hers."

He unzips his bag. "I appreciate you digging into this, but I need you to be careful, all right? I wouldn't want you putting yourself in danger now."

I nod.

"Hopefully, this will help us figure out what's going on," he says, taking out a bulky cassette recorder and a suction cup-looking device.

"Is that for tapping my phone?"

"Technically, this isn't a tap; it's a recorder." He moves to the counter next to the phone and starts fiddling with my phone wires. "A tap? I'd need a judge to sign off on a warrant, and we don't have time for that. This is going to give us all we need right here. This here—" Plough holds up the suction-device. "—is a microphone." He sticks it to the phone receiver. "And I called the phone company already, so if you keep her on the line for at least sixty seconds, we can likely get a trace on her location, too."

"Okay," I say. "What do I have to do? Just press record?"

"Don't worry, you don't have to do a thing. As soon as you pick up the receiver, this'll start recording. Just keep her talking."

"So it—it will record anyone who calls me?"

Plough turns and raises his eyebrows at me. "Why? That bother you?"

"I'm just thinking about my brother," I tell him. Which is the truth.

"Wouldn't mind getting a trace on his location, either," Plough says.

"I don't want him to get arrested, though, for Mitch's shooting." I swallow. "I feel awful for accusing him."

"Now, don't be counting your chickens before they're hatched," Plough says. "Just because some whackadoodle calls you and claims to be the shooter doesn't mean she's telling the truth."

My brow wrinkles. "Why would she lie about it?"

"Beats me. But false confessions happen all the time."

He finishes clipping wires with alligator clips and tests the setup by calling the station. When he replays it, the tape is fuzzy but intelligible. Reminds me of my eight-track recorder in the studio, gathering dust.

"Okay, you're all set." Plough packs up, zipping his tool bag. "Just answer like normal and keep her talking."

"Sure. Thank you."

"You're welcome. And—oh." Plough pulls a business card out of his pocket and hands it to me. "This has my home phone on the back of it. Anything comes up, call me, day or night. Understand? No more driving around playing cops and robbers."

I nod.

"And I worry about you being here alone. Anything suspicious, you reach out."

"Don't worry. She's not after me. And anyway, I have Mitch's hunting rifle." I fight a yawn and a hot sting of tears at the same time.

"Get a good night's sleep, Kit. Talk soon."

"Later."

I lock the door and set the chain. I check every window, peeking out at the pitch-black night. Then I change into my pajamas, grab the hunting rifle, and tuck into bed. It's haunting and awful to be alone. I can't wait to fall asleep and forget my loneliness.

I'm almost asleep when the shriek of the phone snaps me to attention. I sit up in bed, hand over my palpitating chest. Dread washes over me because, somehow, I know just who it is.

Here we go.

I get up and tiptoe quickly down the dark hall. The closer I get to the phone, the sicker I feel. Nervously, I review what Plough told me to do—keep her on for at least sixty seconds.

"Hello?" I say into the receiver.

A beat passes, an ocean of static.

I swallow, listening to the sound of someone breathing. I close my eyes and brace myself.

"Hi," Gloria says. "It's me again."

28

I sink into a stool at the counter, a chill passing over me. The wheels in the tape recorder turn. I pinch the bridge of my nose and ask my adrenaline to please remain calm.

"I won't bother you," she says, voice shaking, warbling from emotion or intoxication; I can't tell which. "I just need you to know I'm sorry. I keep—I keep thinking about how nice you were to me. And what you told me about your parents. And I just ... I just wanted to say to you, I hope you can move on in your life. Have a good life, like you told me to. That this one tragedy doesn't define you. That's all."

Afraid she's going to hang up, I blurt, "Are you ready to tell me what Mitch did?" Sixty seconds. I need to keep her on for sixty seconds. "I'm dying to hear the full story. I'm his wife. Don't I deserve to know?"

Upon hearing her *sniff-sniff*, fireworks burst inside me. I'm frozen with dread, afraid of what's next. Afraid, most of all, I'm going to hear a click in my ear, and this call will amount to nothing.

I glance at my watch. Fifteen seconds has passed. I need forty-five more for Plough to trace the call.

I take a different tactic and sprinkle sugar in my voice. "You know, I've tried to find you. Just tonight. I went looking for you."

She takes the bait. "Looking where?"

"The address you had on file at Breakneck Bay." Twenty seconds. Twenty-one, twenty-two. "The one on your job application. I called the phone number, too."

"Oh," she says with a light laugh. "That. You're never going to find me."

"Well, I just talked to the police."

"Did they believe you?"

She asks it as if she's genuinely curious.

"Because they didn't believe anything I ever told them," she says. "Neither did the FBI. 'We'll look into it.' Bullshit."

Thirty seconds down, thirty to go.

"If they had," she goes on, slurred speech making me wonder if she's drunk or on pills, or if it's something even harder than that. "Maybe I wouldn't have needed to shoot him. Or trash his office to get their attention."

It's official: She's the one who trashed his office, too. *I knew it.* I rest my elbows on the counter. Thirty-five seconds have passed.

"You ... did that to his office," I say, watching the tape churn, imagining Plough listening to this later. "Can you tell me why you did that?"

"I wanted to show them."

Twenty more seconds.

"You put the blood there," I say.

"Mmm-hmm. That part was ... gross."

She sounds sleepy, almost as if she's nodding off. Fifteen more seconds. I clear my throat loudly.

"Gloria, I—I'm sorry for whatever it was Mitch did to you." I get up and pace the short few feet the phone cord allows. Pain balloons in my chest. "If he was—inappropriate with you." Ten more seconds. I need to keep her on. I inject my tone with sympathy, even though I'm trembling with rage. "Or whatever might have been going on between you two. I can see now why you framed him and came after him."

Her voice sharpens and creeps closer, as if she's pressing her lips to the receiver. "Your husband is a *serial killer*. Do you really not know? Are you actually this stupid?"

It's like a meteor fell from the sky and demolished me on impact. This accusation is so bizarre, so unexpected, and so massive I forget how to breathe. When I remember the old inhale-exhale, I force a bitter laugh out of my throat. I'm dissociating. I'm watching myself react to what she said from outside my body.

Five more seconds. I can't find my words. I'm so gobsmacked that I squat on the ground, afraid I'm going to faint.

"I'm sorry about two things, Mrs. Blue," she says. "First, I'm sorry because you're a victim in your own special way, too. And second? I'm sorry I didn't aim better and kill him when I had the chance."

The click sounds in my ear at the exact second that my watch registers one minute passing.

"Shit!" I yell.

I clatter the phone on its cradle so violently, part of the mouthpiece cracks. The tape stops rolling, coming to a stop.

And I look at my empty house of shadows and scream at the top of my lungs.

29

By the time the morning sun slices through the blinds, I've barely slept. My head pounds. I keep replaying Gloria's words, that horrible final line, like a skipping record.

I'm still in my bathrobe when my phone rings. The sound of it makes me flinch.

"Hello?" I say.

"Morning," Plough says. "We got a hit."

Relief floods me. Thank God. I've been afraid I hadn't kept her on long enough. I worry she'll never call back again, and I missed my chance. Now we can finally figure out where she is and how to find her.

"And?" I ask.

"Took longer than I wanted," he says. "But Pacific Bell traced the call. She stayed on just long enough for them to get a routing number."

I can barely breathe. "Where?"

"Here's the kicker: public phone." He exhales. "Payphone outside a Greyhound station in Sacramento."

That throws me. "Sacramento? She's that far?"

"Could be. Or she could've made the call while passing through. We got an address on the station, but no way to tell where she went after."

I grip the edge of the counter. "What now?"

"I've already called Sac PD. They're on the lookout for anyone matching her description." He sighs. "Big 'if,' but it's something. Better than nothing. And if she calls again—now we know she's willing to talk."

I nod, heart racing. Sacramento. A payphone. She's not a ghost. She's real.

"What about what she said about Mitch?" I ask, nauseated by the thought. "She's accusing him of being a serial killer."

"It's an interesting motive, but I'll be honest, Kit—she sounds delusional more than anything else. But next time you get her on, ask her about it. Try to keep her talking. And think long and hard about whether anyone you know might have information on where she is, so we can catch up with her."

"Okay." I twist the phone cord. "I'm going to work today. Who knows, maybe I'll learn something new."

"All right. Take care, you hear?"

"Wait, hold on a sec," I blurt, remembering something. I run and grab my piece of paper where I've been jotting down notes and return to the call. "Still there?"

"Yep."

"When she called the other times, she mentioned city names and dates. Medford, 1970. Olympia, 1971. Does that mean anything to you?"

"Not off the top of my head, but fire 'em off and I'll look into it."

I list them off, paper shaking in my hand.

"Good work, Kit. Talk soon."

We hang up, and I get ready for work.

Last night, I barely slept. The conversation with Gloria kept repeating in my mind, the words *your husband is a serial killer* looping like a song from hell. I closed my eyes and heard the beeping of Mitch's heart monitor. Guilt strangled me for not being there with him, for even listening to such utterly ridiculous accusations from a possibly psychotic teenager. I couldn't sleep. All night, my mind was on fire, jumping from sickening thought to sickening thought. Every year that Mitch came and went—the mystery that surrounded him, even at our closest—could he ... and then, how dare I even entertain the thought? How dare I? When I finally snatched an hour or two of sleep, who did I dream about?

My father.

The man my heart disowned long ago, the man I push from my mind whenever he lurks there—because no matter how many bear hugs he gave me, no matter how many times he pushed me on a swing or kissed my tear-stained cheeks, he was also a monster who could yell and pull hair and threaten to kill us all when he snapped. And I've never been able to reconcile my father the man and my father the monster.

But I shake off the nightmares and head to Breakneck Bay —not stopping at the hospital like I usually do. Leaving Mitch there alone. Telling myself I needed some time to digest everything, that I needed a day of normalcy, and that I'll stop by after work.

Now that I'm here, though, I'm having a hard time keeping up the performance. I emerge from my car and puke my coffee into the bushes. Then, I make my way down the stairs to the admin building and clock in.

"Hey Bluebell, how's it shaking?" Dwayne asks as he punches in next to me. He's wearing his sunglasses inside and seems extra laid-back—guessing the job's been a breeze lately with his boss out of commission. "You hangin' in there or what?"

"By a thread," I mumble back.

I recall what Rhonda told me about Dwayne and Gloria yesterday—was it only yesterday? God, I've aged ten years in a week. I grab the sleeve of Dwayne's neon shirt as he turns to head to the coffee machine.

"Can we talk?" I whisper.

He glances behind him, as if he thinks I'm talking to someone else.

"Sure," he says. "Something wrong?"

"Everything's wrong." I can't help the words coming out of my mouth, so I sweep them away with a forced laugh. "Just—I have a few questions."

"Yeah. Totally. Where do you want to go?"

I nod toward Mitch's office, and he follows me inside. The group of employees laughing and smoking cigarettes on the couch stops their conversation to watch us, and I fake I don't notice. I'm learning how to live with this cloud of suspicion surrounding me. Closing the door, I nod toward Mitch's desk. I step over the carpet that still smells new, trying to forget the sight of blood and teeth. I plop into Mitch's chair with a shiver, and Dwayne sits across from me.

"Meet the new boss," he sings into an invisible microphone. "Same as the ..." Then he seems to remember my circumstances, and his smile melts. He pushes the sunglasses up on his forehead so I can see his bloodshot eyes. "Uh ... so what's up, dude?"

Sitting here, folding my hands, I study him. I let the silence percolate, first because I'm not sure where to begin. But then I notice his squirming. The way he jiggles his leg and keeps glancing at the door. And I can't explain it—I sense that there's a reason he's nervous and wants to get out of this room as fast as he can.

"I want to know everything you know about Gloria," I say.

The plastic grin on his face melts, and his brow furrows. "Gloria? Why?"

"You don't need to know why. Just be honest with me. Do you know where I can find her?"

He's taken aback, clearly. The nervous energy I sensed before morphs into bewilderment. He scratches his head. "I don't know where Gloria is, man."

"Was there something going on between her and Mitch?"

Dwayne makes a noise as if I just socked him in the stomach. "I—uh—I don't know. I really don't, like, wanna get involved with your marital problems—"

"Just *tell* me," I bark in a voice that doesn't sound like mine.

He swivels in his chair once, all the way around.

"Look," he finally says. "Maybe. There might have been. No one *told* me about it, though."

"Do you know anything at all?" I ask, voice climbing. "Please. I'm begging you, anything. I need to find her."

"Dude, the last place I saw her was when she was at work that day." He puts his hands up. "Swear on my mama's life."

I ball up my fists and fight the urge to scream. But I did enough of that last night after Gloria's phone call. I'm still hoarse from it. I rake a hand through my hair and suppress the volcano in my chest. Dwayne watches like he fears me, which he should. Because I don't know how long I can keep myself from exploding.

But wait a minute. Wait just a minute.

My mouth drops open.

"Everything okay, Mrs. Blue?" Dwayne asks uneasily, cracking his knuckles.

I point a finger at Dwayne and narrow my eyes. "You're lying."

"I'm not! I would never swear on my mama's life if I were lying." Dwayne checks behind him nervously. "Look, you seem kinda stressed out. Maybe you should, like, take a sick day—"

"You told everyone that you saw Gloria at a payphone the night she disappeared. And that was the last time you saw her."

His expression is dumbfounded. I can tell he completely forgot about that. He swallows and nods. He picks at his cuticles on the table, as if they're the most interesting thing in the entire world. "Right. I meant—I was talking about—well, like the last time I saw her in *person*."

I reach across the table and grip one of his hands with such force he winces. I don't let go, either. I squeeze harder, all my desperation channeled into this moment.

"Ow, Jesus—" he starts.

"Dwayne, if you don't tell me exactly what the fuck you know, I will go to Creighton and get you fired. I will tell everyone you lied. I will go to the cops and tell them you're dealing weed."

"I don't deal!"

"I don't care," I say, gritting my teeth, squeezing so hard he's tearing up. "I'm not kidding. I will ruin your life before it's even fucking started."

"Fine. I didn't see her, okay? Let go of my hand, you crazy bitch."

I relent, pulling my hand back. Only now do I realize my heartbeat has turned into machine-gun fire. Dwayne scowls and shakes his hand, eyeing me like I've lost it. Which I have. Who is this Kit? I don't recognize her. I'm a little triumphant; I twisted important information out of Dwayne. Plough would be proud.

"You didn't see her at the phone booth?" I ask.

He's still rubbing his hands. "Don't tell anyone," he says, a worried expression on his face aging him backward. I'm looking at a sheepish child. "I panicked, okay? I—I didn't want him to get in trouble."

"Him who?"

"*Mitch*."

The word cuts through the air. The sound of his name guts me. Mitch. *My* Mitch.

"Why would he get in trouble?" I sit back. "I don't get it."

Dwayne blows a sigh out. Under the table, his leg is jiggling so madly it's tapping the desk. There's a bead of sweat on his brow. The usual half-stoned, carefree teenager is now a worried, frazzled boy who looks completely lost.

"Just tell me, Dwayne. I swear I won't tell anyone."

He purses his lips, thinking hard.

"Swear on my mama's life," I tell him with a tiny, encouraging smile.

Dwayne doesn't need to know my mama no longer has a life to swear on.

"I told her where the spare keys to his office were," he says, so quietly I lean in to hear it. He keeps his eyes on his fingertips. "I didn't know why she wanted them. Didn't know she'd go nuts and do what she did and mess it up so badly. I freaked out when the cops came and started asking questions. I said I saw her because I—I didn't want Mitch getting in trouble. I didn't want them thinking he did something to her when it was a prank or whatever. But I knew I'd get fired and my ass would be grass if people found out the whole thing was my fault. So, I didn't tell anyone about the keys. I figured she was fine. I just pretended I'd seen her to get Mitch off the hook."

"Why do you care so much about letting Mitch off the hook that you'd lie to the police for him?" I ask, baffled.

"Because ... well, him and Marrs are tight. And, like, after everything with Pamela last summer ..." He closes his eyes and puts his head in his hands. "I just wanted to work a summer job, man. I just wanted to make some dough and get to see chicks in their bikinis, and ride waterslides for free. Why's this place got to be so crazy?"

"Pamela?" I repeat, my head feeling like it might pop at any second. "What does Pamela have to do with this?"

"Oh, man," Dwayne says, putting a hand to his face and hanging his head. His voice drops to a mumble, almost more to himself than to me. "Why do I keep getting drawn into this shit, man?"

The room is still. Deep in my gut, a maggot of doubt squirms, telling me something's rotten. I really, really don't like how often Pamela Bronson's name has come up.

"Dwayne, out with it. Finish what you're saying about Pamela."

He moves his chair back and forth like an impatient child.

"I'm on your side," I remind him.

Nothing. Not a whisper.

I try a different tactic, inviting a quiver into my throat. I sniff. "I'm trying to figure out who the hell shot my husband."

Dwayne's hand drops from his eyes. "Aw, man. Don't cry, Mrs. Blue."

"Help me!" I beg him softly. "I'm in the dark here."

And the fake tears manifest into real ones. All at once, they're spilling and I'm not performing anymore. I ache with my ignorance. I crave answers so badly. Mostly, I just want my husband back. For Mitch to come back here, in this chair I'm sitting in right now. Whole. Unhurt. Harmless. The way he was before.

In some ways, it's like he died already. Whether or not he's breathing, I'm chasing a ghost.

"Mrs. Blue—like, um." Dwayne scrambles up hastily and comes over to me. "Don't cry. It's going to be okay."

I shake my head, too choked with sobs to respond.

"I—I—" He runs his hands through his shaggy hair, exasperated. Then, he tries to come behind me and pat my back. "Shhh. It's okay. He'll be all right. Right?"

I can hardly take a breath. Finally, I strangle out the words, one by one. "Nobody will tell me the truth. About anything. Pamela or Gloria, or anything."

Dwayne crouches down, eyes wide. "Don't cry. I don't know about Gloria, okay? I told you what I know. Pamela—the Pamela thing—that was—I don't know, shit, it wasn't anything." He swallows. "All it was—Marrs asked me for a favor. He said he needed to keep Mitch out of hot water. The night Pam went off Scream River... she was with Mitch." He puts his hands up. "I don't know what they were doing, Mrs. Blue, all I know is that it was after closing time. Maintenance found her body the next morning, and Marrs pulled me aside and told me that if any investigators asked, I had to say that Mitch left when I did. That Pam must have stayed behind alone. Because otherwise, Marrs or Mitch might have been held liable for her mistake, you know?"

I wipe my eyes. "What mistake?"

"Riding Scream River after the park was closed. You know. Operating it when no one was around. I don't know. Employees aren't supposed to do that kind of crap."

This information is a knife to the gut. My mind flickers with faint memories of last summer, when this happened. I was in LA. Mitch was here, working. I remember having a hard time reaching him, and every time we talked, he sounded stressed and breathless because of the tragedy that happened at the park. He never *once* mentioned that he was there the night she died. He told the story the way everyone else did: that Pamela must have stayed after the park closed and ridden Scream River when no one was around. That someone found her body on the hillside the next morning, skull bashed in. Paramedics helicoptered her out. She hung on in the hospital, then she died. Mitch told the story like it was just another waterpark accident. Like he barely knew her. Mitch was more preoccupied about the park getting investigated than anything else.

But is that what he was *really* worried about?

My face feels like it's slathered in dried glue from all the crying I've done. "Is that what you think happened?"

"That's what they say."

"And you believe it?"

He scoffs. "Who cares what I believe?" He scratches at a scuff on top of the desk. "Marrs gave me five hundred bucks to keep my mouth shut. He'd have my ass if he knew I told you this."

Poor Dwayne. He's still more of a kid than an adult. This is a lot to put on his scrawny shoulders.

"Didn't you know Pamela?" I ask softly. "Didn't you feel bad keeping that to yourself?"

"I didn't know her *well*. She went to my school." His voice drops, softer, still focused on the scuff on the desk. "It was an accident. I try not to think about it."

There's something about him at this angle—the fall of his dark hair around his face, the bony elbows, the beaten-up Chuck Taylors. He reminds me of Freddie. Not bad-hearted, just misguided. Not stupid, just unwise. A boy on a rocky path. All at once, I want to hug him.

"Listen, it's okay," I say. "I appreciate you talking to me. I feel a lot better. I really do."

Dwayne looks up at me, brown eyes glassy. "Yeah?"

I nod. "We'll keep this between us. Don't worry."

He stands up slowly. "Cool. Okay." He glances at the door. "Can I go now?"

This must be what the school principal feels like after pulling a student into their office to give them a talking-to. I offer a little smile.

"You're a good guy, you know that?" I tell him. "But can I give you some advice?"

For a moment, time warps. I'm talking to my brother, years ago, before he went off the rails. Before he decided nothing was worth following rules for, telling the truth for—living for. "If something in you tells you something isn't right … be guided by your own light, you know? Always listen to your intuition."

Dwayne blows out a sigh and lets his sunglasses down over his eyes. "Thanks. Right back atcha, Mrs. Blue."

As he walks out, the words echo in my ears.

What is *my* intuition saying?

I look around at Mitch's office—his wood-paneled walls without decorations. No evidence of him anywhere in here. A box in a corner erupting with neon shirts. The brand-new carpeting. The wooden desk that used to belong to Creighton. And it's like I'm in a waiting room, or a stranger's office. The realization hits me with a new velocity.

Maybe I don't know Mitch at all.

Hill Valley Gazette
August 1981

BREAKNECK BAY EMPLOYEE DIES WEEKS AFTER WATER SLIDE TRAGEDY

Pamela Bronson, 17, succumbed to her injuries this week after spending nearly three weeks in critical condition following an accident on Breakneck Bay Waterpark's notorious Scream River slide.

The Hill Valley teen, a seasonal employee at the park, was discovered unconscious by maintenance staff early August 1st, long after the park had closed for the night. Sources say she suffered traumatic brain injuries and multiple fractures, and had been unresponsive since the incident.

Park owner Creighton Marrs issued a statement expressing condolences to the Bronson family while emphasizing that Pamela "should not have been on the ride after hours," calling it a "personal decision, not a park liability."

Officials have declined to comment on whether foul play is suspected. The investigation remains open.

Pamela's family describes her as "bright, headstrong, and full of promise." A memorial is scheduled for this Friday at Forest Glen Chapel. Breakneck Bay has announced it will observe a moment of silence during park hours.

30

Working in the humid Ouch Shack goes by fast today.

I show up, hoping there will be time for me to ask other employees about Gloria, but everyone I confront says they barely knew her. Even the Rapids crew, which is where she worked, has nothing new to tell me. I open every locker in the Ouch Shack, just in case I've missed something, but find nothing.

It's the thick of July, and work is as busy as it gets. I count how many people come through today: sixty-six. Sixty-six people bruised, battered, sliced, half-drowned, heatstroked, concussed. Mitch always defended this place using Creighton's rhetoric. That Breakneck Bay is for the "fearless." It's "high-risk"—and so this place is special. But it occurs to me for the first time, as I reflect on grown men crying for their mothers and women wailing about being scarred for life, that maybe this is just dangerous and irresponsible, period. The editorials in the paper, the ones that say this place shouldn't exist—they may have a point.

After my shift is done, I head to the parking lot. Then I

hear, "Mrs. Blue! A moment, Mrs. Blue!" Rhonda comes running after me up the stairs.

"Hey Rhonda," I say, exhausted. "It's been a long day—"

"I just wanted to update you," she says breathlessly, a hand on my arm. "Last night I was studying the file, and—"

"Can we catch up tomorrow?" I ask. "I'm filthy, and I still have to go home and shower before I head to Creighton's for dinner."

"It'll only take a minute. I promise. You'll find this worth your time."

I wait, tilting my head, thinking that Rhonda doesn't know how much I've learned since our foray into Riverwood yesterday, and there's nothing in that file she could tell me about that I don't already know.

"I'm an avid subscriber to *Reader's Digest*. It's one of my favorite publications."

Where the hell is this going?

"And when I was studying Gloria's file closely, I ran across something that immediately piqued my interest. First off, I think her driver's license isn't legitimate. There are font inconsistencies with the birth date and her name. I can't prove it, just a hunch."

"Okay, thanks—"

Rhonda's eyes sparkle with excitement. "But the more interesting clue I found was her social security number. 078-05-1120."

She memorized the entire number?

"And?" I ask, glancing at my watch.

"*Reader's Digest* published a fascinating article about that number in a back issue. In the 1940s, a wallet manufacturer issued a fake social security card with that social security number on it. It was some kind of marketing gimmick. Since then, thousands of people have been using it. It's one of the most commonly abused social security numbers in American history."

My head feels like a balloon ready to float away. This just keeps getting weirder and weirder.

"So, her phone number doesn't work, her address doesn't exist, and her social security number is fake." I rub my temples. "I don't get it."

"I don't either, Mrs. Blue. Maybe you and I could go over her file again together?"

"Rhonda, I'm sorry, I don't have time. Like I said, I have to go to Creighton's for dinner. And I need to stop by the hospital, too."

"Oh. Okay." Rhonda looks disappointed. "Another time, then. Shall I call the police with this information?"

"No, I'll tell the detective the next time we talk. I appreciate you figuring that out." I smile at her. "You have a bright future ahead of you as an investigator."

"Investigative reporter," she corrects me. "And thank you. Have a good evening."

The entire drive, all I can think is—if all of Gloria's information is fake, how can I trust a word she says?

I visit Mitch. I still stink like sweat and chlorine. Sitting next to him, observing his still figure, I clutch his warm and ringless hand. I whisper to him I love him and that I can't wait for him to bounce back. But inside, I'm blank. I'm at a wake; the only mourner. I'm occupying a room with a person who is no longer here. I glance at my watch again, debating if I've held vigil long enough. Then I kiss his temple and rise to leave. An unusual feeling washes over me.

Relief.

Beep-beep-beep.

I pause in the doorway. There's something almost comforting about seeing him lying there, helpless.

Did I actually think that?

What is *wrong* with me?

Days ago, all I wanted was for him to wake up, be okay. For him to answer me and tell me what happened. I'm all upside down. Now, the thought of him fluttering his eyes open makes my stomach turn.

"Bye, baby," I whisper, and I don't look back.

31

Driving to Creighton's for dinner tonight, I should be developing an appetite. Instead, I'm chewing my cheek and filling up on dread.

The sky darkens, the trees thicken, and I wind farther up the mountain into a wealthy enclave known locally as Valley View. Here, the houses are not houses anymore—they're estates, tucked behind wrought-iron gates and decorative hedges. Occasionally, the wink of a distant swimming pool or an emerald vineyard catches my eye. I've only visited here on a handful of occasions in the past few years. Every time, I get carsick as a passenger on these hairpin curves. But right now, as a driver, it's strange how my stomach clenches up. Despite my dread, I'm able to hold it together.

"Kathy!" Kimber says, coming up behind the servant opening their front door, giving me a one-armed hug. She wears a kaftan and holds a martini with four olives in it. Her hair is Lucille Ball red, swept up in a Brigitte Bardot style, with a face made up to rival Baby Jane—although she's probably only a decade older than I am. Kimber freaks me out a bit. Is it the eternal, stretched smile, courtesy of her plastic surgeon? The heavy, false eyelashes? Her syrupy demeanor? I don't know. But regardless, anyone who has to put up with Creighton Marrs in sickness and in health, for better or worse, 'til death do they part, has my sympathy. Even if she can never get my fucking name right. "Kathy, how *are* you?"

"I'm okay. Good to see you."

She steers me inside, arm still around me. She smells like perfume that's much too expensive for me to identify. Somewhere, I hear the scream of a pet parrot. The living room décor is gaudy chaos: a gold statue of a deer in the corner ; a TV so big it looks like it belongs at NASA; an aquarium with a leopard shark; a rug that looks like Muppet skin. And a servant standing in a uniform that resembles a French maid Halloween costume.

"I can't *believe* what happened to Mitch," Kimber says in a gossipy tone.

"Yeah."

"What *happened?*"

"He—"

"Sorry, I don't mean to jump in. You need a drink, don't you? Want a drink?"

"I—"

"Biance Maria, get our guest a drink," she nearly shouts to the woman who stands three feet from us. Kimber turns to me and asks, sweetly, "What'll you have?"

"Iced tea?"

Kimber snaps her fingers at Biance Maria, who spins on her heels and leaves. I cringe. I don't understand how those with money treat others like they're beneath them. It's something I will never accept.

Kimber takes my elbow and leads me into their living room, where there's a blazing fire in the fireplace even though it's eighty degrees outside and the AC is blasting. "Oh my *God*. I can't *believe* what you're going through, you poor thing."

"Look who it is!" booms Creighton. He comes in through the sliding glass door from the patio and puts his hands up in a hallelujah gesture. He wears an apron that says BEEF. IT'S WHAT'S FOR DINNER! and clamps a set of tongs like they're his claws. "Kimber talking your ear off? Don't bombard her, Kim."

"She just came in, you oaf," Kimber says.

"Lemme guess: she already signed you up for her Jazzercise class. Am I right?" Creighton chuckles. "Jesus, Kimber. Give her a second to breathe."

"You're the one who won't shut up," Kimber says, then downs the rest of her martini.

I haven't even taken my jacket off yet, and I already want to go home.

I follow my hosts out the patio doors and try to focus on appreciating their lovely yard. The landscaping is lush as a tropical jungle—ferns, waterfalls, baby palms. The view from the deck brags a twinkling, faraway strip of lights that is downtown Hill Valley and, to the left, the serpentine swirls of lit-up waterslides and rainbow curls that make up Breakneck Bay. That's why Creighton loves it here, I think. He sits out on his deck and swears he can see everything going on at the park.

"It's fun," he said once as he peered through his binoculars. "Like being a kid and looking at your ant farm."

I'll never forget that.

"How's Mitch?" Creighton asks as I take in the view, my eyes falling on the guest cottage below where Mitch used to live. Creighton rests a hand on my back.

"No change yet," I say.

"Been meaning to go visit him, but I know Mitch. He wouldn't want anyone seeing him like that."

"Probably not."

"He'll be all right." Creighton sips from his beer bottle. "That guy can survive anything."

I coax my lips into a smile. "I sure hope so."

"Well, I've known him longer than you. I promise—he's gonna be okay." Creighton opens the grill and turns some sausages with a cough in the escaping smoke. "I've seen him survive jumping out of a moving car. I've seen him set himself on fire and stop, drop, and roll. I saw him get shocked by an electric fence once. He's a goddamn superhero."

I nod, though to me, Mitch has always just been a man. A mostly wonderful, sometimes confused, mysterious man. It pains me to know that Creighton's known Mitch so much longer than me, that he has access to years I don't.

Dinner is fine. It's hard to mess up sausages and potatoes. We eat on the deck and swat at mosquitoes. The sky darkens, the city lights glitter even brighter in contrast, and I try not to make it obvious that I keep checking my watch. Kimber has four martinis and drones on about the life-changing practice of Jazzercise and how much she hates Jimmy Carter. Creighton guzzles about six beers and eats four sausages and doesn't seem fazed. When Kimber goes inside to answer the phone, I'm relieved to have a break from her high-pitched, nasal voice and energy. It occurs to me the world was spared when Creighton and Kimber decided to forgo having children.

"You good?" Creighton asks.

The night's fully set in now, a moon grinning above his head. Creighton lights a cigar and sits back in his chair, studying me.

"Yeah. Thanks for having me."

"Is everyone treating you well at the Bay? Getting along with Rhonda okay?"

"She's been helpful. Thanks for lending her to me."

I swallow and watch Creighton. He adjusts his aviator-shaped eyeglasses. Kimber's inside the golden window, animatedly talking on the phone. If I'm going to ask Creighton anything important, now's the time. I roll my thoughts around, going over my conversation with Dwayne earlier. It's like someone dumped a jigsaw puzzle on the table, and I'm trying to figure out how this colorful mess is supposed to fit together.

"Creighton?"

"Yes, sweetheart?"

"Can I ask you something? Would you be honest with me?"

"Me? I'm always fuckin' honest, you know that. To a fault." He chuckles. "Just ask Kimber."

Blunt doesn't mean honest.

I choose my words carefully. "Did Mitch have something going on with Gloria Wilson or Pamela Bronson?"

Creighton rocks back and forth on his chair, making it squeak agonizingly. The whole time, he puffs his cigar and stares back unblinkingly. He does it so long I wonder if he heard my question. "Pamela Bronson," he finally says. "Why are you asking about Pamela *Bronson*? That was ages ago."

"Tell me, Creighton. I want to know."

He lets out a long sigh. He swivels his chair around to face the view, then turns it back around to face me again. An owl hoots somewhere. Crickets chirp; frogs sing.

"You want to know," Creighton says slowly, leaning in and stabbing his cigar in one of Kimber's forgotten martini glasses. It extinguishes with a hiss. "You want to know?" Creighton raises a bushy eyebrow at me. "Kit. Honey. Haven't you learned? Sometimes the safest place to stay's in the dark."

My mouth goes dry. I reach for my glass, but it's empty. Creighton and I stay still, watching one another. Something quivers in his eyes. I'm not used to whatever it is. But when I recognize it, it's even worse.

It's pity.

Creighton Marrs is *pitying* me.

"I'll tell you this," Creighton says, sitting back. "I learned a long, long time ago that if you're going to love anyone unconditionally, you've also got to be blind as a goddamn bat. I love Mitch. We're tight, like Starsky and Hutch. Anytime I've needed someone to help me with my half-baked ideas and ask no questions, bam, he's there." Creighton smiles. "And I'm there for him, too. It's unspoken."

I nod, my heart skipping erratically. I don't know where this is going.

"I probably know that guy better than anyone. Still, he surprises me all the fuckin' time. I don't think he has life figured out. I don't think he knows himself." He puts his hands behind his head and leans back, taking in the frenzy of constellations above our heads. "Do any of us really know each other? Do any of us really know ourselves? There's the fuckin' question."

I sneak a peek at my watch. Two hours I've been here. I remember Dwayne earlier. *Can I go now?* I get it, Dwayne.

"He's a good guy, mostly. Sure, he's done some shit. We've all done shit we're not proud of. He called me, needing my help. He's asked me for favors when he hits a tough spot. Once he started crying—I'll never forget it. A year or two ago, maybe. I told him to marry you, that you'd keep him out of trouble. He thought you were too good for him. He didn't deserve you."

"Really?" I ask softly, tears pricking. The stars flare momentarily as my eyes water.

"Yeah. He said he wanted to be a good man, but he struggled." He chuckles. "Don't we all, though?"

Creighton's eyes narrow on me, a razor-sharp focus. I shiver as if I'm in the crosshairs. For just a second, he looks blank, deadpan—and unrecognizable.

"What?" I ask, unsettled by his gaze.

"I just remembered. I, uh … I have something for you. Wait here."

Creighton steps inside. I wait on the porch, watching him stalk across the living room. There's something gorilla-like about his stomping feet, brooding expression, and fixed jaw. He comes back a minute later with a cardboard box under his arm.

"Here," Creighton says, plopping the box on the table. "Mitch left this shit here from when he was staying in the guest house. I've been on his ass to pick it up for months now."

Strange timing, but okay.

"Oh. Okay," I say. "What is it?"

"I don't know. Papers, mostly. Kimber wants to turn the guest house into a Jazzercise studio, so we need to clear the place out." He snorts, pulling out a sepia-toned photograph of him and Mitch ten or fifteen years ago. They're shirtless, grinning, with full beards and Jesus hair. You'd think they were twins. "Look at us. Man."

"Wow."

He tosses it back on top of the box. "Yeah, good old days."

"I'm sure Mitch forgot this all existed. He's not one to hold onto stuff."

"Then burn it, I don't give a fuck. But I'm wiping my hands clean of it." Creighton smiles at me, and his gold tooth winks. "It's his stuff, not mine. Last thing I need is Detective Roy Rogers poking around here for evidence."

The remark makes my eye twitch. Evidence?

Now I'm dying to know what's in the box.

He's not who you think he is, Gloria's voice pipes up. *Your husband is a serial killer. Do you really not know?*

Creighton brings me back to the present moment by slapping the moth between his hands and wiping his palms on his shorts.

"He loves you; that's all that matters. Whoever the fuck he

is." Creighton pulls himself up out of his chair. "I think we got some shit to make sundaes. Cherries and the whole nine yards. Want one?"

"I'm okay," I say. "I should get going."

Creighton gives me a cologne-stinky hug in the entryway. Kimber's still arguing drunkenly with what sounds like her mother on the phone and waves vaguely at me from the living room. I step out into the darkness, to my car, and head home.

"Will I ever know?" I ask the rearview as I take the curves on the unlit roads, surrounded by shadows and black branches.

I hit the steering wheel repeatedly. *Bam, bam, bam.*

"I don't understand what it all means. What does it all fucking *mean?*"

For the first time, the most terrible thought occurs to me: that I might never know.

That Mitch could die before I get the chance to find out who he truly is.

HAWK

1975

The room at the police station is as bleak and slate-gray as Hawk's inner state. Bare, nothing but a table where he sits. He ogles a wall in disbelief as he waits for the detective. And calculates.

Should he have come? Should he have refused? Should he deny everything? Say he doesn't know the girl in the photo, never saw her? Or keep a little truth to flavor the lies? What emotion do they want to see in an innocent man? Rage at the accusation, worry about the consequences, intrigue about the missing girl?

It's important to nail the emotion right because there's a smudged mirror to the side of him. An audience is watching him, maybe. Who knows? Because this is the first time police have questioned Hawk.

There's a panic inside him, rattling around like a screaming monster behind a door. He's trying to fend it off. He keeps pushing thoughts of prison out of his head—an unending concrete nightmare he couldn't survive. That's not an exaggeration, either. Because what would happen there would be his own personal hell: to be trapped inside Hawk with no prey to hunt. The urge would build and build and build and never find release.

He'd rather die.

So, as he sits here, he envisions a world where there is no Hawk. Makes up a story and goes over a few simple details he will stick to. Yes, he saw that girl. She was having car trouble, and he gave her a ride to the service station up the highway. That was the last he saw of her. Dropped her off and kept going. *Why?* Here, he'd lean in, widen his eyes. *Did something happen to her?*

The door opens with a metallic groan that reminds him of what a prison gate would sound like.

"Thanks for waiting," the detective says. He's got a crew cut and a daze in his eyes like he hasn't had a good night's sleep since 1950.

"Of course," Hawk says. "Though I've got to get to work soon. How long do you expect this is going to take?"

"What kind of work you do?" The detective takes a seat across from him and doesn't answer his question.

"Odd jobs. Landscaping, handyman work, stuff like that."

"Ah."

"I'm still not understanding why I'm here, though."

"Well, this young lady never came home last night."

"She hasn't even been gone twenty-four hours. You really go looking for every girl who doesn't come home?"

"No, but her fiancé is a sergeant here in the department, so we're helping him out."

You've got to be kidding me.

That woman was engaged to a cop.

The detective slides that same photo of the girl on the table. Hawk peers at it, trying not to think about what her face looked like after he bashed her teeth in. One of her canine teeth is sitting in the ashtray of his car right now.

"Highway patrol found her vehicle on the interstate late last night, and her fiancé is concerned something happened to her." The detective takes a pack of cigarettes out of his front pocket and lights one. "I'll cut right to the chase, young man, because I don't want to waste your time, and I sure as hell don't want you wasting mine. Someone spotted her getting into your vehicle."

Who? How did they put two and two together so quickly? But Hawk nods, deciding the best tactic right now is unwavering commitment to his story. A full-on performance. "Yes, I saw her pulled over on the side of the road and asked if she needed help. She said she ran out of gas, so I drove her to the service station. That was it."

"Drove her to the service station—then what?"

"That's it. Just dropped her off. She said she'd do all right from there. I thought she was going to use the phone to call someone."

The detective pulls out a spiral notebook and begins jotting notes. "What time was this?"

"Ten or so."

The detective sits back. "And then where'd you go after that?"

"Straight home."

The detective clicks the retractable pen about a dozen times before asking his next question. "What did you two talk about when she was in your vehicle?"

Hawk forces a laugh. "Barely spoke a word the whole ride. Took about three minutes."

"Hmm." The detective frowns at his nearly blank page. "Can I get your name and contact information in case we need to follow up?"

"Of course."

Hawk gives it to him. Spells it carefully, letter by letter. For a blink, he's so committed to this story that he tricks himself and imagines he wants to help the investigator.

"And—just in case we need it—is there anyone who can verify your whereabouts?" the detective asks.

The moment hangs, unnerving. Hawk can't tell what's going on behind the detective's unblinking gaze. Sweat threatens to break out over Hawk's body as his mind scrambles for an answer. *Alibi!* The word flashes in his mind like a liquor store sign. He knows this is the fork in the road where he teeters on the edge of Last Person Who Saw Her and Suspect.

"Yeah, I do, actually," he says. "A friend of mine I went to the bar with. He met me back at my house afterward. We drove separately, but he was right behind me. I stopped to pick that girl up, dropped her off at the station, and met my buddy back at my house just a few minutes later. He followed me the whole time and saw everything. We played a round of poker at my house afterward." He snorts. "Got my ass whooped."

The detective nods. "Your friend got a name?"

And Hawk tells him.

———

Hawk's first brush with law enforcement shakes him up. He used to be invincible. He convinced himself that his innocent appearance protected him. He could blend in, fade to a background character, escape notice. He thought strategically. He discarded clothing and burned fingertips to make identifying the bodies difficult. He moved often and traded his cars in. He grew his hair out, then cut it again, and sported a variety of beards. He was a shark: restless, untouchable. The fact that he had no criminal record protected him. He was slippery. He was smart.

But is he?

The question doesn't just rattle him from the inside out; it attacks him.

A wicked case of the flu swallows him in the days after the police interview. He's convinced it isn't a normal flu, but a spiritual flu. Because, during a restless, delirious night in his sticky sheets, the ceiling of his bedroom peels back. A white light shines in. And God's deep, bass voice asks, *Are you the devil's shadow, or is the devil yours?*

The nightmares he wrestles with over the next feverish twenty-four hours are a timeless hell. Blood thunders in his ears. Walls of pulsing flesh surround him. When he examines the throbbing palms of his hands, canine teeth are growing out of them. Distantly, he hears choking noises. He is reminded of werewolf movies he watched as a kid, the horrid transformation that consumed these normal men when the full moon undid them. And he can see a future where he is Hawk, he is only Hawk, there is nothing but Hawk, where evil has won, and he sobs and curls up in a fetal position and begs for death.

But death declines the invitation. The delirium passes. The rushing rivers of blood fade into the cheerful twinkling of birdsong. Sunlight turns the pulsing walls of flesh into familiar wood panels. His palms are smooth and pink. He sits up, quivering, catching his breath in the quiet music of morning. In the mirror, he beholds a human being. He gets on his knees, prays, and weeps with gratitude.

"The devil is my shadow, Lord," he repeats.

He writes it down in his notebook: left-handed, like a promise, in all caps:

THE DEVIL IS MY SHADOW

He packs up and moves again, vowing to start fresh. He's

not around when the waitress's body is found by the river. He's two states away, digging trenches, growing a handlebar mustache. He lives in a guesthouse near the beach. He attends church services. He calculates that, with enough intention, his good deeds can make up for his bad ones.

He donates spare change to the homeless; the devil is his shadow.

He carries his elderly neighbor's groceries, he drives by the bar but does not stop, he leads a weekly Bible study; the devil is his shadow.

He feeds tuna to a stray cat that scratches at his back window. He circles his hands around the cat's soft neck but does not squeeze; the devil is his shadow.

He picks up pretty hitchhikers with flowers in their hair and delivers them to their destinations; the devil is his shadow.

And yet, there's a nameless, unsettling quality to this time of his life—the Hawkless period. Like he's in a school play that never ends. He's acting a part. He's directing it, too. Watching himself unendingly and evaluating his performance. Living in a permanent state of dissociation. Empty. A mask.

Months roll by like tumbleweeds.

Life is a bright, smiling nightmare.

The itch returns. Just a wiggle under the skin at first, small enough to ignore. His eye twitches. His palms burn. He salivates when he passes a high school. He has dreams about a teenage girl at his church. He still has his pouch with teeth in it, locked in a box in his closet, and sometimes he takes it out to fondle them, to smell the iron tang of them.

He puts them away; the devil is his shadow.

As the months stack into a year, the itch becomes harder to bear. It's like the summer heat cranking up, degree by degree, and suddenly he's sweating. The urge makes him irritable and unfocused. His work suffers, and the pastor at his church asks him if something is wrong. He sits Hawk down and asks odd questions about sins that make him wonder if his pastor thinks he's homosexual. He leaves shaking, stops at a pub to calm his nerves, and ends up calling his friend sobbing and drunk at 1 a.m. His friend tells him it's too late to call, he's got a girlfriend he's shacking up with now. Hawk's never felt so lonesome in his life.

There aren't many hawks where he lives now. There are pigeons and seagulls. But one morning, while building a deck in the canyon, he hears a familiar cry in a nearby oak tree. He cranes his neck and spies a nest with not one, but two hawks—and his friend's new relationship rings to mind, and the pastor's words do, too. Suddenly, a ray of light shifts right onto him, like a spotlight. He laughs. An old line comes back to his mind: *The hawk rips into his screaming dinner with love in his heart.*

Even Hawk has love in his heart.

It's over two years after his last kill when he picks up a hitchhiker with thick brown hair and feathered bangs, a guitar strapped to her back. The beach highway is empty and dark, quiet except for the sighs of the ocean. His pulse races as she climbs into his passenger seat. He inhales the perfume of her strawberry lip gloss and the salty hint of the sea. Her cheeks have a pink glow to them, and though she says she's in her twenties, she could pass for fifteen. Hawk's adrenaline surges, and his ears ring. The urge swells up in him like it's never swelled up before—and twists into something new. Almost unrecognizable.

He's back. Hungrier than ever.

But the devil is no longer his shadow. He's behind him now. He's gone.

He turns down the radio. He tells her how gorgeous she is.

He drops his name—his real name. He asks her if she'd like to go dancing.

There's more than one way to catch a girl.

32

I wake up pining for my apartment in LA.

It was a crap one-bedroom with mold in the bathroom and stained carpet, but it was in wild, happening Hollywood. It was walkable to my diner job, the record store, and the Whisky a Go Go. Sometimes, Freddie would show up wasted on my doorstep and sleep on my couch. I stayed up late and made music alone in my living room. I went to the beach with my dog. That place was mine from floor to ceiling—my posters, my scratched-up records, my funky secondhand furniture.

Sometimes Mitch would stay for a week or a month. Sometimes he just called or wrote me postcards from the road—he was always off doing odd jobs for Creighton, and summers he spent at Breakneck Bay. I imagined it would be so great, so perfect, when we merged our lives and made it official. Everything would improve. I'd have a baby, and we'd be a family: a new-wave Ozzie and Harriet. Foolish girl. What I wouldn't do to blink my eyes and go back in time and be there again. To trade this vast, terrifying wilderness for the comforting, concrete city.

When I'm at a red light, blinker on, about to turn toward Breakneck Bay, for one split second I imagine turning the other way toward the 101 South. Glancing at my wedding ring and tossing it out the window. Never looking back.

What a horrible thing to think.

I force myself to turn into the park. It's not my shift I care about, though I need the money. I want to get the file back from Rhonda so I can pass it along to Plough. I know Gloria's file is full of lies, but it occurred to me that maybe there's something there that could be evidence, that could lead us to her. A fingerprint, even.

I'm beyond desperate.

"Good afternoon," Rhonda says, coming into the Ouch Shack on her lunch break.

It's been hectic as ever today, but right now it's just the two of us.

"Hi Rhonda," I say, mopping up margarita vomit. "You just missed the fun."

She wrinkles her nose and hands me a manila envelope containing the papers, which I stash in my purse. "How's Mr. Blue?"

"Oh, you know." I swallow. "On the precipice of death, but thanks for asking."

I clamp my hand over my mouth when I say it. The words are so harsh, so sharp, it's like they didn't come from me.

Behind her glasses, Rhonda's eyes are wide and bright as silver dollars. "Mrs. Blue, I'm so sorry," she says. "Has he—has his condition—"

"I shouldn't have said that," I sit on the stool, studying my lap in disbelief. I'm off, so detached. I'm not myself. "Nothing happened. He's in the same state."

"Phew," Rhonda says.

I wrench up my face, misery rising with such intensity I might cry. But it's like trying to juice a raisin—nothing's left.

"You're worrying me," Rhonda says. "You … don't look well."

I close my eyes. My heartbeat throbs all the way up in my skull. Am I going to have a stroke? An aneurysm? Is this how it feels?

Rhonda puts her chilly hand on my arm. "Do I need to get someone?"

I open my bleary eyes and shake my head. "That's okay. I'll live."

In awkward silence, we ready the shack for business. Rhonda sweeps while I restock supplies. My mind combs over my dinner at Creighton's on Saturday night. Something's nagging me. The box he gave me—it was mostly random stuff I've never seen. Cheesy records: Jackie DeShannon, Dusty Springfield, Lesley Gore. But Creighton's name is scrawled on the album covers in black marker. A few shirts and hats I don't recognize. A shoebox full of postcards and photographs from a random assortment of strangers. I can't help but wonder if these things don't belong to Mitch at all … but why would Creighton give them to me if they're his?

And then there's Gloria, the girl who apparently doesn't exist but who somehow shot my husband.

I have a million ghosts in my head, tuning in and out like a staticky radio station.

"Your husband is a serial killer. Do you really not know? Are you actually this stupid?"

"Rhonda," I ask as I take the industrial bottle of iodine out of the storage closet. "You told me you're into cold cases."

"Yes, studying them is one of my hobbies."

I fix a funnel into the top of the iodine spray bottle. "You said Ted Bundy stayed in Riverwood."

"Yes, according to the folks who run the Sleeping Inn."

A chill rattles me, from the bottom of my spine to the top. I pause a moment to make sure it's over before pouring the iodine. "Have there ever been any—other serial killers in this area?"

"No, not that I can recall," Rhonda says, kind of sadly. "That's the one and only."

As the rust-red liquid *glug-glug*s into the bottle, I breathe a little deeper. Gloria's full of shit. Mitch is harmless. No serial killers are around here. I'm losing my mind from lack of sleep, that's all.

"Though for a moment there, when the FBI was here? I wondered if—" She stops herself, clearing her throat. "Never mind."

"Wondered what?" I stop my pouring and put the jug on the station in front of me. "Tell me."

"I'm trying to be respectful," she says.

I narrow my eyes. But Rhonda can't stay respectful for long.

"The teeth," she says. "The prosthetic teeth in Mitch's office? Followed by an FBI visit? Well, my first thought, of course, was the Canine Killer."

A second passes. Then two. Instinctively, my hand flies to my mouth, where I press my index finger to my sharpest tooth. A sick, electric wave washes over me—that weird, backwards déjà vu.

"The Canine Killer." I clasp my hands and squeeze so hard my knuckles crack. "Who's that again?"

"He's never been caught." Rhonda stands on her tiptoes with the broom to sweep a cobweb from the ceiling. "One article I read estimated he murdered at least a half-dozen girls. He got his moniker because he rips out a tooth as a keepsake. I think he's on the Most Wanted list."

My neck prickles. "And he's from around here?"

"Well, no. But in surrounding states, and all in locations off the highway." Somehow, I know what she's going to say before the words even come out of her mouth. "Olympia, I think? Medford, Oregon. Somewhere in Colorado ..."

"And Omaha," I say.

All at once, I think I'm going to hurl. I turn toward the wall and accidentally knock over the industrial jug of iodine, which falls to the floor with a plastic *crack* and sprays everywhere. It's like that horror scene in Mitch's office all over again. Rhonda gasps. I shut my eyes and swallow a dry-heave. Not here. Not now.

"Mrs. Blue?" she says.

"No," I say, refusing to open my eyes. "No, no, no."

"Mrs. Blue," she says, sharper, more alarmed.

This poor girl, watching me self-destruct. The pollutant, metallic stink of iodine is so overpowering, I might faint. Finally, I open my eyes and turn, almost slipping as I make my way through the puddle of chemicals and toward the door.

I burst outside. The sunshine is blinding.

Despite the heat, I shudder as I race down the stairs.

"Uh, are you okay?" Stacey calls out from the ice cream shack.

"Whoa," says a headphoned employee scrubbing graffiti from the side of it.

I wave my hand dismissively and sprint toward the parking lot.

"What happened?" the twins say in unison as I run past them.

I have no words. I shake my head.

It's all crashing together in my mind, the pieces merging into a picture so awful I hate myself for even entertaining it.

What if—*if*—Gloria's right? And Mitch is the Canine Killer?

Could he be?

No. Crazy.

But—is it?

Mitch was a nomad. He's been to all fifty states. He traded in cars and careers for years. He—

You're spiraling. Stop.

I hate myself for thinking this. For even considering it for a second. But I can't—

I can't unthink it.

I stab my keys in the ignition and buckle my seatbelt extra tight before I floor it out of the parking lot.

33

Mitch showed up at my apartment last fall, clutching his duffel bag and backpack. He was tan as leather, greasy-haired, with bags under his bright eyes, smelling of sweat and earth. The sight of him was as shocking as the downpour of rain that had come that afternoon, darkening the skies and shaking the palm trees.

"I've tried it," he said simply. "I can't."

I crossed my arms in front of my chest. "Can't what?"

"Live without you."

I wanted to shut the door in his face. He had disappeared on me for the last time. I was finally moving forward with my life and accepting that this on-again, off-again boyfriend of mine would never get it together. He was a drifter. He drank too much. He was terrible at staying in touch. All his loyalties were in the wrong places: to Creighton Marrs, who treated him like a dog. To Jack Daniels. To a summer waterpark job that seemed to bring him nothing but stress.

"Face it, Kit," Freddie had said to me once, probably from a sleeping bag on my living room floor. "Your boyfriend's a loser."

Coming from him, this insult was a real doozy. That wasn't the problem, though. Losers I could handle—case in point, my brother. No. The problem went deeper than that.

Mitch was as unpredictable as my father.

"Come in," I said icily, stepping back on the carpet to let Mitch inside, hairs on my neck standing up. I couldn't explain it—the ghostly feeling that came with inviting him in when I knew I shouldn't. "Freddie just left. I feel like I'm running a motel. You need a towel for the bath, sir? A mint on your pillow?"

I tried not to look at Mitch because it hurt too badly. He wasn't ever going to be the man I wanted. He'd disappointed me one too many times. The nail in the coffin had come at the end of the summer when he dropped out of contact. When he finally called me from the road, drunk at a rowdy bar, I told him how pissed I was that I hadn't heard from him. He laughed a low, devilish laugh, one that turned my stomach.

"You don't know how lucky you are," he said.

He didn't sound like himself—his voice hardened into a low, weird growl—and it scared me.

I swallowed.

"I could have hurt you. I could have. But I didn't."

"You're hurting me right now, asshole," I said to him. "I'm done, Mitch. Not doing this anymore."

I hung up. I fell apart. I built myself back together again.

And then, months later, he was here in my apartment. Daring to come back, and me, predictably, letting him right back in. It was like watching my parents' abusive relationship all over again.

"Kit, I'm not leaving this time," Mitch said, putting his bags down.

I crossed to my kitchen. "You want tea or something?"

He followed me in, hands in pockets. He reminded me of a sheepish little boy under the mop of hair he'd grown out. "I'm serious."

"I have chamomile and peppermint," I said, turning to the cupboard.

He came behind me and wrapped his arms around me. I froze, playing dead while standing up. It hurt where he touched me because I was so hungry for it. I hated that Tiny Kit was running around joyously inside me. I hated that my fear of being alone was so great that even this man's occasional attention felt like a spell of desert rain.

"I've given up drinking," he whispered into my ear. "I'm done with it. It makes me a monster."

"Even tea?" I joked as I faced the cupboard.

His lips went to my throat, kissing me. I blinked away tears.

"I won't be that man anymore, you hear me?" he whispered.

"Mitch—"

"Don't let this ruin us." He inhaled my hair. "Remember? You're unbreakable."

His grip around me was tight, so tight. I relaxed under its force. We stood there for a long, still moment. My mind raced. My eyes swam. I knew, somehow, this was a crossroads. Here, in my tiny kitchen with the ugly yellow fridge and peeling linoleum tiles, a life was going to take shape. Mitch squeezed me once more, and then I felt his arms slacken. For one split second, I flinched, fearing a blow to the back of the head. I didn't know why this was what came to mind. Mitch had never raised a hand to me before. It was a sickening thought.

Instead, when I turned, Mitch was on one knee. Tears in his eyes.

"Please, Kit," he said.

It sank my heart to see him like that—begging. Hands

clasped. But then he showed me the ring balled up in his hand, the sparkle of diamond.

"Make me the happiest man in the world," he said. "I promise I'm a better person. I'm not the old Mitch anymore. I'm going to do right. Wherever I go, you go. I'll be good. I'll be good."

I gasped. This was the last thing I expected, yet everything I'd wanted for years. It was the proposal I'd given up on. Mitch wasn't the "marrying type." He didn't "like kids." He didn't want to be "tied down." The remorse in his face was tangible. His chin quivered. His eyes pleaded. I wanted to believe him. I wanted to believe that, at their hearts, people were mostly good. That light conquered darkness. That men can change.

I chose to believe.

Within six months, we were married and packing a moving truck with boxes. I was babbling on about having babies and smiling at the wink of my wedding ring. Decorating the cabin and convincing myself I loved it out in the boonies. Working at the Ouch Shack and telling myself I was having the summer of my life.

My whole life, I've prided myself on my loyalty.

But maybe my loyalty is my downfall.

I sit on the floor of my closet. The cold hardwood makes my tailbone ache. I'm desperate for answers. The only place I think to look for them after leaving Breakneck Bay earlier is here—in this meager corner that holds Mitch's few possessions. His backpack and sleeping bag, which he's taken on many camping trips. A fishing pole. And now, this random box Creighton gave me. I pull out some things I haven't studied yet: a notebook, a velvet pouch with nothing in it. Some bird feathers, polished stones, arrowheads, and a big blue button. I lay them on the floor. These items must mean something to him.

They mean nothing to me. I flip through the notebook, filled with random jottings—jumbled poetry.

THE HAWK RIPS INTO HIS SCREAMING DINNER WITH LOVE IN HIS HEART

someone wrote in ballpoint pen on page one.

A shiver vibrates down my spine, from the floor all the way to the top of my skull.

That's not his handwriting. And I've never seen Mitch write in all caps.

I pull out the records again, with Creighton's name in the bottom right corner. All caps—but much neater.

Did Creighton give me a box of his stuff, trying to pass it off as Mitch's? If so, why?

Creighton's voice echoes as I chew my cheek. I flip through the pages of the notebook, all nonsense words and snatched song lyrics and odd maps. I don't know what I'm looking for—some evidence tying him to the cities Rhonda and Gloria mentioned. Omaha, Medford, Olympia. But Mitch didn't keep a journal. There's no *dear diary* here, just weird, cryptic phrases like THE DEVIL IS MY SHADOW. And it all dead-ends into blank pages.

I shut the notebook with a sigh. Even if I had stumbled upon something that lined him up with the cities a serial killer was in—so what? That isn't enough to be certain. Freddie rambled around the country for years. Creighton had failed real estate projects and businesses in half of the US. Does that make them serial killers?

Swallowing, I let that thought expand for a single second.

Maybe it was Creighton all along.

Creighton—the man who respects no one. Who looks at

people as expendable. Who always convinces other people to do his dirty work. Creighton, the man who wanted to dump the employee files in the first place and who is now trying to pretend this box belongs to Mitch. Is there a reason he wants to be rid of this stuff that he joked was "evidence," a reason he's pretending it's Mitch's? What if Creighton is the Canine Killer? What if he's sensing justice circling him and is just trying to cast doubt elsewhere?

I need to call Plough. The files, this box—he'll know what to do.

Then I hear the shrill shriek of the phone ringing. I get up and hurry down the hall, past the entryway where, if I stare too long, I see Mitch's body lying there. The phone rings again, and fear flickers—so fast, hot, and awful it's like a strike of lightning.

What if Mitch dies?

What if I never know the real story?

I cross the dark kitchen and answer the phone on the last ring.

"Hello?" I say.

The tape recorder automatically starts turning its wheel.

"Hi," Gloria says.

Her voice is raw and gutting. She sounds like she's calling from some place unimaginably far away: the moon, maybe. The bottom of the sea. Maybe this time we'll be able to trace the call and finally find her—or maybe she's just calling from another pay phone, another dead end.

"Gloria, why do you keep calling?" I ask her. "What is it you want? You already shot Mitch. You already got your revenge, or whatever it is you want."

"But I've been lying to you," she sniffles. "To everyone."

I wait, watching the tape roll. Relief washes over me so intensely I close my eyes and savor it.

She was lying about Mitch. He did nothing. All that serial killer bullshit—none of it was true.

But that's not what she says at all.

"My name isn't Gloria," she says. "My name is Cynthia Carpenter."

34

I lean against the wall, sliding down to a cross-legged position on the floor. My stomach clenches. I brace myself for whatever's next—this madwoman whose name I apparently don't even know.

"Okay." I blow out a breath slowly, trying to maintain control. "Who the hell is Cynthia Carpenter?"

Her breathing is heavy. There's the sound of her drinking something, followed by a long exhalation—smoking, maybe? My face rushes with pins and needles. I'm holding back so many emotions I might break out into a full-blown rash at any second.

"Stop playing games," I say.

"I mean, I'm Gloria to you. I went by Gloria at the park. The girl you remember as Gloria? That's me. But that's not my real name. I was born Cynthia."

The tape recorder churns on, a comfort. Plough will love to hear this call when we're done. Not will we be able to trace her location, but now we've got her real identity. "And?"

"When I first got a job at Breakneck Bay, I knew it wouldn't do to use my real name. Just in case. I didn't want him to know me."

"Him? Who? Mitch?"

"Yes. The man who almost killed me."

I ball my fists up so tight that my fingernails dig into my palms. One part of me wants to rip the phone out of the wall. The other needs to hear this, because it's everything I've feared. "Fine, I'll bite," I say flatly. "When did this happen?"

"I was nine when he attacked me," she says.

Sobs roll out of her. If they're real, they are gutting. If they're fake, they fill me with rage. I don't know how to feel. I just close my eyes and listen.

"I grew up right outside Medford, Oregon." She breathes in and out once, raggedly. "In this tiny, shitty trailer right next to a peach farm. Every morning, the school bus dropped me off and picked me up near this ... patch of woods. I walked the rest of the way home from there, along a trail that led to the trailer park. There was a highway across the road there, and a little fruit stand. I can still picture it—I can see it as if I'm there."

I want to yell at her to hurry, but I bite the side of my tongue.

"Well, one afternoon, the bus dropped me off. I started walking home from school through the woods. And suddenly, out of nowhere, this man steps out from behind a tree. Scared the shit out of me. He was whistling this tune ..." She clears her throat and hums it. A low, sad song, one I recognize right away. One that floods my entire body with goosebumps.

It's Jackie DeShannon's "Take Me Away." One of Mitch's favorite songs.

It's not an incredibly popular song, either. The only other person I've ever met who's a fan of Jackie DeShannon is Creighton. In fact, one of her records is in the box Creighton gave me ... with *his* name on it.

I'm suffocating.

Gloria—*Cynthia*—whispers, "I'll never forget that song."

My eyes burn. I pinch the bridge of my nose.

Her voice shakes. "The man had his hand in his jacket pocket. He stepped closer to me and said, 'Hey there. I just caught a bunny. Want to see?'"

I shake my head, trying to wake myself up from this nightmare. Wake up. Wake *up*.

"It was a rock," Cynthia says sharply. Her voice changes, void of emotion, as if this is a story she's told so many times she doesn't quite feel it anymore. "And he hit me over the head with it. I fell on the ground. And then he—he unzipped his pants—"

"Stop," I say, pressing my hand to my sternum. "I can't listen to this."

"Why? Because then you might have to face the fucking music? Because you might have to accept the fact that you married a pervert and a killer?"

"There's no way Mitch would do something like that."

"I got away that day. Played dead, and then I somehow got up and ran toward the highway. He grabbed me, but I bit his hand so hard that he let me go."

"I'm so sorry this happened to you," I say, softening my voice. "But it's likely you've mistaken Mitch for someone else."

"Believe me—when someone steals your innocence and almost murders you, you never, ever forget them."

My head is swimming. What she's saying is heartbreaking, but I can't buy it. "Mitch doesn't look like he did back then. He —" I stop speaking, pressing my fingers to my lips. Remembering that photograph in the box Creighton gave me, how the two of them looked like twins. "He looked like every other rambling, long-haired man."

"No one ever caught the guy who did that to me."

"I'm sorry to hear that, but that doesn't mean Mitch did it

to you. And what does any of this have to do with the Canine Killer?"

"Because years later, I saw the Most Wanted sketch on a telephone pole. Instantly, I recognized him." She scoffs. "I guess I should consider myself lucky. His other victims didn't get away."

This is unbelievable. It's such an absurd reach. How can I trust this woman's instincts? But deep down, I wonder what it would mean if she is telling the truth. And that thought is so devastating that I peel away from my consciousness, floating above myself and looking down at the woman hunched on the floor on the phone. This isn't my life. This isn't real.

"People looked at me with pity everywhere I went," Cynthia says. "I was raised by a single mom. She spiraled, drank herself into oblivion, blaming herself for my attack. Lost her mind from guilt. By the time I was fifteen, she had died of cirrhosis, and I was living in a group home in Eureka." She sniffs. "You know what those homes are like? They're training grounds for criminals. I had to sleep with one eye open every night and bribe my roommate to not beat me up. We were stuck in this ... shit house with shit staff eating shit food all day long. Once a year, we went on a field trip. Lucky us. When I was seventeen, guess where we went?"

I swallow and whisper, "I don't know."

"Breakneck Bay," she says with a flourish.

I flinch at the words. Here I am, apart from myself, a ghost separating from my body. I wish I could disappear. Make it all stop.

"I was standing in line when I saw him," Cynthia says, her voice sharpening with emotion. "He was training someone—a pretty girl—and he had this flirty smile. The instant I laid eyes on him, I felt like I was going to puke." I hear a gulping sound, as if she's downing a drink. "But I told myself, no. Wasn't him.

Over the eight years that passed since he assaulted me, I saw him everywhere. He starred in my nightmares, and he was every man I passed on the street during the day. Everyone could be him."

See? She just admitted what I was thinking this whole conversation.

"But as I waited there in line," Cynthia continues, "I kept my eyes on him. The girl he was training left, and he stood there watching her. Watching her walk away like a lion watches an antelope. And he walked the other way, whistling a song—*the same one* that had haunted me for years. And the *second* I heard it, I knew." Her voice rises and she shudders with a sob. "That song was like a key. I'd never heard anyone sing it before, and I haven't heard anyone sing it since. There wasn't one doubt in my mind. It was *him*."

"Then why didn't you go to the police?" I challenge.

"Oh, I did. Bet your *ass* I did. But they don't listen to girls with juvenile records. They don't listen to girls who spent months in an institution. They took my 'tip' and did nothing."

"Maybe they did nothing about it because there wasn't enough evidence," I say.

"That's when I took matters into my own hands," she says, ignoring me. "I got out of the group home this past spring. I moved right outside Hill Valley. And I landed a job at Break-Your-Neck Bay." She makes a shuddering sound. "Being around him made me sick. But I pretended to be interested in him, just to ask him questions about his life, to make sure it was absolutely, positively him. And sure enough, all it took was me batting my eyelashes at him like he was James Dean, and he spilled to me about his years on the road. Ever been to Omaha? What about Olympia? Colorado Springs? Yep, he'd been there. All the places the Canine Killer had left bodies over the years."

I remember what Rhonda had said about their *chummy*

talks. How Mitch described them, too—he said Gloria had asked about road trips. My heart sinks at the synchronicities.

"So I framed him," she says, her voice taking on an edge. "To make the world see him for the killer he is."

"And look how that turned out," I mutter.

There's a long, static silence. The intense emotional whirlwind fades, and what I'm left with is a numb gravity. Gloria—*Cynthia*—weeps openly and wetly on the other end of the line. For one moment, I allow myself to fully let this possibility into my head. To imagine that behind Mitch's façade, there's a predator. That he's done horrible things to young women. I think of news stories and the smiling faces of serial killers that looked so disarmingly human. I think of my father and the twinkle in his blue eyes.

"Do you believe me?" Cynthia weeps. "Please tell me you do. I thought you, of all people, would, after what you went through. You were so kind to me that day— when you told me about your parents? About how rough you had it when you were young? I felt like—I felt like maybe you would understand."

I can't bear to give her what she wants, even though I ache for her. Everything lines up. But my heart just can't fall in line.

"Where are you, Cynthia?" I ask softly.

"Why? So you can call the cops? Go ahead. By the time they find me, I'll be gone."

"Where are you going?"

"I'm going to shoot myself," she says in a shaky voice.

Suddenly, she sounds like exactly what she is: just a teenage girl pushed to the edge.

"Don't do that," I say. "That won't make anything better."

"Evil always wins."

"Cynthia. Whoever did this to you—whatever happened—they've taken enough. Don't let them take your life, too."

"I don't want to go to jail," she sobs.

I sigh. I don't know how this has turned into me comforting her, but I fall into it so naturally. It's instinct.

"Trust there's more for you," I say. "Believe me—" I choke up for a split second, remembering how broken I was after my parents died. How I didn't think I could go on. "You can survive this. You can learn to look at the bright side. You can put it behind you. You can get to a point where you go an hour, then a day, then a week without remembering the bad things that have happened to you. I promise. Don't give up. It's going to be okay."

Tears fall down my cheeks. Am I talking to her or to myself? I don't know anymore.

"You'll be okay," I insist.

I hear a deep breath from her. I swear she's about to say something.

But then the line goes dead.

35

I stare at the phone, the conversation throbbing through my mind. The tape recorder is still and quiet again. I should call Plough, but right now I don't know where to start. The sheer weight of possibilities crushes me. Should I be worried about Cynthia hurting herself? Should I believe anything she says?

What would it be like to go through the things she says she went through?

I bury my face in my hands. Sensing a mental breakdown, Bowie comes running in and licks my arms. I give him a long hug and thank him for his kindness. Standing up, I'm in such shock the house seems to tip slightly, as if it's bobbing on the ocean. I dial Plough but can't bring myself to press the last button. I hang up the phone and pace the house.

Silence has never sounded so oppressive. I open a window to welcome the whispering breeze. Pressing my fingers to my chest, the electric drumbeat of my heart reminds me I'm not actually a walking corpse. God, I wish Freddie was here. I wish *someone* were here for me.

I walk around the house, tremor in my hands, not knowing

what to do with this tsunami inside me. Somewhere, a young woman is sitting with a gun in her hands, and I can't save her. And Mitch—my mind stutters at the thought of him. If I had any contents in my stomach, I would have lost them by now.

I scan the living room with the eerie sensation that I'm standing in a stranger's house. There's no sign of Mitch anywhere. The furniture I picked out, my record shelf, my dusty acoustic guitar in the corner—I never noticed how absent he was until now.

It's like he was never here.

And for one second, I feel so fucking free.

But then reality settles back in, and I might explode. Bowie whines at me like even he knows I'm about to blow.

I burst out of the front door, step outside, and let out a bloodcurdling scream at the pine trees. I'm no longer human. I'm a werewolf. I'm a hurricane. I scream until my throat is raw, until my lungs burn, until my voice goes hoarse.

I could burn it all down right now; I swear I could.

Fueled by a monstrous rage, I stomp to the studio, the stupid studio that Mitch built for me when we first moved here. I thought it was so sweet but now I wonder—was it to keep me out of his hair? To shut me up so I wouldn't keep asking about getting a job at Breakneck Bay? Another attempt to keep me at arm's length? To forever hide who he truly is?

I pick up a rock on the ground and hurl it at the door, making a dent in the wood. But that's not enough. I stomp inside and punch the soundproofed walls until my fists ache. I use my arm to wipe the entire table of my recording equipment, all of it crashing to the floor. I kick the eight-track he bought me for Christmas, unable to help myself. Like a child throwing a tantrum, Tiny Kit has taken over.

A fresh wave of confusion and fury rises. I sob and behold the mess I'm making as if it's not in my control.

"I hate you," I whisper.

I don't know who I'm talking to. To Mitch? Cynthia? Myself? All of the above?

Am I so weak that I'm being undone by a lunatic on the phone? Is my love for Mitch so delicate that she's broken it with these insane accusations?

Stop. I need to stop it.

I slap my face. Get it together.

"She's lying, she's a liar, she lied," I croak in my blown-out voice.

What kind of idiot would I have to be to not know my husband was a serial killer?

What kind of blindness would I have to suffer from?

What does that *say* about me?

I squat on the floor and break down, crying so hard I might as well be turning inside out. Every raw, ugly, hurt piece of me is oozing.

Maybe I'll live the rest of my life never knowing which I am: a disloyal wife who believed the revolting lies of a distant stranger, or the world's biggest fool who didn't realize she slept beside a killer for years.

I stand up, wiping my face. My nose is clogged, my vision is blurred. I'm a void. A ghost. I survey the wreckage, ashamed of what I've done—throwing a fit like a toddler. Ruining my equipment, as if that helps anything. I step to pick up the eight-track, which is worth a small fortune, the fanciest gift anyone's ever given me. And right as I step, I hear a crunch under my foot and wince at the sharp pinch beneath my heel.

I stepped on glass. I sliced my foot open.

Oddly, the pain is a relief—a tangible thing I can focus on instead of my whirlwind of emotions. I peer down at the floor.

No—it's not glass I stepped on. It's wood.

It's the maraca Mitch made me for a wedding present. The

one he whittled and painted so carefully and gave to me on our wedding night.

You'll never know how special you are, he whispered before leaning in for a long, lingering kiss.

And now it's shattered to pieces.

I choke on a sob. I stoop to pick up the pieces—maybe I can save it? Salvage it? Maybe there's some hope still, somewhere, if I look hard enough.

But then I see them.

There. Right there. Next to my bloody foot.

Scattered among the splintered wood.

The beads that were inside the maraca.

They look like—but no. They're beads. Just beads.

I grab one off the floor and peer at it in the light to prove it to myself.

My stomach plummets.

I try to drop it. My fingers won't obey.

I get lightheaded. It takes a full second before the tiny object falls from my hand.

I stumble backward, looking at the mess again with newfound horror.

White. Pointy. Small.

Canine teeth.

My hands tremble at my sides.

No, I'm seeing things.

Hallucinations? Have I officially lost it?

But as I stoop down for a closer look, reality hits me like a freight train.

I forget how to breathe. How do lungs work again?

There's no running from this. There's nowhere to hide anymore.

I married the Canine Killer.

1977

He knows this girl is special within ten minutes of picking her up.

There's a sparkle about her, a kindness she radiates, an instant connection when their eyes meet. She's gorgeous. Stylish. Tight jeans and motorcycle boots and fruity-smelling lip gloss that fills the air and makes his mouth water. She's hip. Early twenties. Chestnut, feathery hair and smoky eyeliner and silver bangles in her ears—the kind of girl who seems out of his league. Who normally he'd be too shy to talk to. He can't explain what it is about this one that is so special. Why he knows instantly he would never hurt her. Maybe it's the guitar. He's never met a girl who plays guitar before. Maybe it's the way she stares right into his eyes like she's unafraid of him.

Or maybe he still has it in him to fall for someone.

Maybe he's not a lost cause.

His heart speeds up as he turns up the radio. In the distance, Los Angeles gleams, a web of bright lights against the mighty mountains.

"I've got the itch to go dancing," he says. "Know of a good place?"

She laughs. "I know about a million places once we get to Hollywood."

His lips curl up shyly. "Well, how about you show me?"

"Oh, you want to take me out dancing, handsome stranger?" The girl laughs. She ponders this for about three seconds. "Why the hell not? But want to know my name first?"

"Oh. Yeah." He shakes his head and laughs at himself. "Sorry. Been on the road too long. I think I forgot my manners."

"Katherine, but you can call me Kit," she says. "You?"

"Mitch."

It feels so good to say it, as if he's just made a promise to the universe. He's Mitch now. He's in control again. Hawk is gone.

"So you've been on the road awhile, huh?" she asks. "Doing what?"

"This and that," he says. "Construction work, handyman jobs, delivery. Whatever I can find."

"You sound like my brother Freddie," she says with a laugh. "He's a roadie for some heavy metal band called Venom Lung. It's always something new with him. I don't even know what state he's in half the time."

Venom Lung. Why does that name ring a bell? Then it hits Mitch—that terrible band he and Creighton saw in Texas.

Wait a second.

"Freddie with long hair and crazy eyes?" Mitch asks. "Heavy Metal Freddie?" He laughs. "Small world, man. I know Freddie. We've crossed paths a few times over the years."

Kit's jaw drops. "Are you serious?"

"Yep."

"What a coincidence!"

He grins. "Or maybe it's destiny that I picked you up."

"Maybe," she says, still marveling.

They end up at a dive bar where he buys her a beer. When he puts a Jackie DeShannon song on the jukebox, she makes fun of him and puts a hand on his cheek in a way that melts him. He makes sure to not drink too much, spacing out his sips. As he relaxes, he imagines what it would be like to have a girl. To settle down and leave his rambling, chaotic past behind. He never thought it was an option, but something about Kit makes him entertain the thought. At the end of the night, her cherry lip gloss is sweet on his tongue, and she writes her phone number on his arm in eyeliner. He promises to call her the next time he's in the area.

Mitch can't get her off his mind. It's puzzling. She's not the first girl he's fallen for in his life, but he's never fallen so hard, so fast. He calls her from his temporary home in Hill Valley, where he's working to help his best friend, Creighton, open a waterpark. He writes her letters that he drops in the mail. While he's at work building eccentric waterslides or on road trips for materials, she's on his mind constantly. There's something so soothing about having these kinds of feelings for someone—wanting and loving her in a way he never thought he could. Maybe it's possible for him to put Hawk to rest for good and live a normal life. No one will ever know. He could be a better person, make up for his sins.

Kit seems to be the key.

Slowly, over the course of the next year or two, he woos her. It's like a hunt—inching closer to her, getting her to open up and trust him, to let him into her apartment, her bed, her heart. There's something about the long-distance relationship that creates a push-pull between them that always leaves him thirsty for more. He visits her every other week. He imagines things he's never had in his life, things he thought were repellent to his identity: a home, a committed relationship, maybe even a family. They call each other boyfriend and girlfriend. They hold hands in public and have pet names for each other. She drops hints about what kinds of rings she likes and how she'd want a beach wedding. And he lets himself consider it. His imagination runs wild when he stares at her there, smiling, her hair blowing in the Santa Ana wind.

But then he sees the sign flapping from the telephone pole behind her. The WANTED poster with a man's face sketched on it—his face. Doesn't have his sideburns, about ten pounds too heavy, but he knows who it is. And a dark cloud blows inside him. Because if she knew ... if she ever found out ...

"What's wrong, Mitch?" Kit asks, putting her hand on his arm.

He shakes his head. He mumbles something about hitting the road. He leaves her again.

This goes on for years. The cycle wears on both of them, but there's something refreshing about making up after breaking up. They never love each other so much as when they think they've lost each other. And she keeps him out of trouble —mostly.

It gets trickier during the summertime when the park is open. Yes, he knows Kit's back in LA, impatiently tapping her boot and waiting for him, but there are teenage girls crawling all over Breakneck Bay every summer. Some of them are his employees. Some of them flirt with him. A few of them, he imagines he could rip apart. He goes to church, and it helps; it does. He volunteers and reads the Bible and keeps his hands busy with whatever new hobby he's into—building model airplanes or fixing cars or fly-fishing. But he can feel Hawk's hot breath on his neck sometimes. And he gets bored and finds himself at the bottom of a bottle more than he likes to admit.

Kit and Mitch are on the fritz when it happens—when he takes a wrong turn one night, flirting back with Pamela Bronson, a girl much too young for him, a girl he supervises. He stays with her late in the Ouch Shack, pretending to give her life advice while stealing glances down her shirt and sharing a bottle of Jim Beam. As she talks about college, some drama about a sorority, Mitch notices he's having a hard time tuning in to what she's saying. He thinks of those Charlie Brown cartoons, the *wah-wah* sound when the grownups speak. That's what Pamela's voice is like to him. There's something about her that reminds him, nostalgically, of his first. The hitchhiker he picked up on that rainy day in Washington before he bludgeoned her with her own chunk of amethyst. And with little warning, Hawk is back.

He's blackout drunk. He can't even fully see her face in the dim light, and that makes what he does so much easier. He finishes the last swig from the bottle. He strikes her over the head with it. The intense wave of power infects him like magic. He takes what he wants from her. And he drags her body out and tosses her down the hill.

The next morning, he wakes up in his bed with the shakes. He thinks he had a nightmare—that's all it was. It must have been. But when he gets to work later that day and sees the ambulance and the fire truck, his knees get weak, and sweat breaks out. His hangover throbs so painfully he wonders if he's going to have a stroke.

"Whatever the fuck this is, we bury it," Creighton says to him quietly in his office. "I don't want to know, Mitch. And this time, I'm not a fucking alibi. Once is all I'll do."

Tears burn Mitch's eyes. All he can see when he closes them is Kit's face. The horror that would paint her expression if she knew who he really was.

"I don't want to be this person," Mitch whispers.

"Buck the fuck up, buddy," Creighton says. "I told that twat assistant of yours to say he saw you leave. It'll be fine. I don't want this to have a *whiff* of foul play, or I'm ruined." He claps Mitch's back so hard Mitch winces. "We look out for each other, right?" He smiles so big, a gold crown winks back. "Now you owe me, big time."

"I didn't want to—"

"Now, shut up, shut up. I don't want to hear it. La la la." Creighton heads toward the door. "Go home. Get some fucking sleep. You look like shit. You smell like a distillery."

Mitch stares at Creighton with bloodshot eyes.

"Want some advice?" Creighton says. "From one dirtbag to another?"

Mitch tents his fingers, saying nothing.

"Marry your girl. Settle down. She'll keep you out of trouble. She'll provide you a refuge, a cover. You can't keep fuckin' up like this, Mitch."

"I don't deserve her," Mitch says.

"Sure, you do. Move her out here; she'll keep you straight."

"You don't get it," Mitch says. "I want to be good. But there's this other part of me. This ... hawk. Living inside me." Tears sneak out of his eyes. "Ripping me apart."

Creighton gives him a long, narrow-eyed look. It's the look of someone who does not know how to respond, who's calculating how much they want to know and how much they want to bury. He forces a laugh, finally, and puts his hand on the knob.

"Stop being a pussy," he finally says.

Mitch soaks the next couple of months with enough whiskey to give him a welcome amnesia. After the season is over, he goes on a long camping trip. He prays to God, and God gives him the cold shoulder. He asks for a sign. Help him choose. He can't keep living his life as two men trapped in one body. He has two choices: He can be a killer, or he can be a lover. He can't be both.

He's hiking when he finally gets the sign. He spends all day sweating and muttering to himself as he meanders up a trail in the brisk morning air. A rattlesnake slithers by, and Mitch is disappointed when it doesn't seem interested in him. At the summit, Mitch surveys the majesty, the three-sixty view. The tiny town of Hill Valley sits nestled between two forests over there. Beyond it, the curls and swirls of Breakneck Bay. The sky is so blue it hurts, and the clouds billow like spun sugar.

There is so much beauty in the world. Such breathtaking highs. Such terrifying depths.

And then he sees it: down below him, about ten feet.

A dead hawk.

It lays face up, majestic even in its death, wings spread out on either side. It's as if it died mid-flight. Its brown and white speckled feathers ruffle, tickled by the breeze. And Mitch knows God finally gave it to him—his sign. The one he begged for.

Ten hours later, after a rainy drive chasing a storm down California, he arrives at Kit's doorstep. She's skeptical when she opens the door, but she lets him inside.

"Kit," he promises, voice full of emotion. "I'm not leaving this time."

And for once in his life, Mitch keeps his word.

Hawk is finally dead, for good.

"Killer Chronicles," by Rhonda Wegman

For nearly a decade, the so-called "Canine Killer" terrorized America, leaving a trail of vanished girls and eerie, unexplained crime scenes. Police linked the killer to at least eight disappearances between 1972 and 1978, but after that, it's like he vanished into the trees. The killer targeted young hitchhiking women and was known for extracting the canine teeth of his victims. But in recent years, the trail has gone cold. No confirmed sightings, no new victims—just silence. Some believe he's dead, others say he's in serving time in prison for other crimes. A few whisper that he's still out there, watching, waiting. After all, monsters don't just disappear… do they?

36

I back out of the studio, gaze still locked on the—the *teeth* on the floor—the pointed canines that belonged to real women.

Real women, who my husband murdered.

It doesn't sink in. My mind is still bewildered, as if there's been some mistake, but what that mistake could be, I couldn't say. I have fully separated from myself at this point. There's Kit's body, moving, and Kit's mind, floating a few feet above. I'm in such a state of shock that I'm calm. I am in the eye of a hurricane right now. I cast one last look at the teeth on the floor—seven; I counted—and turn away. I step outside into the twilight air and pull the door closed behind me.

I cast a look upward. The golden burst of light in the canopies, the innocent trills of birdsong—nothing adds up. A maple leaf catches the wind and gracefully falls to the forest floor. How can the world be so beautiful and ugly at the same time?

As I step onto my front porch, my palm hovers over the knob, my stomach clenching. It's like I'm about to enter a haunted house. The dread is overwhelming. I can't face evidence of our life in there, built on lies. I can't.

What if it's more than teeth? What other horrid trophies has he been hiding? Locks of hair? Jewelry? Clothing? My wedding band? I pull it off and hurl it into the woods, as if it's a spider crawling on my hand.

Then, without thinking, I crack the door open just enough that I can reach inside and snatch my car keys from the mantel. I jog to my car and buckle myself in. The stuffy silence swallows me.

"You're going to get through this," I say in a hollow voice as I start the engine. "You're going to be okay."

I back out of the driveway, hands quivering on the wheel.

"How were you supposed to know?" I ask, eyes stinging. "How were you supposed to figure this out? You were doing the best you could with what you had."

The light is blinding, and I block it with my hand as the wheels crunch over leaves and rocks. I glance back at the house just once, imagining it on fire. I'm disappointed when I blink and the flames disappear. Turning the car in a three-point turn to face the highway, I stall for a moment with my hand hovering above the blinker. I inch the car forward onto the road. I don't know where I'm going. Do I turn right and go to Hill Valley and tell Plough what I found? Do I turn left and head out of town to flee this nightmare? I don't know which way to go.

And then, in a split second, life decides for me.

"Oh shit," I yell, spotting the truck speeding around the bend, straight toward my side of the car. It's too late. It happens too fast for me to even react.

The world spins, tumbles, crackles, sparkles, crunches, crushes, aches, and finally goes black.

And then—sweet nothing.

37

"Mrs. Blue, can you hear me?"

"Katherine, stay with me, honey."

"Can you open your eyes?"

"Look into this penlight."

"Do you know what day it is?"

"Who's the president?"

"Katherine Blue. Katherine Blue, stay awake here."

Who are these voices talking to? They swirl around me like a dream. Then I feel a chilly hand tapping my cheek—a gentle slap. My memory comes into focus.

Me? I'm Katherine Blue. They're talking to me.

I'm trapped inside my body, eyes closed, and they're talking to me. It takes every ounce of strength to open my eyes. Bright lights everywhere. White ceiling, white coats, white floors, beeping sounds I recognize. A song I've heard before.

Beep-beep-beep.

"What ..." I croak, throat parched.

My head is heavy, wrapped in something, throbbing. My arm aches, too.

"Why am I ..." I start, trying to sit up.

A nurse comes and *shh*s me, coaxing me back to a supine position. "Honey, you were in a car accident. Don't worry. Sit tight. You've got a concussion, and a broken arm, but you and your baby are going to be just fine. The doctor will be back in a moment."

Her heels click away. I hear her voice murmuring in the hall over the beeping, the occasional bumps of wheels, and the quiet breath of air conditioning in the vent. I lie here, staring at a crack in the ceiling for a good minute, letting the reality that I am in a hospital and that I was in a car accident reverberate around my brain. And then suddenly, I sit up, cringing at the pain in my left elbow.

Wait a second. Wait one fucking second.

"*Baby?*" I shriek.

<h1 style="text-align:center">38</h1>

"Congratulations. Looks like you're about six or seven weeks pregnant, Mrs. Blue," says the doctor, coming in and giving me a smile big enough to rival a politician.

"But ..." I stare at the cast on my arm. "I don't understand how."

"You—don't understand how?" the doctor repeats with a slight grimace.

"No, I mean, obviously I ... I just wasn't expecting this." I place a hand on my belly, covered by a star-spangled hospital gown. My head still feels thick, swollen like a balloon. It hurts to blink. My ears are ringing. I'm adjusting to this new reality here, this backward reality where I'm the one in the hospital bed. Distantly, alarms are ringing inside me—something is wrong, something is very wrong, I was running from something —but all I can process right now is the fact that I'm pregnant. "You're sure?"

"We're sure. And we did an ultrasound already—the baby is just fine. Wish I could say the same about your radius. We're going to put a cast on you soon and give some instructions on caring for it, but that arm will not be seeing the sunshine until summer's over." The doctor pats my head and gets up from the stool with a squeak. "Do you have anyone we should call for you? We tried calling your husband, but he didn't pick up."

The words *your husband* sink me like a pile of stones.

"My husband is in a coma," I whisper. "In Intermediary Care."

"Here? At Hill Valley General?"

I nod.

He flips open my file again, squinting at it. "Well, I'll be damned. He's one floor above you."

My eyes blur.

"That's unfortunate. I'm sorry to hear that." He gets up and adjusts the stethoscope around his neck as if he wishes he had the words to comfort me, but there's absolutely nothing he can say right now. "Well, what a miracle that you survived that crash, and that your baby did too."

That's one way to look at it.

They want to keep me overnight for observation. I have so many questions. Where's my car? Is my dog okay? All they can do is give me vague reassurances about looking into it. The nurses bring me ice water in a plastic pitcher and pills for my pain, then leave me to rest, shutting the door. Soon I'm left alone with the beeping machinery. I think of what the doctor said: Mitch is one floor above me. I lie here staring at the ceiling, running my tongue along the sharp edges of my canine teeth. I can still see them there, sharp fangs twinkling from my studio floor.

My hand rests on my belly, rising and falling. I'm going to have a baby. My husband is a serial killer in a coma, and I'm going to have a baby. This should be the worst thing in the world, and yet somehow it doesn't feel that way—it feels like dawn peeking over dark hills. It feels like a drink of water after a long, hot day. Somewhere inside me, there's a being. She didn't ask to be born. She didn't invite herself into this cold, unpredictable world. She doesn't know that her father is a monster. But here she is—pure light, just wanting to live.

"I know the feeling, little one," I whisper, tracing a circle around my stomach.

I breathe in deeply. I try to center myself, get practical. I don't think deeply about the mess back at the studio and all it means—it's there, lurking like an impending storm, but I can't face it head-on right now. Instead, I fix my eyes on the future. I get practical. I'm pregnant. Alone. My car's totaled. I have no way to get around. I hate my job—there; I admitted it. I thought it out loud. I hate Breakneck Bay, the Wild West of waterslides, the manifestation of Creighton's greed at the expense of other human beings, where teens crack their heads open and drink illegally and even go missing, and no one cares. I don't want to go back there again. I imagine myself, potbellied and pregnant and spraying sobbing grown men with a bottle of iodine. No, thank you. Not the movie I want to star in.

My heartbeat picks up speed as the painkillers kick in, and my headache quiets. I have to think about the inevitable. I have to consider what the hell I'm going to do with the horror show I found. I remember the crack of the maraca underfoot and wince—like stepping on a baby bird. And then the sharpness under the sole of my foot, the sharpness that was *other women's teeth*. A wave of self-hatred comes over me—how could I have not known? What kind of fool am I? But for the little one's sake, I stop. I can't let hatred into my heart when she's sharing it with me.

"Options," I whisper, sitting up, folding my hands in my lap.

There's the obvious: call the police. Let them come and tear my house apart to pull every bit of evidence they can to build their case against Mitch. From there, Mitch will either wake up from his coma and stand trial, or he won't wake up. Then what happens? Then there's no resolution for anyone. No answer from him. The world will remember Mitch not as the man I thought I knew, not the gentle, mysterious rambler, but as a coldhearted serial killer. And the baby—the baby will grow up with the shadow of her father's crimes looming over her. The baby will grow into a girl who wishes she could forget the man she came from, who will grow into a woman who seeks the wrong kinds of men to patch a leak somewhere in her soul.

A woman just like me.

I want so much more for her. Can I even imagine how free I would have been if I had never known my father? If, somehow, when that horrid atrocity happened, I had been blissfully ignorant, my slate wiped clean?

What mercy it would have been.

If Mitch is caught, I see it now: there will be months of investigations, maybe years. My face will be all over the newspapers. People whispering, how didn't she know? What kind of wife marries a serial killer and has no idea? Forever and ever, that's who I will be. Not Kit the mother, not Kit the musician, not Kit the sister. I will be Kit, the idiot wife. Kit, the monster enabler. And my baby—people will look at her with pity.

Life is not math. As much as people like Creighton Marrs have tried to reduce people down to a number you can put on paper, a dollar sign you can pay off, a check ripped from a pocketbook, people are more than a sum of the injuries they've incurred and inflicted. But sometimes, it's hard not to think that there is *some* kind of math involved. A man like Mitch lives a life and takes at least a half-dozen others' away. Cynthia tried to wipe him off the earth because she thought the world would have been better without him. That's another kind of math, but is she wrong? Or was she on to something?

Would the world be better if she had succeeded?

I weigh my options for a long time, hand on my belly as the night darkens and the stars blink on, one by one, through the window. I close my eyes and beam every bit of love left in my bones to the little creature inside my womb. I'm sorry I was blind for so long. I'm sorry I ignored the signs. I'm sorry I looked at the bright side when the shadows deserved just as much attention.

But I know what I have to do now.

39

The next morning, I steal into Mitch's room quietly. I was brave on the elevator ride up, but now I'm weak in the knees as I stand in the doorway. I can't bring myself to look at him. I can only glimpse the shape of his legs under the white blanket. Reminds me of a white sheet draped over a corpse.

Gathering myself, I reluctantly take a seat on a chair about five feet away from him. I tote a paper bag with my old clothes —the ones I wore when the ambulance brought me in yesterday. Dropping it beside me with a crumple, I cross my legs. I scratch my cast, still itchy and strange. Like every change life throws at me, it will take getting used to.

Beep-beep-beep.

I exhale a long breath out my nose, fighting the lump in my throat. Not a lump from sadness—a lump that is my permanent nausea every time I think of Mitch. I put a hand on my stomach, under my sweatshirt, and sit up straighter. The tears brim, burning like acid. I wait for the right words.

"I don't know who you are," I say.

I allow my gaze to float up to his left hand, where that white strip of skin reminds me where his wedding ring used to be.

"I trusted you. I defended you. I slept next to you. It makes no sense, I—"

I stop myself because my chest is tightening so badly that I need a moment to breathe. I close my eyes, gather myself, calm the rage. Skyrocketing blood pressure can't be good for the baby.

Opening my eyes, I wipe my face and try again. This time, I'm brave enough to look him in the face. His swelling has gone down. The dressings are smaller. There's just an eyepatch and a bandage over his cheek. His hair is greasy and grown out longer than I've ever seen it. I hate how I fight the urge to brush it from his forehead, like it's second nature. Who shaves him? Who clips his fingernails? The nurses who come in here every day and tend to him—the surgeons, the doctors working hard to bring him back—they are comforts he doesn't deserve.

"The key question I have," I say, leaning in to whisper it to him, hoping he can hear me. "Is why me?"

Beep-beep-beep.

"Why did you kill them, but somehow love me?"

Beep-beep-beep.

"Did you ever look at me from across the dinner table, or watch me sleeping at night, and think about killing me, too? Why didn't you? I don't understand. What is it about me that made you—because you can't love people. Right? You're—one of those psychopaths with something wired wrong inside you. You can't love. Or can you?"

Beep-beep-beep.

"Did you target me? Did I have some—some—invisible sign hanging over my head that promised you I was a gullible idiot? That my dad was a fucking murderer, too?"

Beep-beep-beep.

The more I speak, the angrier I become. I choke up and look away, unable to stand the sight of his face anymore because it's nothing but a mask. Finally, I force myself to address him again.

"Were you sorry? Did it eat you up inside? Is that why you were so—so … all over the place? Erratic? Why you disappeared and drank too much, and … why did you have to drag me into this, Mitch?" My hands tremble in my lap. "What kind of sick mind game is it to give me these *women's teeth hidden in a gift* on our wedding night? Did it make you happy to know that you had me that fooled? I remember you acting like it meant so much to you. It puzzled me at the time—yeah, I saw you'd whittled it and painted it, but you've always been good with your hands."

The double meaning hits me like a bus. I dry heave instantly and eye the empty trash can in the corner, wondering if I can hold in the hospital food churning in my gut.

Beep-beep-beep.

I breathe steadily, eyeing him, wishing Cynthia had better aim.

Cynthia. I think the name with a pinch. Poor girl. Poor fucking girl. I hope she pulled through, wherever she is. Mitch stole her life from her before it even started.

And she was right. The world would be better without him.

"I'm pregnant," I tell him, looking down at my baggy sweatshirt, still hardly able to believe it's real. "Somehow, I just know it's going to be a girl." I lean in and whisper, "And you're never, ever going to meet her. She's never going to even know you existed."

I stand up, legs shaky. I glance behind my shoulder at the closed door.

Beep-beep-beep.

I stare at the mountains and valleys of his heartbeat on the machine.

Beep-beep-beep.

I step closer to him. My breath hitches as I touch his cheek, surprised at its warmth.

Then I pull my hand away. I reach over to the machine, pressing the mute button. The beeping stops.

In the silence, I see his eyelids twitch.

I can't breathe for a second, shock stealing my air.

His eyelids flutter. *He's trying to open them.*

Oh my God. Panic explodes inside me.

Somewhere in there, he's fighting to wake up.

But I can't let that happen.

I gently take the pillow from under his head.

I raise it in the air.

And that's when his eyes flutter all the way open.

He's looking at me. I'm looking at him.

I gasp at the sight of that lagoon-green color I haven't seen in days, the way his stare widens with recognition even as his face remains still.

My eyes water. My hands holding the pillow remain frozen in the air. An entire lifetime seems to transpire in a single moment as our gaze is locked. The night he picked me up on the side of the road. Dancing and laughing in a dark club, his arms around my waist. The pull of his kiss. Our wedding, bare feet in the warm sand. But I blink the tears away.

"Sweet dreams," I whisper.

I lay the pillow on top of his face, covering him up, relief pouring over me as soon as I don't have to look at him anymore.

I lean my weight down on it with even force, holding it there while I focus on the amber burst of sunshine in the window.

He doesn't move. Not a peep, not a thrash, not a single

twitch—it's as if he's already dead. A dead man with a heartbeat.

I stay still for a long time in disbelief, waiting for resistance, for a fight.

But all I get is the line leaping on the heart monitor—faster, then slower, and then finally flatlining. A dial tone.

I can't believe it. Just like that.

It's over.

He's gone.

I relax my grip and pull back. My hands fly to my face. I wipe my nose and eyes. I fear what he looks like under there. The shock is paralyzing me, but I hurry. Lifting the pillow up, I allow myself to study him one more time. His eyes are shut now. I was expecting something gruesome—a blue face, blood coming out of his nose. But he looks ... peaceful. He just looks asleep. I tuck the pillow back under his head. I loved him.

I loved the man he pretended to be.

I let out a sob and kiss his cheek once before turning to the door and throwing it open.

"Help! Please!" I yell into the long, white hall, and suddenly I'm so heartbroken to lose him, so shattered by his ending, that I almost believe I had nothing to do with it. The panic in my throat is real. "Nurse! Something's happened to my husband!"

40

It's hard for me to wrap my head around the fact that I've been a widow for a month now. *Widow*—the word is so severe. I used to associate it with old ladies and venomous spiders. But now, like many things I never asked for, it's become mine.

I've been trying to steady myself by being here and now. Practicing mindfulness while I accomplish the practical tasks at hand: signing paperwork, burying my husband. Burning everything he owned in our fireplace. Packing my belongings into boxes. Reading Dr. Spock. Bailing my brother out of jail in Reno.

Me and the Big Empty have become ... *chummy*; that's a good word for it. I've learned over the past month that I can exist within the wild and the quiet so long as I surrender to it. Make friends with it. Let it hold me as I inch through every day. The Big Empty says, don't think about Mitch and monsters and the men in this world you can't control. When I fix myself in this moment, undistracted by the pain behind me and the uncertainty ahead, I'm okay. I'm always okay.

This is what I tell myself as I stand atop the stairs in the employee parking lot, surveying the park below. Here at Break-neck Bay, life goes on. The rapids churn, the artificial waves ebb, and the rivers scream on. It's not even nine-thirty in the morning, and I can already smell burgers. I blow a breath out and clutch the railing as I make my way down the stairs. I haven't been here in weeks. I never wanted to come back here again—but Creighton made me promise I would swing by on my way out of town and say goodbye.

As soon as I walk through the doors of the admin building, it's as if I stepped out of a time machine and the summer's just starting again. The coconut scent of tanning lotion, cigarette smoke, and burnt coffee all hit me at once. Stevie Nicks' hypnotic vocals are bleeding from the boombox, and Creighton's voice is somewhere out of sight, yelling, "Goddamn regulations, as if it's my fault this area has rattlesnakes. Are you fuckin' kidding me?"

But the energy of the room screeches to a halt the second I step inside. Dwayne turns to me, cigarette dangling from his lip. One twin gasps and slaps a hand over her mouth. Billford nearly spits his coffee out on the carpet. And then, stage two, the one I'm not quite used to yet: the pity. The head-shaking, heart-clutching pity, as if the mere sight of me is gutting.

Me, the widow.

"Hi everyone," I say with a shy smile. "Nice to see you."

It is. I didn't realize until I said it aloud that a *tiny* part of me will miss Breakneck Bay. As ludicrous, dangerous, and immature as this place is, it's got personality. It's a wet pocket of the Wild West, lawless and insane, run by teenagers. And I'm never going to return again as long as I live.

Everyone comes over, gathering to greet me and shell out condolences and pepper me with questions. Since Mitch died, they've sent cards and left me messages, but this is the first time I've shown my face.

"You coming back to work?"

"Is it true? Are you leaving Hill Valley?"

"Where are you heading next?"

"Did you know that detective guy's looking for you?"

I swallow, overwhelmed by the attention. I run a hand through my hair and laugh nervously. "No, I'm not coming back to work. Yes, I'm leaving Hill Valley. I'm going back to LA, where I lived before—my old apartment building has a unit open. And yeah, Detective Plough? We've been in touch since Mitch passed. The case is closed now."

In fact, he swung by just yesterday to grab his recording equipment—and the blank tape I put inside it.

Dwayne pushes his sunglasses up, revealing bloodshot eyes. "Dude, I'm so sorry about Mitch."

Everyone murmurs in agreement. I wince, my pulse skipping a beat.

"Did they ever find out who did that to him?" asks one of the twins.

I sigh and shake my head. "We might never know. For all we know, it was self-inflicted." I swallow. "I'd really rather not talk about it."

"Man, stop being so nosy," Dwayne says, jabbing her in the ribs.

"It's okay." I wipe my eyes preemptively, knowing tears are coming. Focus on now. Stay here now. Mitch is gone. It's over. It's behind me. I put my hand on my belly—behind *us*. Not that my former colleagues here at Breakneck Bay have any idea I'm pregnant. It's my little secret with the universe for now. "Can I talk to Creighton?"

We are all ignoring Creighton in there, who is still in his office shouting, "Am I God now? Did I invite that snake to bite that tourist in the ass? Because that's what this bullshit is claiming!"

"Sure, he's in his office," someone says.

"Thanks." I smile and walk to his office, trying to ignore the awkward way this entire group is staring at me, as if I'm a Martian who just landed in their waterpark.

Creighton's door is ajar, so I push it open. He's seated behind a desk, berating a man who sits across from him. The man wears a wrinkled suit, face pinked with shame.

"What the fuck am I supposed to do? Hire a rattlesnake hunter?" Creighton yells at the man. "You know those dirty hippie environmentalists would crawl up my ass in half a second—" Creighton notices me and his eyes widen. He stands. His voice changes completely, ice melting. "Kit, honey, come on in. Don't just stand there. Come here and gimme a hug."

I walk toward him uneasily, the argument still lingering in the air.

"Get the fuck out of here, I'll deal with you later," Creighton barks at the man in the suit. "You want Chinese for lunch? Tell Rhonda; she'll order some for you."

The man scrambles out of his chair as if he'd love nothing more than to leave the room.

"Shut the goddamn door. Where'd you grow up, in a barn?" Creighton yells after him.

Slam.

I stand in front of Creighton, who shakes his head. "Those city inspectors are such gutless rats, my God." He opens his arms, showing off his Hawaiian shirt covered in flamingos. "Bring it in. I can't believe it, I can't *believe* it."

I accept his embrace stiffly at first, inhaling his spicy cologne, but soon I relax into it. He smacks my back with his hand as if I'm a baby he's burping.

"I'd have bet my right ass cheek Mitch was gonna pull through," he murmurs to me. "It just—it blows my mind. I didn't know how bad it was. I really should have visited him. I feel like a genuine piece of shit, you know?"

"It's okay," I say, pulling back, throat tightening. "He wasn't there at the end, anyway. He'd probably prefer you didn't remember him that way."

"He was my best fuckin' friend." Creighton shakes his head. "My oldest fuckin' friend."

Your only fuckin' friend, I think.

"Well, where to next?" Creighton asks in a brighter tone, as if the perfunctory mourning is over and now we can move on.

"Back to LA."

"The Smog Farm. City of brown-nosers. You really want to go back there?"

"I was happy there." A lump grows in my throat. "I wish I'd never come here."

He scoffs. "Oh, come on, shit happens everywhere."

"Creighton," I say, giving him a look. "A disproportionate amount of shit seems to happen here."

Creighton's eyes narrow. "Yeah, well. What are you going to do about it?"

An icy breeze seems to have blown over the conversation. He peers past me at the door, as if he can't wait for me to leave.

"Anyway," I say with a nod. "I just wanted to say goodbye."

"Sayonara," he almost shouts. "Thanks for stopping by." He snaps his fingers. "Wait a second. Let me give you something. Hold up one minute."

Creighton circles behind his desk, slamming open a drawer and smacking a checkbook on the table. He sits down with a squeak in his chair and uncaps a pen, writing out a check with a flourish.

"Oh!" he says, stopping suddenly and tapping the table with his pen. "Guess who the fuck I ran into?"

"Who?" I ask.

"That little flake who ran away ... Gloria. The one the cops kept sniffing around here, looking for? The one everyone was up in arms about, thinking Mitch—" He makes a noise like the *Psycho* soundtrack, *reek-reek*.

I flinch at both the information and the reference. Then his words sink in and my mouth drops.

"Wait ..." I say.

"I told everyone. I told everyone not to worry, that Mitch didn't do anything. She was just a deadbeat who bailed on her fuckin' job. My God, the resources that were wasted on that little tart."

"Where did you see her?" I ask, coming forward, heart in my throat. Adrenaline hits as the possibilities firework in my brain. Cynthia is alive. I will my mouth to not smile, to react properly, because I don't know how to feel—but I know that somewhere in there, beneath the pain and confusion and the mess I carry, there's joy that she's still on this planet.

"At a fuckin' frozen yogurt place. Have you heard of this stuff? Frozen yogurt? It's like ice cream, except it tastes like shit. Kimber's obsessed with it, made me drive with her out to the mall in Raven's Landing to get some. And guess who's working behind the counter? She tried to act like she didn't know me, but it was her." Creighton rips the check out of the booklet. Then he frowns. "I'll bet she pissed in my sundae, now that I think about it."

"Wow," is all I can think to say.

Creighton gets up. "Yeah. I informed the entire staff at our last meeting. Made sure everyone knew I saw her. I don't want some pubescent hussy dragging Mitch's memory after he's gone."

I nod. "Oh, good," I say, though the words feel wooden and meaningless.

He crosses to me and hands me the check. "Here you go. Don't spend it all in one place."

When my eyes fall to the number he's written, my jaw drops. It's more zeros than I've ever seen on a check written to me in my whole life.

"Creighton, I can't—"

"Consider it a parting gift for helping Breakneck Bay keep its good name," he says, clapping my shoulder, beaming a smile that shows off that gold tooth.

I nod, dizzy, still staring at the check. It sinks in: He's buying me off. He's scared I'm going to badmouth Breakneck Bay. Because there's no such thing as generosity for Creighton Marrs, only bribery.

But I take the bribe because, after everything I've suffered through, I deserve it. This is a crib, a changing table, and the start of a college fund right here. I fold up the check and tuck it in the pocket of my jeans.

"Thanks," I tell him.

Creighton walks me to his door and waves at me once. Then he turns back to his office and forgets I exist. I give the twins and Dwayne a wave from across the room and head toward the exit—but I'm stopped by the creak of a door opening. The door I've been trying not to look at this entire time, the door I've been ignoring as if it were never there.

Rhonda comes out of Mitch's office, startled at the sight of me. She's got a visor on that matches her neon shirt, and she's wearing a lanyard that says *General Manager*. Glancing up at Mitch's door, I see her lanyard matches the title there, too. *Rhonda Wegman, General Manager*.

Good for her. She earned it.

"Hey, Rhonda," I say. "How are you?"

"Mrs. Blue—" She stops herself, fingers flying to her lips. "I'm sorry. Do you still go by Mrs. Blue?"

"Kit. Just call me Kit."

"Right. *Kit.* I've been wondering how you are. Did you get my card? The one with Garfield on it?"

"I did, thank you. Very sweet."

"I love Garfield."

"He's cute."

A silence expands.

"I was just swinging by on my way out of town," I tell her. "I'm moving back to LA."

"Los Angeles! How exciting! I'm applying to UCLA next year. They have a magnificent journalism program."

I smile. "Well, good luck."

"Perhaps I could ... look you up? See how you're doing?"

I was thinking I was going to leave this place without a trace of me—sever all connections. Erase Hill Valley and Breakneck Bay from my maps and move on. But the eager expression on Rhonda's face makes me think, what the hell. I can make one exception.

"Yeah, sure. I'll call you when I get my line set up. How does that sound?"

"Marvelous. Wow. Thank you, Kit."

She doesn't seem like the hugging type, so I shake her hand.

"Nice working with you," I say. "Thanks for everything."

"Of course. At your service."

Our goodbye is just as awkward as every other encounter we've ever had. But as I head outside and make my way up the stairs to the parking lot for the last time, it hits me that Rhonda was the closest thing to a friend I had here at Breakneck Bay.

I make my way over to the rental truck parked in the corner, climbing in the passenger's seat. Immediately, I smell weed, and my irritation flares.

"Freddie," I say. "Don't smoke pot around me when I'm pregnant. Come *on*."

He turns down Black Sabbath, sucking a lollipop. "Don't worry, I've sobered up already. You were gone for, like, an hour."

"It was not an hour."

"I gave up cigarettes. Give me a break, I need to smoke *something*."

"Actually, you don't," I say, clipping my seatbelt. "Are you good to drive?"

"Yes. Jesus, what is this, the Spanish Inquisition?" he says in a British accent.

I give him a look. The same look I've been giving him since we were kids. The same look I'll be giving him until we're both old and gray—if we're lucky enough to get old and gray.

"Just drive," I mutter.

He revs the engine.

"You're lucky I'm here, Kit," he says, with just a flicker of hurt in his expression. "I mean, for shit's sake, you tried to have me arrested for murder."

My heart throbs at the memory. "I know. I've told you how sorry I am."

"Yeah, yeah, I get it. They had a warrant out and it looked bad, but ..."

"I should have trusted you."

"It's okay," he says, always eager to forgive. "You thought I beat a woman up at the time, I guess it makes sense." He shakes his head. "That chick was so crazy. I'm so fuckin' glad she dropped the charges."

"Me too. You should have told me the full story. If I had known she attacked you and you were just defending yourself—"

"Don't worry about it. If, if, if," he says. "What's the point of 'if?'"

He turns up the music, and off we go.

As we make our way through the forest, Freddie's too busy trying to harmonize with Ozzy Osbourne to hold a conversation. Which is nice, actually. Gives me time to think. Gives me a moment to process everything: Breakneck Bay shrinking in the rearview, Creighton's check, and the glowing relief I experience knowing that somewhere, the girl who called herself Gloria is still alive. She'll keep going. With a little luck, she'll grow up and become a woman and have a million stories to tell, and a few to keep all to herself, too. It's the strangest thing in the world, but I'm grateful for the girl who shot my husband. She woke me up. She showed me a mirror when I didn't even know I needed one.

I turn to Freddie. "You know, I was thinking about naming the baby Cynthia."

"Cynthia," he says dramatically. Then he nods. "I like that, sis."

"I don't know." I shrug. "We'll see."

I look out my window at the eternity of pines, the wild woods that swallowed me up and spit me back out again. There's a darkness lurking. Shadows, pitfalls, and jagged rocks we pass on our way down the mountain. A dead deer in the road, a vulture picking at a carcass on a shoulder. I know they're there. But I choose to look past them. I choose, instead, to look at the bright green leaves and the baby ducklings and the waterfall that glints in the sunshine.

I choose the light.

Want to know what happens next—from Cynthia's point of view? ᐧ ᐧ

ONE MORE THING ...

If you enjoyed *Breakneck Bay,* good news: I have other psychological thrillers I think you'll like, too.

How about *The Mirror House Girls,* a psychological thriller about a cult led by a charismatic psychologist?

You might also check out *Like It Never Was,* an unhinged psychological thriller about a female friendship plagued by paranoia and revenge.

Maybe try *They Are the Hunters*, a psychological thriller about a family with some deep, dark secrets.

Or give *The Second Life of Ava Rivers* a read! It's a psychological thriller/mystery about a twin who comes back after twelve years missing with no memory of where she's been all this time.

I also have a collection of psychological thrillers all set in the same universe. They're called **The Jolvix Episodes**.

NOTE: These standalone novels can be read in whatever order you want, but *Eve in Overdrive* is technically a prequel to *The Slaying Game.*

- **THE PREDICTION:** A newlywed woman's smart device begins offering chilling predictions about her husband.

- **VIOLET IS NOWHERE:** A kidnapped woman and a stranger on the end of a phone line have one week to figure out how they're connected or their lives are over.

- **WHAT JANUARY REMEMBERS:** A dysfunctional family and their sentient companion bot gather for the holidays for the first time since their last Christmas together—which ended in attempted murder.

- **PEARL IN DEEP:** The love of one woman's life turns out to be a psychopath with a disturbing talent for deepfake video.

- **EVE IN OVERDRIVE:** An outspoken journalist buys a cutting-edge car only to find herself at the mercy of a vengeful internet troll.

- **THE SLAYING GAME:** A former Jolvix employee ends up at the center of a serial killer's deadly game.

A NOTE FROM THE AUTHOR

If you got this far, thank you for reading and supporting my work. As an indie author, I put a ton of effort into each book—not just writing, but editing, marketing, and everything else it takes to guide a book through the whole process from a glimmer in the brain to a real, actual thing you can hold in your hands.

If you enjoyed it, please consider leaving a review. Reviews truly make an author's world go round. If you're interested in keeping up with book news, please join my newsletter or follow me on social media. And I love to hear from readers anytime at <u>faith@ faithgardner.com</u>.

As always, I tried my damndest to fix every typo, but alas, I am only human. If you spot an error, please let me know! I appreciate every reader who makes me look smarter.

ACKNOWLEDGMENTS

Mom, this time you deserve double thanks. Not only did you read and help me edit my draft, you did it twice after I made some major changes. You are truly the best mother—and best editor—I could have ever asked for.

Micaela, thank you for beta reading and always making me laugh with your comments. You're the best sister ever.

Noelle Ihli, Steph Nelson, and Caleb Stephens—your feedback for this book was so crucial. Thank you for your honesty, your amazing suggestions, and your endless support. I can't believe how lucky I am to call you talented writers my friends.

Dad, thanks for your excitement when I told you I was writing about a 1980s serial killer. I've never known anyone so joyful to go out to lunch and talk about the Green River Killer. You're so smart, so full of true crime knowledge, and you're one of my favorite characters on earth.

To the rest of my family, I love you and I'm so grateful for every single one of you. Special shoutout to Jamie, the best partner I could have asked for. I love you and appreciate everything you do more than words could say.

My bright, brilliant, beautiful daughters Roxie and Zora, for always being proud of their mama and her "dark books"—even if you're way too young to read them.

To every reviewer, supporter, Bookstagrammer, TikToker who has helped boost my books: without you, none of this would be possible. So much appreciation and respect for all you do for us writers.

And thank you, dear reader, for spending a little time with me and my book.

ALSO BY FAITH GARDNER

STANDALONES

The Mirror House Girls

Like It Never Was

They Are the Hunters

The Second Life of Ava Rivers

THE JOLVIX EPISODES

The Prediction

Violet Is Nowhere

What January Remembers

Pearl in Deep

Eve in Overdrive

The Slaying Game

YOUNG ADULT NOVELS

Perdita

If You Can Hear This

How We Ricochet

Girl on the Line

THAT ONE TIME I WROTE A ROM-COM

Make Me a Double

ABOUT THE AUTHOR

Faith Gardner writes suspense novels. When her head isn't stuck in a book, she might be playing music, cooking, or playing with tarot cards. She's also a fan of documentaries and scary movies. She lives in the Bay Area with her family. Find her at faithgardner.com.